The MoDERN

The MoDERN

Anna Kate Blair

SCRIBNER

First published in Australia in 2023 by Scribner, an imprint of Simon & Schuster Australia
Suite 19A, Level 1, Building C, 450 Miller Street, Cammeray, NSW 2062

Sydney New York London Toronto New Delhi
Visit our website at www.simonandschuster.com.au

Scribner and design are registered trademarks of The Gale Group, Inc.,
used under licence by Simon & Schuster Inc.

10 9 8 7 6 5 4 3 2 1

A catalogue record for this book is available from the National Library of Australia

9781761421242 (paperback)
9781761421259 (ebook)

Cover design by Laura Thomas
Typeset by Midland Typesetters in 12.5/17 pt Adobe Garamond Pro
Printed and bound in Australia by Griffin Press

The paper this book is printed on is certified against the Forest Stewardship Council® Standards. Griffin Press holds chain of custody certification SCS-COC-001185. FSC® promotes environmentally responsible, socially beneficial and economically viable management of the world's forests.

for arts workers and motherless girls

1

Anthea told me she went to the bathrooms in the basement, by the cinema, when she needed to cry at work. Joanna recommended the stairwell behind the librarian's office. I just sat silently at my desk, staring hard at my computer screen, rubbing my eyes as if they were smarting from all the data entry.

I was lucky to be here, checking measurements and shining the sentences that would appear on object labels. The open-plan offices felt like a new-age monastery; we showed our devotion through our long hours and low salaries, our gratitude and obsession with our work euphemistically called *attention to detail* in all the job advertisements. These offices were almost always silent save the soft clatter of our keyboards and the occasional ring of the elevator doors opening when somebody left for the galleries filled with bright, white light, where the crowds gathered to take photographs of endlessly reproduced images, paying homage to our gods, to modernism.

I wanted to stay, forever, because of the paintings. I wanted to stay forever because of Frank O'Hara, who worked as a curator and wrote poems on his lunch breaks, and Grace Hartigan, his friend and mine, who was the only woman included in *The New American Painting*, organised by the museum in 1958. I could see Grace as my friend only because I worked here, researching her relationship to the museum. She had died when I was twenty-one; I had first encountered her name in an *Artforum* obituary.

In another year I shall be thirty, she wrote in 1951. *Time to begin to fulfill the 'promise'.*

I was about to turn thirty. I didn't know how this had happened. The century had gradually grown teenage and I was an adult, remembering the period when we'd all calculated time by adding up the years before and after the turn of the millennium. The time since seemed to have vanished, disappearing into a rush of cities and museums and schools and universities and aeroplanes that blurred and abstracted the earth, creating neat frames for chaos.

I was on a short-term contract at the museum, with a half-forgotten PhD and no meaningful publications or exhibitions to my name. I googled myself, sometimes, and found only a journalist covering events for a paper in Tulsa, Oklahoma. I wasn't sure I had achieved anything beyond having left Australia, where I'd first studied art history through slides projected in a darkened lecture theatre. I had not yet fulfilled my promise, if I had any, but I had fulfilled that undergraduate dream, wandering through the canon of modern art each morning before the museum opened. I had not fulfilled my promise, but I could forget my past and future in this cerebral space; I could lose myself to looking.

It was winter. I went to work, hung my coat on the coat-hanger beside my cubicle and hoped for a blizzard that would blanket the sculpture garden with snow. Robert sent out applications for tenure-track jobs and postdoctoral fellowships quickly and without anguish, formatted chapters of his PhD as articles and sent these to academic journals. On weekends I walked west to the Whitney Museum or caught the subway to exhibitions uptown. Robert cycled around Manhattan, restless, and made plans for warmer weather. In the evenings, we met for dinner in small restaurants with short menus.

I liked winter. It was restful. We had spent too much of the previous summer in the Hudson Valley, visiting Robert's family, attending weddings and hiking almost every weekend. I had been surprised to find summer weekends so busy in New York. I hadn't realised that Robert knew so many people who were getting married and I hadn't expected to be invited alongside him. I saw weddings as something academic; they were the subject of Grace Hartigan's paintings, made in the 1950s, or an essay topic for an undergraduate in gender studies, not an event in twenty-first century life. There was a certain type of American on the East Coast, though, who still closed their twenties with an expensive wedding.

The weddings were almost always outdoor, dogged by professional photographers who refused to direct people. These photographers rarely bothered with most guests, gravitating to those who already seemed like stars, with their own inbuilt flash, with moisturised skin that caught the light in a particular way. The world beyond became a mess of gloaming colours, yellow lights and white flowers blurring into a charcoal sky. It seemed, that year, that nobody wanted much depth of field in photography. Everybody wanted reality as it was felt, not seen. Everybody wanted their weddings softened, shown as dreams.

'That's not how I work. I'm documenting,' these photographers said, when elderly relatives asked if they might get some nice shots of the youngest grandson before he spilt his orange juice on his shirt. They lowered their cameras and turned away, disappointed, when guests tried to arrange themselves into meaningful clusters, smiling.

I wasn't one of the people that the photographers circled. I spent the weddings wishing myself invisible, flinching at questions. I was always asked where I was from, what I was doing in New York.

'I have a two-year fellowship,' I said. 'At MoMA.'

'You're so lucky,' cooed strangers.

'Yes,' I said, usually.

I knew that it would be rude, disingenuous, to refute this idea. I hated, though, the ways in which luckiness flattened out everything, acknowledging neither my own achievements nor the cruel indifference of the institution itself, which asked absolute allegiance whilst offering precarity and little acknowledgement. I felt as if I were searching for a sign that my work was valuable, that I had a future which extended beyond my contract's end, and coming up always with the universe's indifference, with the hard facts of probability. I was lucky; the dice had rolled and I had landed at MoMA, but I knew that that didn't say anything about the past or the future, that – every modernist knew at least one line from Mallarmé – a roll of the dice would never abolish chance.

I remembered, each time an acquaintance or stranger told me that I was lucky, my first day at the museum, on which a woman from Human Resources had told the four fellows that we had been chosen from over a thousand applicants. This had been the first of many moments in which the institution said, under the guise of compliment, that we were disposable. There was not a line of people waiting to replace us so much as a crowd, clamouring. HR, of course, had negotiated the best employment deals for their own department; they had open-ended contracts and left each day after only eight hours in their offices.

'What will you do afterward?' somebody would ask.

I was trying not to think about this question. I was Australian, so I would have to persuade any potential employer to sponsor a visa. I had a PhD, but every job – or at least every arts job in New York – seemed to require more than this and I lacked both academic publications and managerial experience. I was overqualified, in the minds of many, yet I barely scraped the minimum requirements for most jobs.

I didn't like weddings, or at least the weddings that summer, because I was always asked about life after MoMA, if I'd be getting married or going home.

I saw my friends at these events, occasionally, but they had questions, too. In Cold Spring, Lucy, who had been an undergraduate with Robert before graduate school with me and who worked, now, at the Metropolitan Museum, pulled me aside and pushed a glass of wine into my hands.

'So,' Lucy said. 'Robert. How long has it been now?'

'Um,' I said. 'Five years?'

'I know this sounds a bit cheesy,' Lucy said. 'But is he the one?'

It felt, sometimes, as if friends learnt how to make small talk from films that failed the Bechdel test. I suspected Lucy had asked about Robert because she wanted to avoid talking about her own employment anxieties; she was on a two-year contract and had applied for dozens of jobs with no luck, despite having chosen the Met from five fellowship offers two years ago. It was strange, I thought, that we accepted a curatorial job was a rare thing, precious and unlikely, and yet still believed, when asking after relationships, some sort of permanence might be possible, might not be too much to ask in the romantic realm.

I couldn't, remembering summer from the end of winter, distinguish one wedding from another. It seemed as if every bride had worn white, as if every bride had married a groom, as if every group of girls awaiting a toss of flowers had encouraged the same nudge from an elderly woman, the same *could-be-you* comment even as I skirted the ritual. I could recall neither rain nor yellowed grass. How was it that not even one September wedding had been marred by flash floods?

There were always groups of older men gathered around Robert.

'What kind of pack are you carrying?'

'Osprey Exos. Internal frame, about fifty litres.'

'I'll tell you what: it was tougher in our day. Huge packs. None of this ultra-light shit.'

'I'll bet,' said Robert.

Robert had an easy, Ivy League confidence about him, which I envied and sometimes resented. Robert knew that he would secure a job, but for him a job was simply something that facilitated hiking and reading – in more ways than one, as he had written his dissertation on narrative structure in texts about walking.

'And what comes after that?' somebody would ask.

Robert wasn't afraid of questions about the future. I lived in fear of the pace at which I had to flip the pages of my calendar, while Robert planned everything in advance. He had known for years, since before we met, that he would spend the summer after he finished his PhD on the Appalachian Trail. He had told me this very early in our relationship, before it was really a relationship. Robert's desires never seemed to fluctuate but followed a neat plan.

'Maybe the Continental Divide,' he said. 'But I'll have to see. Depends where I'm working.'

'What about Sophia?' somebody sometimes asked.

'She doesn't mind hiking,' he said. 'Still trying to get her onto long-distance, though.'

The older men would look over at me, as if sizing up my potential, and laugh.

I envied the wedding photographers, who could use their cameras as an excuse, as a tool to mediate everything and everyone. I thought about the way in which a photographer might focus the camera on Lucy, capturing each strand of hair in sharp focus, blonde and glowing against the shadows of the indistinct trees behind her. I considered the way in which a photographer might use the flash, freezing Lucy mid-question, smiling, and yet also capturing, with the longer exposure, the motion of the dancers nearby and the shudder of the fairy lights in the branches above. I saw photographs like this, that winter, when everybody who had been married in summer uploaded albums to Facebook.

I spent a lot of time, at the Museum of Modern Art, thinking about what *modern* meant. In staff meetings, we spoke about modernity as a central concern guiding acquisitions, exhibition proposals, educational programs and interactions with journalists. It seemed to be the only interest that connected our separate and often antagonistic departments. We all wanted to be modern.

We began with the assumption that there were three central ways of being modern. It was possible to be modern simply by having been born into or produced by the world that came after the Industrial Revolution. It could be a matter of style, of pushing forward into the future, of being avant-garde. In some cases, *modern* just meant *new*. We usually went further, though, borrowing vaguer and more poetic definitions from Friedrich Schiller and Charles Baudelaire. *Modernity is the disenchantment of the world*, I thought, often, paraphrasing Max Weber in my mind. My fellowship focused on researching the museum's own history, so I was never far from the word.

In 1944, the museum had held an exhibition entitled *Are Clothes Modern?* It was a question that couldn't really be answered, more seductive than analytical. Somebody, upstairs, in Architecture and Design, was planning a sequel, tentatively titled *Is Fashion Modern?* I started to pose almost everything as a question that followed this formula. *Are Clothes Modern?* became *Are houses modern?* and *Are children modern? Is travel modern? Are rats modern?* It could be a prompt for serious contemplation or a joke, but it was always with me, a frame through which I considered the world. I thought about the question and I thought about the many definitions for *modern*, and I thought of myself, again and again, because there was no way of avoiding the obvious question: *was I modern?*

Grace Hartigan, on whom my research focused, was known as an abstract expressionist, but her strongest paintings weren't abstract but representational. *Grand Street Brides*, her most famous painting, resembled a portrait of European royalty filtered through the mid-century neon that might advertise a candy shop. Grace had painted a group of six women, or dressmakers' dummies, facing forward against a dark grey backdrop, slabs of white, pink, turquoise and yellow colliding with one another beneath sharp black lines that ballooned outward below the waist. It was clear that these were figures posed in a window, perhaps prostitutes or mannequins, dressed in silks and tulle, and yet the lines were so spare and the colours so lavish that I felt, each time I looked at it, astonished that Grace had managed this balance without rendering everything illegible. *Grand Street Brides* seemed like evidence that ghosts had existed in the 1950s; it seemed like an antidote to images of suburban families.

I found it hard to approach Grace's work intellectually, though I'd been hired to do so. I spoke and wrote of her as *a woman who played a significant role in a movement often described as 'masculine'*, as being *unique in her ability to combine the techniques of abstract expressionism with imagery drawn from a range of historical sources*, but at night, lying in bed on the Lower East Side, I felt a strange combination of exhilaration and fear, as if the figures in *Grand Street Brides* might spill from the painting into my subconscious, as if I expected to be haunted by Grace's bright pageant girls with hollow cheeks and eyes like scratches. I spoke about the painting to Robert, sometimes, but he fell asleep easily and was never eager to continue conversations after I turned off the lights.

Robert, when it wasn't late at night, asked questions about Grace Hartigan in the same way that I had skimmed Henry David Thoreau and Annie Dillard's books to humour him. We were interested in the same areas, generally, but approached them in different ways. Robert was fascinated by wilderness, by what lay beyond the city, and I was always reading about modern art, modern life, about creative people who had come to New York to make sense of the times in which they were living. Robert approached everything with scholarly detachment, picking apart narrative construction, while I looked for artists with whom I might fall in love, following desire, not reason. The city had swollen, in the 1950s, with artists and writers, with potential; Robert saw this as the past, while I saw it as history, as mythology, as the foundation of contemporary life. I wondered if other couples had conversations like our own, messy with references to cultural figures with whom the other person wasn't familiar and culminating, often, in furious judgements about New York City. We agreed that New York was modernity's centre, but argued about whether the air we breathed was full of utopian dreams or just automobile exhaust and rotting garbage, about when or whether we might leave.

Grand Street was no longer a bridal thoroughfare; the Lower East Side streets were lined with greengrocers, poorly regulated bus companies and millennial-pink cafés. There was one store, though, with a window of dresses that reminded me of Grace Hartigan's painting. Behind the mannequins, shadows gathered like layers of grey paint, obscuring the interior. I walked past, often, on the way to the subway and glanced curiously at the door. I was never sure if it was open and I did not want to try it, to open myself up to the presumption that I was engaged or that I wanted to be. This store was compelling in a gothic way, appearing almost abandoned, save that the dresses on the mannequins switched occasionally.

———

On the Sunday before Robert flew to Georgia, we went to an event at an art space in Brooklyn. There was an artist using a laser to write names on bowls of rice and an astronomy club in the garden; I looked through a telescope and saw a planet but wasn't sure which one. I fell in love, upstairs, with a scrap of newspaper reporting on Robert Smithson's *Island of Broken Glass*, a project cancelled after protests by environmentalists. The short article had been pinned on a wall, presumably as inspiration, by an artist creating an installation which itself wasn't yet finished. I wondered if the most beautiful artworks were always the ones that I couldn't see – projects cancelled or not yet realised – and if the best thing an artist could do was conjure an image that could be embellished by the imagination. Robert, more environmentalist than artist, frowned slightly at the article, but said nothing.

We went around the corner for dinner and Robert commented on the chill in the air; it still felt like February, though it was March. It was strange to think that winter would segue into spring so soon, that it already felt like spring in Georgia. I was still hoping for a second blizzard, for a chance to wear the gumboots I'd bought only at the end of January.

'Do you mind that I'll be gone for five months?' Robert asked.

'I don't believe in relationships where one has to ask permission,' I replied.

'I'm not asking for permission,' he said. 'I'm just asking if you mind. I want to know how you feel. You could still come, too, if you wanted.'

He had already asked and I had already declined. I couldn't and wouldn't leave the museum before my contract finished. I wasn't really interested in spending five months in the forest, looking at the ground so as to avoid tripping on rocks and roots, instead of looking at painting and photography indoors, on flat surfaces. Robert had told me that most people expected that it would be the physical difficulty that made it hard to hike the Appalachian Trail, but it was rather a feat of psychological endurance centred upon repetition.

Robert made it sound as if this were somehow noble, but silently I translated this into my own words: it was hard to hike the Appalachian Trail because the Appalachian Trail was boring. It was 2,190 miles of trees and more mountain summits than anybody bothered to count. It would take three months to get through the Louvre if one spent thirty seconds looking at each painting, per popular wisdom, but art historians knew that that wasn't the way to approach art, with a timer and a goal, emerging exhausted, having seen everything but appreciated only the first few rooms. I would, we had decided, join Robert for a few days here and there, taking trips on long weekends when possible.

'You know I can't come,' I said. 'I have work. And you're leaving tomorrow. It's nice, anyway, that we have separate lives. It's healthier.'

He nodded, though I wasn't sure he really agreed, and then we drank more wine and ordered tiramisu for dessert and then coffee martinis and I laughed at how unhealthy it seemed, getting drunk two days before hiking the Appalachian Trail, and Robert told me that I had the wrong idea about hiking, anyway, and then I said something about art and he said something about love and we smiled at one another across the table as if we'd been dating for three months, not six years, and then suddenly Robert asked me to marry him and I, without thinking, said 'yes'.

2

We didn't speak much the next morning, but hovered around one another, hungover. I'd taken the day off work. On the subway to the airport, we sat on pale blue benches; a young girl opposite us cradled a backpack the colour of a peach emoji, like a post-modern personification of spring. In Long Island City, the train rose out of the tunnel and into the air, past new buildings glittering in the sun, still tenantless. Robert held my hand and I felt glad that he hadn't bought a ring. I imagined it cutting into the palm of his hand, creating a space between us.

'I'm going to write you a lot of emails,' he said.

It felt strange to accompany him on the airport bus after the subway, stretching out the departure, muttering phrases that we'd been repeating for weeks. Robert had told me, before, that he would send emails; I had reminded him to take photographs. I had a list of dates on which to mail boxes containing supplies he could not carry and addresses along the trail to which the boxes should be sent. It was too late to start conversations we couldn't finish and so we sat in silence, speaking only when the months ahead felt frightening, too wild and unknown.

I thought that I loved airports, but I realised, when Robert left me at La Guardia, that actually I loved the travel that they signified, the anticipation of my own departure. After Robert's plane left, the airport was simply a mall with a small selection of shops charging five dollars for bottled water. I felt a strange sort of emptiness, at once momentous and hollow, as if I were at the edge of a ravine, but I was just standing on a curb, waiting for a bus to take me back to the N train. Lucy had told me to message her if I wanted company for dinner, but I was still hungover, underslept, and needed to find a way to process the last twelve hours.

Robert and I had seen each other almost every day since we'd met in graduate school at a party. It had turned out that we lived in the same housing complex; our second meeting was in the kitchen, a few mornings later, where I'd been trying to make and drink coffee before I spoke to anybody. Robert was returning from a run, so I mistook him for a scientist. I didn't know any humanities students who were outdoors before eight am.

When we'd travelled separately, we'd texted one another constantly, worked out the time difference for telephone calls. Eventually, I'd started accompanying Robert down to New York to visit his family for holidays, explaining my absence to my own family as practical, given the cost of flights. Robert had come with me to Australia, once, and I liked seeing the country through his eyes. I felt happier visiting tourist destinations with him than I had felt, as a teenager, being dragged by my classmates to drink behind woolsheds. We'd posed for a photograph in front of the Big Merino, driving down from Sydney, and it was framed now, sitting on Robert's bedside table. I couldn't remember the last time we'd been apart for longer than a week.

We would, in theory, still be speaking while Robert was hiking, but I knew that cell reception was likely to be intermittent. Robert was planning to keep his phone on aeroplane mode, too, to save the battery, and I didn't know what our conversations would be like. I didn't know if we would wait until we were in the same place before we talked about the engagement.

I didn't feel, on the bus home, as if I was in New York. The scale of everything was different, somehow, in Queens. The city spread horizontally rather than vertically. I couldn't imagine Grace Hartigan and Frank O'Hara on Grand Central Parkway, choked with trucks. I couldn't even count the lanes; there were too many. I kept checking my phone to make sure I didn't miss the stop that linked up with the subway, didn't stay on the bus as it merged with the interstate, soaring across to Randall's Island. I kept glancing out the window, trying to match my surroundings to the dot moving on my phone.

I was, at once, engaged and alone. Robert and I hadn't really talked, that morning, about what it meant. I'd woken, or half-woken, after Robert placed a cup of coffee on my bedside table. I murmured gratitude and he folded back into bed beside me, and slid his hands beneath my t-shirt, slipping it over my head as I lifted my arms. I tried to kiss his lips, my eyes half-open, and kissed his ear instead; I sensed him shifting to pull off his boxer shorts. I slipped my own shorts off, kicking them out the side of the bed.

'Do you think sex will be different once we're married?' Robert asked, pushing inside me, and I kissed his neck, because it was too early for sentences.

I felt myself melting, becoming liquid, and wrapped my legs around Robert, my feet catching one another behind his back. I liked feeling small and flexible beneath him, and I liked that the movements I made reverberated through him. I shifted my legs and ran my hands down his body, gripping the back of his thighs and feeling him tense inside me, compelling me, in turn, to arch and push myself toward him. I opened my eyes properly and met his gaze and held it, for a moment, before everything felt too intense and I closed them again, tensing my jaw.

I didn't think this counted as a conversation about marriage.

I wondered, as the train wound across from Queens and down through Manhattan, about the question that Robert had posed that morning. If we hadn't been in a hurry, afterward, and then on our way to the airport, I might have tried to answer it.

We'd spoken a lot, in the beginning, describing fantasies to one another during sex. I liked to think of women, to create scenarios in which I slept with women without losing Robert, and he liked this, too, and lent it his narrative talents. It had been exciting to learn that my attraction to women was something that could draw us closer rather than pushing us apart.

'Do you consider yourself queer?' Robert had asked, though, once, as we walked along the Charles River. I had been detailing some shifts in gender roles that had occurred after World War II, frustrated at ways in which bisexuality had been erased.

'I guess,' I'd said, startled that this was, two years into our relationship, a question.

'Oh,' he'd said.

'What else would I be?' I'd asked.

'I didn't realise,' he'd said. 'I mean, I knew you'd slept with girls, but that was in college.'

I'd imagined another version of myself, one who confidently retorted that 'in college' didn't change anything, one who asked why he'd whispered descriptions of me fucking other women in my ears if he didn't think that I was queer. I'd thought that it was obvious, something that didn't need to be labelled, and I hadn't withheld anything, and yet Robert had read my sexual history as youthful experimentation. With Robert, I was almost indistinguishable from a straight girl. I thought that 'almost' mattered, but perhaps I was caught on a technicality.

I wondered if Grace Hartigan had ever been attracted to a woman. If she had been, history had left no trace of it, and perhaps that would be true for me, too.

I'd worried, after this conversation, that I might be betraying myself when Robert and I indulged in our shared fantasies, as if detailing my desire for women was titillating to Robert only because he didn't really perceive women as a threat. I wasn't afraid, anymore, that Robert would fall in love with somebody else; I was afraid, instead, that I was complicit in the reduction of queer female desire to something performed for a male gaze. I became more tentative; I feared that if I told Robert I had political misgivings about our sex life then the fantasies would disappear, destroyed by analysis, and I didn't want this, but I also couldn't engage as fully as I had in the beginning.

Instead, I focused on the motion and sensation of our bodies, on how it felt when we touched one another. I liked the tenderness of it, that we held hands, sometimes, or locked our gaze into one another's eyes. If I closed my eyes, I imagined moving through the landscapes of which Robert reminded me; I pictured mountains and valleys, shadowy clouds and rocks, roads winding through forests that suddenly burst out upon spectacular vistas.

I wondered what the next phase would be like, though I'd never been primarily motivated by sex. I was motivated by love, often, and occasionally by the desire for security or for escape. I had all these things, with Robert, who would take me to windy mountaintops and hold onto me so that I wouldn't blow away.

I instinctively checked my phone for a message when I emerged from the subway, though Robert was still in the sky. I pictured his journey, his descent into Atlanta. He would stay overnight near the airport before catching the MARTA, the next morning, to the last stop, where somebody from a hiker hostel would pick him up and give him a lift to the Southern Appalachians, to the trail that led to the trail itself.

In the flat, that evening, Robert's favourite chair sat empty, the wrinkles in the leather catching the fading sun. There was a couch opposite, a small table, more books than I could count arranged between two black bookshelves. Robert had left a small stack of books that he thought I would like on a side table, beneath a lamp; *Eros the Bittersweet*, I read, on the cover atop the pile. There was a line of collared shirts hanging in the wardrobe, a cereal box in the recycling bin and a pile of newspapers neatly stacked beside the door.

I felt a sudden, peculiar sadness and wondered if I'd been thinking about our relationship all day so as not to think of Robert's absence, of the emptiness of our apartment. It seemed pointless, now, to have all this space; I didn't want to cook, with nobody to eat whatever I made, so I slipped two pieces of frozen bread into the toaster. I looked at the magnets on the fridge and the dishes in the drying rack – all Robert's, originally. I owned magnets and mugs, too, but they were in a storage locker on another continent, awaiting a permanent visa to justify the cost of shipping. I wondered if I could justify it now.

I had never been interested in hearing about the Appalachian Trail when Robert was clamouring to talk about it, but I looked it up on the internet that evening. Robert would begin, tomorrow, at Amicalola Falls State Park. There was a large lodge there that looked more like the countryside campus of an expensive liberal arts school than a place where hikers might stay. I skimmed the description on the lodge's website and scrolled down, looking for pictures or information about the trail itself.

Instead, I found a picture of a windowless room filled with round tables draped with white tablecloths, labelled *Meetings*, and a picture of a woman in a white dress holding a bouquet, her eyes closed. *Weddings*, read the text below. I stopped scrolling and considered it. It was sunset, in the image, and a man, occupying only a fifth of the frame in which the woman was centred, was kissing her on the cheek. The man looked a little like Robert, neatly dressed and earnest, with floppy brown hair, but the woman looked nothing like me. If I clicked on it, I knew, I could read more, but instead I closed the browser window and went to bed.

3

On Tuesday, everything was the same as it had been on Friday, before Robert had proposed, before Robert had left. I was glad, arriving at the museum, to have no ring; when Anthea asked about my weekend, I could just say that I'd been to Pioneer Works, had dinner in Red Hook, drunk a little too much. I could turn the conversation back toward her, to the film she'd seen at Lincoln Center and the housemates she always ran into at Rite Aid, buying ice-cream and beer, but rarely saw at home, where all their doors stayed shut. I could, without a ring, ask questions rather than answer them.

The galleries and the curatorial offices loosely mirrored one another. I could, through the first layer of glass, look down and across the sculpture garden. Beyond that, reflections of the grey city played like an experimental film on the museum's own glass façade; through those shapes, I could see the staircase leading up to the Marron Atrium.

There was somebody lying on the stairs, amongst the tourists' feet, with a security guard directing the flow of visitors. The figure appeared to be a woman and was upside down, her head below her body, knees bent and one arm outstretched, angled downward, toward the sculpture garden. She looked elegant and broken, as if she had fainted, as if she were not strong enough to withstand the chatter of tourists with their gaudy t-shirts and the dirt they tracked in from outdoors. Her jumpsuit matched the grey of the stairs and her sneakers were the same shade of white as the walls, MoMA white, and probably unscuffed.

There were other bodies in the museum, draped on other staircases and across the Marron Atrium, dressed in identical grey jumpsuits and white shoes. These bodies had been slowly tumbling for a week and were scheduled to continue for another month.

I didn't need to think about marriage at the museum; I needed only to enter measurements and mediums into our electronic cataloguing software. It was the sort of task that strained my fingers but not my mind. I usually thought about Grace Hartigan, about the museum's history, about my silent colleagues and the mysteries of their email inboxes. I didn't need to think about marriage right now, I reminded myself, but I couldn't seem to keep my mind off it.

I didn't want to be somehow caught thinking about marriage, either. It seemed deeply embarrassing. I'd always resisted talking about Robert at work; I didn't want my colleagues to assume that I was straight. It was impossible to avoid mentioning him completely, though; everybody wanted to know why my rent was so cheap.

On Instagram, the bodies multiplied, hashtagged under the performance's title, *PLASTIC*, and the name of the choreographer, Maria Hassabi. It was almost always the bodies that read as women that visitors photographed. In their images, these figures were inverted, prone, crumbling across the atrium, clinging to the floors, the stairs and the two grey sofas. I wondered what it meant to make somebody the subject of another person's photograph. I wondered, too, why we deified the female body that did not show strength, did not meet our gaze, but appeared to fall in slow-motion while we focused our cameras.

Grace Hartigan, impulsive, married her first husband at nineteen. 'I married the first boy that read poetry to me,' she told somebody, later, in an oral history transcript which lay on my desk. She married to escape suburbia, to travel to Alaska, to live a life outside middle-class conservatism. She couldn't have regretted it completely, I thought, as she had married again, three times, and spoke of each marriage flippantly in the interview, yet still I thought of the son, from this first marriage, who Grace had abandoned in order to paint. Grace hadn't thought of him often, or, if she did, she didn't speak or write of it; she thought primarily of art.

Grace's relationship to marriage was puzzling. She hadn't married three of the partners who were most significant to her – Ike Lane Muse, Al Leslie and Walt Silver – though she'd lived with and worked alongside each of them for much longer than the men she had married. She didn't have elaborate weddings, simply signed legal documents at the city clerk's office. Grace's marriages seemed prompted by a desire to leave; with the first, she went to Alaska, while her second marriage facilitated a stipend to live in Mexico. The only time a marriage stuck, she moved to Baltimore for a man she'd known three days, trading the New York art world for financial security.

I didn't envy Grace. I didn't believe that she'd been happy.

I wondered what it would be like to be married to Mark, the Assistant Curator, who had the desk diagonal to mine. His wife ran a popular lifestyle blog, posting pictures of their kitchen and their small child. Mark was on a permanent contract at the museum and seemed more comfortable than the rest of us, cringing at the other departments, turning to tell us stories. I pictured his wife preparing and photographing meals as he built furniture on the weekends; I pictured his child drawing in the kitchen, which I knew from the blog was full of light. I wasn't sure it would be possible, in the art world, for a woman to live like Mark. He was the only person in the department with a child.

Lunch? Anthea emailed.

We had developed a habit of meeting in the cafeteria and eating in the sculpture garden the previous summer, and it was finally warm enough to resume this. I felt more comfortable with Anthea, who worked in Architecture and Design, than I did with the other fellows; she, like me, had grown up elsewhere, was not trained in North American optimism, was still willing to admit her love for New York City.

Jessie, from Prints and Drawings, who joined us sometimes, had grown up on the Upper West Side. She was the youngest of the fellows, twenty-four and near the beginning of her PhD. Jessie was the only child of two Columbia professors and still lived rent-free in their apartment. I had met her for the first time at a drinks reception at the Whitney's new building downtown, where I commented on the Statue of Liberty, visible in the distance, and she just looked at me, obviously unimpressed, before turning to talk to somebody else.

'My girlfriend's parents are taking us on a family trip to Fire Island next weekend,' said Jessie, today, sitting down. 'Might be awkward.'

'Where's Fire Island?' asked Anthea. 'Why is that awkward?'

I wanted to say something to show that I understood. I wanted to forge some sort of bond.

'It's a gay vacation destination,' said Jessie, taking out her lunchbox. 'They're trying to be supportive, but, well, you know . . . it's a weird place to go with your girlfriend's parents.'

'Frank O'Hara died there,' I said.

'I forgot about that,' said Jessie. 'He was hit by a beach buggy, right?'

'Who's Frank O'Hara?' asked Anthea.

I tried to imagine a marriage to Anthea. I pictured the pair of us sitting gloomily in a disorganised kitchen, drinking beer and complaining about power structures, each of us occasionally explaining things to the other, our pessimism multiplying as we talked. I would tell her about painting and poetry, about the history of the museum, and she would tell me about contemporary architecture.

I was intimidated by Jessie, by the apparent ease with which she moved through the world. I couldn't imagine, coming from a farm in Australia, what it must have been like to grow up in the easiest city, at the easiest time in history, to be queer. I wasn't naïve enough to think it totally unfraught, but I still looked at Jessie and wondered what my life would have been if I'd been born six years later, in Manhattan, with social media. I couldn't imagine marrying Jessie, because I thought of that first glance, that evening at the Whitney, and the way she turned away, saying nothing. I knew that Jessie would have all the power.

PLASTIC undercut those first glances, those photographs, that suggested that the female body was weak, that the body could easily be read. The figures looked as if they had fallen, as if they were grasping for something, but the trick was that they were not falling, that they needed nothing. These were dancers holding their bodies in an imitation of collapse. They had absolute control. They were counting beats to unheard time, moving gradually. They embodied the feminine vulnerability that society found seductive and yet, when we looked closely, as they compelled us to, we found they did not embody any of that at all.

I took my thought experiment further, after lunch, imagining what it would be like to be married to one of the senior curators, somebody who had an office with a door that closed and an assistant to forward phone calls. Most of the men were gay, of course, and most of the women were exhausted.

I pictured, anyway, what life might be like with Antoine. I imagined myself staying just out of frame as he took a photograph at the opening of some new museum, glassy and inaccessible to his hundred thousand Instagram followers. It wouldn't work because I'd be bitter, thinking of the curatorial assistant back at the office writing a catalogue essay that would bear Antoine's name, though Antoine would have done little more than strike out three lines and add an opening sentence. The CA would be typing a description of the work she'd done for the acknowledgements, downplaying her contributions, abstracting them so that she wouldn't seem the primary author, to which Antoine would add an adjective. *I am grateful to Sally Boyd, Curatorial Assistant, for her careful work on this catalogue and exhibition.*

I imagined myself married to Doreen, who had the next office over from Antoine. She was more like a grandmother than a lover, though not like my grandmother, who was always covered in mud and outdoors, early, feeding the pigs. I remembered finding Doreen in the elevator one day that winter.

'Thank goodness you're here,' she'd said. 'I've been waiting for you!'

I blinked at her, scrunched my forehead.

'I forgot my ID, so I can't get the doors to open,' she said. 'I've just been riding up and down.'

I imagined a marriage much like an assistantship, spent organising Doreen's life. She had no patience for practicalities. Doreen's mind was filled with history, with the particular walls where particular paintings had been hung in exhibitions held decades before my birth, even when the walls in question were long gone.

Joanna, the most energetic of the curatorial assistants, walked through my field of vision, and I reminded myself I had other things to do, though there was nothing pressing. I didn't have many responsibilities. I was at a slight remove from my colleagues; my position was funded by a large organisation named for a robber baron, rich with mining money, that funded fellowships in cultural institutions. The scheme was supposed to provide early-career art historians with museum experience whilst furthering the museums' access to academic research on their collections and institutional histories. It was fine, really, just to work on turning my dissertation into a book, but I wanted museum experience; I knew that I would need it to get another job. I tried to find work around the department, volunteered to help with exhibitions when the curatorial assistants were frazzled. It was strange to be thinking about marriage when my professional future was uncertain.

I tried, at my desk, to remember what it had felt like when Robert proposed. It felt like rock candy dissolving on the tongue, shards of pink and blue sparking a rush of sugar, a diabetic spike. It felt electric and childish and bad for my health. It felt like a banquet, like the onset of gout. It felt like cake and good wine, like a lot of wine, like giggling, like a ride home in an Uber, a glass of water and a tumble into bed, and like waking up the next morning with a headache.

I flicked through photographs of *PLASTIC* on Instagram as I waited for the subway home that evening. I imagined the ways in which I might compose an image, the points at which I would crop the bodies. It would be almost too easy to take an image that worked, visually, but these women were not mine to photograph, or at least not from the distance that the image would require, which was close enough to feel intimate, close enough to see the delicacy with which the eyes shut, the softness of the lids, to make out eyelashes against cheeks, sense the readiness of limbs. It felt like a transgression to make an image at such close proximity – perhaps this element of transgression was, in fact, what made it intriguing. It would be socially acceptable and yet intrusive.

It wasn't until I was on the subway that I dared to imagine what it would be like to marry Sally. I didn't plan to run through everybody in the department – the preparator, the department manager, the interns, the administrative assistant, the curators and curatorial assistants with whom I didn't work closely. I had to think about Sally, though.

I had been fascinated by Sally, the Curatorial Assistant with whom I worked most closely, when I'd arrived at the museum. I remembered googling *workplace crushes*, feeling comforted to learn that 'everybody' had them. I had painted my nails neatly before work; I had opened incognito browsers to search her name. I envied those who had been there longer than me, who knew Sally better, had cheered her on in the New York Marathon and met one of her sisters.

She was just Sally, now, a favourite colleague rather than a woman around whom I held my breath. She was Sally, infuriatingly bad at delegating, polished yet childlike. I had thought Sally unfriendly, at first, but then learnt that she was shy and perhaps as intimidated by me as I was by her. She ventured jokes cautiously and seemed delighted when I laughed.

'You make a great team,' Antoine had said, once, to Sally and me. I clung to the memory.

I imagined marrying Sally would be like a second childhood; Sally was doll-like, with her neat fringe and large eyes, sack dresses hanging on her small frame. I imagined we would bake cakes together and trade clothing. It was like a fantasy because it *was* a fantasy. I couldn't know what life would be like with Sally, but told myself that some part of it would be envy, overwork, lacking time for one another, miscommunication and inequalities of affection. I couldn't be myself with Sally; I cared too deeply about her opinion. I needed to feel that the stakes were lower, which they always somehow were with men.

I felt on edge, scrolling through pictures of *PLASTIC* on the internet. I was thinking of what I could take from the idea of falling, of cracking, of bending and twisting. There was something voyeuristic about my response to *PLASTIC*, about everybody's response to it. The performers summoned a sort of looking that could challenge the status quo, created a kind of glance that forced me back into myself. It felt taboo, almost pornographic, to look at these images of bodies on the internet, even clad in jumpsuits, and looking at these figures across the sculpture garden and through the glass was like seeing all the pictures on the internet all at once. It was almost too much, which was why I kept them in the corners of my eyes.

I tried to imagine, finally, what it would be like to be married to Robert. I supposed that the only real change would be to my sense of time; I would be forced to think about the future. I would be committed to him in a more permanent way, though we already lived together. Our lives were entangled, but this had happened slowly, and the proposal felt like a jolt, a point at which I had to consider who I was and what I wanted. I thought of Emily, my undergraduate best friend and flatmate in Australia, telling me, a decade earlier, that she would never speak to me again if I got married.

'Why would you think that I'd get married?' I'd asked.

I'd been firmly against marriage, then. In arguments about legalising gay marriage, Emily and I had always insisted that it was an archaic tradition, that reform would lend marriage a legitimacy that it didn't deserve, that we should dissolve marriage completely rather than extend it further.

I wondered if Emily's stance had softened. I hadn't spoken to her in years, now, because neither of us were good at sending emails or arranging Skype dates. It was healthier, anyway, I'd thought, to distance myself from Emily, who'd never loved me as much as I'd loved her, who'd always overshadowed me with her brilliance.

I still cared about Emily's judgements, even if they existed mostly in my mind.

I wondered if I had a stance on marriage. I wondered if it was a question that tied me to Emily, to the symbolic order of our undergraduate years, even as it was supposed to be about Robert, about the present and the future.

Robert would be organised and considerate in our marriage. He would take my dirty clothes to the laundromat each week and collect them, later, clean and folded. He would encourage me to stop working on weekends and to go for walks. He would teach me the names of birds. He would suggest eating out, several times a week, and I would wonder if we needed to be a little more careful about our finances, if we were saving enough. He would reassure me that everything would be fine. I could relax.

I had tumbled into my relationship with Robert. He had decided on me and I had stayed passive, yielding rather than chasing. I wanted more from marriage. I wanted to have chosen it, rather than to have woken up one morning and found myself engaged and hungover, unsure of the precise machinations through which I had entered this state, unable to trace the contours of the conversation. That didn't mean, though, that I hadn't chosen it. I just wanted, like Maria Hassabi's dancers, to slow life down. I wanted to fall into marriage as the dancers fell down the stairs, deliberately and with precision, each step considered.

4

Robert's first email, which I read on the subway, was surprisingly inane; the mountains were steep, he told me, and he had blisters. The only interesting part was a short digression on the concept of trail names. *This idea of being given a new name by those around you when you start hiking goes against the whole idea of the individual in the wilderness, the solitary journey,* he wrote. *You're literally named by the community – you become who they decide you are.* Robert mentioned people called *Jelly* and *Headache*, which made me cringe.

How's it all going in New York? He finished. *What have you been up to?*

I tried to type a response, but couldn't articulate anything. What had I been up to? It had only been four days. I didn't want to write something boring, so I sent a photo I'd taken the day before, showing a tourist asleep on one of the benches that lined the museum's second-floor corridor, arms splayed off the sides, while a child played on a phone attached to a nearby charge point. This was, I thought, how it was all going in New York.

The Museum was focused, at the moment, on a vision of the future in which I wasn't included. The Nouvel Tower, into which the museum would expand, grew slightly taller each time I walked past the construction site. It wouldn't be finished for another few years, but everybody in Curatorial was tense, aware that management saw the new galleries as opportunity to change things that didn't need to change, were intent on making decisions that ignored the ways the Departments preferred to work. We'd been, historically, a set of six separate worlds – Painting and Sculpture, Prints and Drawings, Film, Architecture and Design, Media and Performance Art, Photography – stacked happily atop one another, working alongside one another, creating separate shows using our separate expertise.

The 1960s show, currently being installed, was an experiment in collaboration. The curatorial assistants had to work together and yet were expected, by each of the curators, to ensure that their own department's interests won out. The spaces for the 1960s hang had historically belonged to Painting and Sculpture, and at our last curatorial meeting, Antoine had talked about the dangers of setting a precedent.

'We'll lose autonomy if the departments move around,' he'd said. 'We'll have to compete for space. We'll have to negotiate everything with the whole museum.'

I wasn't really involved in this, but I registered the atmosphere of uncertainty. It felt as if the 1960s show had, in bringing the

Departments together, inflamed dormant disciplinary tensions. Anthea told me that Architecture and Design didn't think Painting and Sculpture were modern at all. They saw our department as retrograde, seeking to maintain the primacy of outdated mediums in a museum dedicated to newer forms. I knew, from arguments with the fellows over lunch, that Photography and Film saw it in this way, too. Prints and Drawings, who seemed to ignore disciplinary boundaries entirely, curating distinctly conceptual shows, appeared dismissive of the entire discussion.

It wasn't something that we talked about as much, really, in Painting and Sculpture, and I suspected that this was because the museum's current hierarchy served us best – the other departments were frustrated because they didn't have our level of support from the administration. I wanted to help Sally with the 1960s show, because she seemed stressed, but when I'd asked Antoine, framing it as an opportunity for me to learn, he'd told me the other departments might be angry if we had too many people in the room.

I spent most of the day in the archives, looking at Frank O'Hara's professional papers. My fellowship involved a research project on an aspect of the museum's history; I'd decided to focus on the role of gender in Frank O'Hara's curatorial practices around Abstract Expressionism, examining his relationships with Grace Hartigan and Joan Mitchell, which tended to be overlooked in favour of his advocacy for Jackson Pollock. It was a luxury to focus on research: it was usually books and articles that secured jobs, not spreadsheets, image permissions and trips to the frame shop. I had time for this, now, because there wouldn't be any more exhibitions opening, other than the 1960s show, until after my contract ended.

I was wondering about the poems in which Frank O'Hara had mentioned various painters. I wanted to connect them to oral histories and exhibition checklists. I'd read an article in which Frank O'Hara's poetry was criticised for being cliquey, deploying references that were only comprehensible to his friends. I was sceptical about the argument, though – Frank O'Hara's work didn't speak to that world so much as summon it, evoke it on the page. The fact that Frank O'Hara didn't explain his references created an intimacy; the poems read as if the reader shared his world and this assumption invited us into it. He referred to paintings and painters of the past, who he hadn't known, as if they were his friends, creating a network that extended beyond the temporal. Frank's poems created a community and allowed readers to transcend the intellectual. We could live within them, I thought.

I wondered if I could use Frank O'Hara as a model for a new form of art history, one that acknowledged love. It wasn't necessary to meet somebody to feel close to them. It was enough, his poems suggested, to connect with their work. I wondered if I would have to throw away all these ideas, later, lest I end up with hagiography.

Emma, who lived in Gowanus, complained about the subway each time that the fellows gathered for dinner. If we met uptown, Jessie could walk home; if we met downtown, I could; if we met in Williamsburg, it was convenient for Anthea. We never met in Gowanus, she'd said, or Red Hook, or Cobble Hill, or Park Slope, or Clinton Hill, or Sunset Park, and by the time she'd finished listing neighbourhoods we'd agreed to go to Gowanus.

Anthea, Jessie and I had caught the subway from midtown together while Emma, who had left early that afternoon for a seminar on post-3/11 photography at the Japan Centre, met us in Gowanus. We crossed the canal on a small wooden bridge with a steel frame painted bright blue; the canal looked beautiful, though it was famously polluted, lined with so much toxic sediment that nobody could check if the rumours of dumped bodies were true. The restaurant, though it was really a bar, was in a brick carriage house a little further along the street. Emma had already found a table, on the back patio, and looked thrilled when we arrived.

'It's finally warm enough to sit outside,' she said.

Emma had invited the fellows from the other museums, too, but most of them had sent excuses. I'd asked Lucy, who lived nearby, if she wanted to join us, but she wanted to focus on work rather than meeting new people.

'My girlfriend's coming,' Jessie said, sitting down. 'She's in Sunset Park. So, you know, you're not the only person in Brooklyn.'

'I'm in Brooklyn, too,' Anthea said. 'Everyone's in Brooklyn.'

Anthea and I went inside to order; I chose a kale caesar salad and copied Anthea's choice of beer. When we went back outside, Jessie's girlfriend had taken my seat. She had short red hair, which appeared natural, and wore a blue collared shirt that looked somewhere between chambray and denim.

'I'm Jem,' she said, as I sat down opposite her. 'You're Australian.'

'I'm Sophia,' I said, unsure of the correct response.

'I have to eat carbs,' said Jem, turning to Jessie. 'If we're going out after this.'

'The burgers are good,' Emma interjected.

'Where are you going after?' I asked.

'Some shitty gay bar,' said Jem.

'You don't know that it's shitty,' said Jessie, to Jem. 'It's a friend's birthday drinks,' Jessie said, to me.

'It's going to be, like, gay men and bachelorette parties,' Jem said. 'I can tell. It's going to be filled with straight girls who go there because they want to dance without being hit on, even though being hit on is the whole point.'

'The point's Tom's birthday,' Jessie said. She looked back at me. 'Jem thinks we need to work harder to be publicly unacceptable.'

I wondered if their bickering indicated intimacy or tension.

'She says that like it's a joke,' said Jem, to the rest of us. 'But it's true. Sometimes it feels like queers are supposed to be, like, a PR campaign rather than real people.'

There was a momentary lull, perhaps because Jem's statements felt like they were directed to a different group, to the set of friends they'd see later in the evening. Emma tapped on her phone and Anthea picked up her jacket, which had slipped off the bench beside her.

I thought of Frank O'Hara, of a poem he'd written, which began *I live above a dyke bar and I'm happy*. I'd gone to visit the building in which he'd lived, on University Place, and found even the small plaque marking O'Hara's presence slightly sad; it made his home a monument, which felt somehow wrong, a little deadening. There was no sign, when I visited, of any dyke bar; there were only students from NYU, the most expensive educational institution in North America, walking past on their way to Union Square.

Jem and Jessie went inside to order. Emma was explaining to Anthea that one of the curators was furious with her because she hadn't been able to persuade Sotheby's to give out the name of a particular collector.

'She hasn't spoken to me in two weeks,' Emma said. 'I don't even bother talking in meetings, now, because she ignores me. It's just awkward for everyone.'

She sighed.

'Anyway,' Emma continued, 'I'm just telling myself that everybody has a bad boss experience and that this is mine. It'll be over soon, which is, like, you know, a good thing and a bad thing. I just want to, like, move to California and be a real photographer or something, quit academia *and* museums.'

'I want to hear about Australia,' Jem said, returning to the table.

'There isn't much to say,' I tried. 'Sydney's got ferries, nice beaches. I'm sure you've heard it all already from the tourist bureau.'

'Soph's very modern,' Emma said, lightly. 'She ignores the past.'

I smiled, but wasn't sure that this was true. I just wasn't really interested in thinking about Australia. I hadn't been interested even when I'd lived there. I'd written my undergraduate thesis, after all, on American art. I'd been relieved, moving to the US, to find Cambridge populated by people who'd attended international schools or universities and who were largely unfazed by national difference. Even the undergraduates I'd taught had often been from overseas.

I'd been more intimidated by the Australians there than by anybody else. Others just asked about Sydney and kangaroos, while Australians assumed common ground, wanted to know me as a person. I'd hated, growing up in a small town, that everybody had known the details of my life, had seen me in relation to that, reduced or explained me through it. Luckily, there hadn't been any other Australians in the art history department at Harvard.

'That's such a problem with modernism, though,' said Anthea. 'The myth of the abrupt break. Like all these European architects took things from other cultures and pretended they were innovations. And talked about the colonies as this *tabula rasa*, just ignoring everything that was there before.'

I nodded vaguely, wondering if it was strange that I devoted so little attention to my past. There was so much happening in New York, though, and life had seemed to start anew, really, each time I'd moved. I'd never really known how to manage distance and had lost touch with most of my friends from Sydney. I double-tapped their Instagram pictures, but didn't know the intricacies of their lives, often failed to think of them on their birthdays. Grace Hartigan, in the 1950s, hadn't talked to Frank O'Hara about New Jersey, I reminded myself. It wasn't so strange.

'Have you met Nell, in Publications?' Jessie asked. 'She's from Australia, too.'

'Do you know what sort of visa she's on?' I asked.

'No,' she said. 'She must have dual citizenship or something.'

'There's that Iraq war visa, right?' said Anthea. 'It's easier to hire an Australian than, like, somebody from Europe.'

It was infuriating and comforting, this deal. I hadn't met many Australians in New York, but they all seemed furious that their lives were made possible by a war that they, personally, had opposed. The agreement had been George W. Bush's way of thanking John Howard's government for their support.

'Maybe,' I said. 'The visa fee's waived, but they still can't pay us less than US citizens. It doesn't help that much.'

'You'll just have to marry an American,' Jem said, smiling.

Anthea expected to go back to the UK, or at least Europe, after the fellowship finished. As far as I knew, she'd never planned to stay long-term. She wanted to have lived in New York rather than to live in New York, maybe, or perhaps she just missed her dog.

The light had faded as we ate. The sky was beautiful at sunset, a pale lavender that balanced the yellow fairy lights strung above the patio. The white trellis caught the shadows of the green plants that climbed it. It wasn't warm enough, yet, to worry about mosquitoes and other bugs. There was a DJ playing inside and the music casually floated out. I felt as if I were on holiday, though it was just a Friday night.

'Ugh, we really should go to this party,' Jem said.

'I hope it's not too bad,' said Anthea.

'It won't be,' Jessie said. 'Jem's just complaining.'

In Sydney, too, the gay bars had been dominated by men, but I missed the queer club nights I'd visited with Emily. I missed smearing glitter on my eyebrows and lending eyeliner to the men that I knew; I missed feeling as if there were infinite ways to exist, that people weren't instantly readable, were more interested in dissolving categories than in explaining anything. I missed feeling like there was a place for me in the world, though I knew I'd never felt like this at all. Instead, I'd worried that I was awkward, a bad dancer, unfamiliar with famous songs. I missed something that I couldn't quite remember, or pinpoint, which I supposed was atmosphere.

'You can come if you want,' Jem said, as if sensing this.

I wanted to take the invitation, but feared that they saw me, or would see me, as one of those straight girls who wanted to dance without being hit on. I thought of another Frank O'Hara poem, 'At the Old Place,' in which the poem's speaker and a friend left a straight bar to go down the street to a gay bar and were delighted to see the same friends they'd been drinking with beforehand, concluding through their presence that everyone was queer.

At Atlantic Avenue, there was a man selling churros, long and crispy, almost the same colour as the painted columns that lined the subway platform. I registered the horizontal lines of the churros, golden brown, alongside the dirty yellow verticals of the columns, but didn't think to take a picture until the train's doors had closed. On the seat opposite me a woman was reading a Lonely Planet guide to Cuba.

'Small change, small change,' chanted a man, walking through the carriage. 'Any small change.'

It was funny, I thought, that at graduate school I'd felt somehow young and brilliant, brimming with potential, as if I could easily do something incredible after my PhD, while at MoMA I felt constantly inadequate. It was hard to know what success looked like, really, when it shifted like this.

When the train rose onto the Manhattan Bridge, offering momentary cell service, I sent Robert a photograph of the Gowanus Canal from the Carroll Street Bridge, the lights of the city twinkling above the dirty waterway, interrupted by a floating orange pipe. I couldn't remember, looking at the picture I'd taken, how the Gowanus Canal smelt. It was a romantic place, I thought.

5

Robert emailed every few days, but we didn't speak on the telephone. I became more alert to the sounds of the street than to those inside our apartment. I grew used to relative silence. Our apartment became my apartment; I draped my coat on the couch, left dishes in the sink, dropped books on the floor beside the bed and nudged them under the dressing table with my foot. Robert would have hated the mess.

I hesitated, one Saturday at the end of March, when my phone buzzed with a call from a private number.

'Hello, Sophia. It's Barbara,' said Robert's mother.

She had never telephoned me before.

'I'm calling about the wedding,' she said. 'Congratulations.'

I was surprised that Robert had told her. I had presumed this would come later, that we would tell people together.

'Oh,' I said. 'Thank you.'

'I'll come down tomorrow,' said Barbara. 'I'll take you out to lunch to celebrate. We can visit some shops, too, start planning. Since you don't have family to help.'

'Shouldn't we wait until Robert's back?' I asked.

'I don't think so,' she said. 'He won't be back for months. These things book up quickly. Besides, Robert's hiking. He's probably covered in mud. He only took one pair of spare socks – did you know that? Do you want somebody with dirty socks planning your wedding?'

'Um,' I said.

'He'll be grateful nobody's asking him about the colour scheme. You're an art historian. You're interested in colour schemes, aren't you?'

I had to admit that I was interested in colour schemes.

'I'll be there at eleven, Sophia,' said Barbara. 'We'll visit some shops.'

I had never been good with *mothers*, with women who wanted to bond with me over handbags and calorie counts, who assumed intimacy from the beginning and told their children to 'send love to Sophia'. I liked Robert's parents, but I avoided them; their regular Skype sessions and care packages alerted me to the distance of my own family. I had not had much practice being a daughter, being cared for in this way, and I distrusted it. I was intimidated by the degree to which older women always seemed to know their own minds.

Barbara arrived at eleven, precisely, and came upstairs for a cup of coffee. She pulled out a printed list of addresses, most of which were in the West Village or on the Upper East Side. I had tidied the flat after her call, but my eyes kept darting around nervously, afraid some detail would give me away.

I planned to acquiesce, following Barbara from shop to shop, smiling and nodding and saying that I would think about things. I had emailed Robert the night before to ask him to talk to his mother about all of this, about waiting until he was back. It wasn't that I didn't want to plan a wedding. It was, rather, that I had never really thought about planning a wedding, that I hadn't yet come to terms with what I might want. As I locked the door of the apartment, though, I remembered the bridal shop only a few blocks away, with the panes of glass arranged in a black grid, the flower boxes filled with heather and the mannequins gazing angrily out the windows.

'It looks a bit sad,' said Barbara, doubtfully, when I suggested we go inside.

There was a bell that rang as the door opened and a blonde girl seated on a high stool behind a counter looked up at the sound. She wore grey trousers, high-waisted, and a faintly Edwardian top, with an elaborate collar and puffed sleeves. Her hair was short, but long enough to tuck behind her ears, and slightly messy, obviously bleached, with darker roots. There was a brightness to her face. She had puffy cheeks that seemed made for smiling, though she wasn't doing so. I wondered about her shoes and socks, hidden behind the counter; I felt sure they would be charming.

'Hello,' she said, summoning a smile.

'Hi,' I replied.

Barbara nodded. 'We're just browsing,' she said.

'Sure,' said the girl.

She gestured toward the racks, which were almost empty. I pretended to examine the dresses, running my hand over scratchy tulle and stiff appliqué. I had wanted to know about this shop and now, after months wondering, I was behind the façade. It didn't feel at all like I was inside a Grace Hartigan painting.

It was a plain room, with dull cream carpet. I felt my curiosity shifting from the shop to the girl at the centre of it, wondering what it would be like to work in a place like this, so removed from the world outside and yet failing to live up to the distorted glamour I'd attributed to the window. I tried to hide my glances at the girl, still seated at the counter, but when I noticed that she was looking down, pencil in hand, I stepped closer.

'I'm sorry,' I said, when she looked up.

'Don't be,' she said. 'Do you want help?'

The piece of paper before her was covered by lines, by contour drawings of faces and flowers, of hairstyles composed of petals, eyes like leaves, branching off noses that might have been the stems of plants. There were women who seemed to double, the neck of one becoming the forehead of another, and fingers that bent sharply, grasping at empty space, and lips that appeared in the spaces beneath wrists. It was a fragmented forest of people and plants conjured from simple, elegant lines like strings that linked details, bursting suddenly into detailed foliage or measuring clearings on the page.

She followed my eyes.

'I scribble when it's quiet,' she said.

'I really like these,' I replied.

Barbara was silent by the door, ready to leave.

'Thanks,' the girl said. She opened a drawer and took out a small, glossy postcard with a list of names in blue print against a pink background. 'I have some work in a show nearby, if you're interested.'

———

The shops that we visited that day, on the Upper East Side, were nothing like the first one. They had large cream couches with cushions, on which I was expected to recline while shop assistants in high heels and pencil skirts brought drinks and dresses, asked about Robert, cooed. I watched their ankles and waited to see if they ever tripped. I let Barbara do most of the talking.

I didn't like the artifice of these shops, where interest in the lives of others seemed a performance for the sake of sales, with love packaged in service of commerce. The costumes and rituals operated as indicators of status and wealth, of conformity and social acceptance. In these stores, marriage appeared to be a ritual sacrificing of women to patriarchy and capitalism; the shop assistants were like classical priestesses encouraging each bride to step forward to appease an angry god who might otherwise claim one of them. I hoped that there was a way to be married that could call these traditions into question, that could reject the tight link with capitalism.

There were, nonetheless, many things that I liked about the Upper East Side. I liked the quiet museums, filled with gilded birdcages and ornate chests of drawers, and I liked the women in fur coats waiting at the crosswalks. I liked the stale look of the diners and delicatessens that did not bother to update their faded signage. This was one of New York's wealthiest, whitest neighbourhoods and I was usually perturbed by extreme wealth and the militant sameness it summoned, but money on the Upper East Side at least registered as feminine; wealth and power took the form of women who wore comfortable shoes and allowed their hair to turn grey, who met other women for coffee and Linzer torte at Café Sabarsky. There may have been men involved with this wealth, but the only men that I saw were doormen, hailing taxis for women who didn't need to stay young. I couldn't idealise the dynamics of race and class in this neighbourhood, but I liked that husbands were irrelevant.

I hadn't thought about marriage before because it hadn't seemed pertinent. *It's for straight people*, I'd thought, but now I wondered what actually distinguished me from a straight person, what would distinguish my wedding from their weddings. I thought of the video I'd seen on Facebook a month earlier, uploaded by some undergraduate acquaintance, showing a group of guests playfully blowing on whistles to drown out a celebrant saying *the union of a man and a woman to the exclusion of all others*, compulsory in Australian services. It looked like a party game; it felt like lip service, empty virtue signalling. It was as if those marrying wanted a disclaimer, a means of distancing themselves from the politics of the institution. But if they didn't believe in that institution's values, why were they getting married at all? It was so easy to blow a whistle across one line. Behind the bride and groom were the wedding party, split and attired along traditional gender lines, bridesmaids in rose dresses neatly arranged beside groomsmen in grey suits.

I understood the temptation, and wanted all of this, perhaps, even as I was repelled by the politics of this image. I might have been disgusted, in fact, because I recognised myself in it. I liked the idea of a party, of smiling and laughing, drinking champagne, of a protest as easy as a whistle. I knew I would choose women as bridesmaids; all my closest friends were women. I liked rose and grey and I had a weakness, though I cringed at it, for white dresses.

—

'How did he propose?' asked the shop assistants, brandishing tape measures.

'Oh,' I said. 'I guess it was spontaneous.'

'Romantic!' they cooed.

As Barbara discussed various cuts and shapes for dresses with these young women, I wondered about the word *proposed*. It was such a strange habit, omitting the actual event that had been suggested. It was always marriage that had been proposed, rather than moving to Canada, walking to the bodega at midnight, making a suicide pact.

'When is he going to get you a ring?' somebody asked, lifting my arm, measuring my chest.

I was impressed by the flawless mimicry of excitement, knew that all these questions had to be routine for these assistants, asked dozens of times each day. I wondered if the boutiques were staffed by all the actresses in New York that struggled to find paying roles on stage. They performed their duties flawlessly, as if choreographed, and each store seemed to hold the same characters as the last.

I hadn't expected, when I was younger, to marry a man. I hadn't expected to marry at all.

I had left Australia after years trying to avoid the question of sexuality. I had been frightened of my own desires, of my relationship with Emily, who never seemed to fall in love with anybody. She felt too little, was unaffected by her adventures, while I felt too much and had no adventures at all. Emily was confident and beautiful, a Californian with dual citizenship who had elected to study in Australia for lower fees. At nineteen, with sharp cheekbones and Hollywood accent, she was a darling of the queer scene.

I had lived vicariously through Emily, listening to her stories and staying silent as other girls in the art history department muttered about her 'being bisexual for the attention'. I didn't want any attention. I was afraid of seeming predatory and Emily wasn't afraid of anything. She wanted to have fun. We had sex, often, and I fell asleep in her bed, too, which might have meant something if it had been somebody else, but I knew that Emily wasn't into monogamy and probably wasn't into me at all. It seemed, in public and often in private, that we were just friends. I wondered what it was that I wanted, given Emily was always sleeping with all her friends, and I didn't know if I could be brave enough to pursue anybody else.

I had expected, when I moved to Massachusetts, to date only women. I had planned to go to parties, to join queer social clubs, to meet lots of people; I had imagined confidence might accompany anonymity in a new city. I had met Robert, though, two weeks after I'd arrived, eager to make friends, and we'd talked for hours about the politics of monarchy, drinking beer, and then he'd kissed me and I'd liked it. We'd kept seeing one another and I'd liked that, too, and I'd thought that dating women could wait, perhaps, until this ended, until my lust for this particular man faded, but I found that it didn't end or fade, that I fell in love with him instead.

If I felt discomfort, it wasn't because my friends in Australia couldn't get married. It was that a different version of myself, the self I'd expected to manifest by the time I turned thirty, still wasn't permitted. I wanted to be braver, to live that other life, without giving everything else up.

I left Barbara at Grand Central and caught the subway back downtown. I didn't feel like going straight home, though, so I alighted at Grand Street and walked south, toward the water, instead of east. I had the postcard that the girl from the bridal shop had given me, advertising a group show, in my hand. I found the gallery in a basement on Monroe Street, marked by a whiteboard above the door on which somebody had written the name in uneven letters.

'What could a girl like that possibly know about weddings?' Barbara had muttered as we left the shop that morning. 'She's just a kid. Her makeup was smudged. And did you see her shoes?'

Barbara's words weren't unfounded. The girl hadn't looked at all like the girls I'd imagined in bridal boutiques, like the polished women we'd met that afternoon. She didn't look as if she wore much makeup, but her eyeliner had been smudged in a way that suggested she'd woken up with it on, that she'd spent the morning crying or that she hadn't learnt to apply it properly but wanted to try anyway, like an impatient child. I'd liked her sense of style, even as I knew that sleeves and a collar like that would look faintly ridiculous on me, on most people.

It was clear, though, looking at the walls of this gallery, that the girl knew rather a lot about weddings. She hadn't told me her name, but I recognised her work immediately because it included photographs of the fabrics I had been fingering that morning, overlaid with line drawings of Catholic saints in black ink on translucent paper. There was a short text explaining the work, describing it as a *meditation on the veil as screen in the age of Instagram*. I liked the work but cringed at the wall label; art students never knew how to write them. Her work was more Jean Cocteau than Amalia Ulman, too sensual and delicate for this kind of theory. *Cara Weathers*, I read on the label, repeating her name to myself.

6

It was nice, in spring, that tears could be hidden behind sunglasses. Anthea was away on a research trip and I stopped buying lunch at the cafeteria, instead walking along Fifth Avenue to the park and taking photographs of cherry blossoms.

I was exhausted by my own invisibility at the museum, by the curators who did not bother to greet me when they walked by my desk on their way to the photocopier. Sometimes, people in other departments forgot to include me on meeting invitations or invited me purely so that I could hold a ruler or take notes. I was tired of walking into the bathroom and waving my hands around, asking to be noticed by the electronic sensor that turned on the lights. I knew, from speaking to the other fellows, that I was not the only person worn down by the museum's hierarchy and silence, by the small, cumulative unkindnesses. There was never a single, reasonable cause for it, so I felt as if I were breaking apart, as if I no longer wished to work in a museum at all, as if to remain would cause me to disintegrate gradually and absolutely. I told myself that the tears were caused by precarity, by my own place in the system. If I were granted a four-year contract, I would remember this sadness only as a rite of passage, something like a hazing ritual.

I was supposed, in Robert's absence, to be certain of all his feelings. Lucy and Anthea laughed when I began my responses to their questions with *I think*.

'You *think* he's liking it? Don't you hear from him?'

'Yes,' I'd say. 'He's sent some emails.'

I wondered how much I could know from an email, if it were really Robert pouring himself onto the page or if he were writing, instead, to follow the conventions of a letter home or a trail diary, to entertain or report. Robert was tired when he wrote and he was writing not just to me, his partner, but also to somebody outside his everyday life, who was not there. Robert was writing to a sceptic who had to be sold on the idea of walking from Georgia to Maine. He was writing to a woman who loved torrid, acid colours invented in laboratories and slathered on primed canvases, who loved industrial surfaces, smooth and processed, textures that couldn't or shouldn't be found in nature. Robert was writing in relation to our differences, and in relation to a tradition of viewing nature with which I was only partially conversant. So, I said: *I think*.

I couldn't know Robert's experiences through his emails. There was a gap that I couldn't close, a degree to which he remained, despite our intimacy, inscrutable. I wondered if it was really possible to know another person. I trusted Robert much more than I knew him; I believed the things that he said, but never verified them.

I tried to remember what it was like to lie in bed beside Robert, but the first moments I recalled were weighted pauses after I asked about his thoughts, before he answered with something that never seemed large enough to fill those silences.

'Nothing,' he would say, often.

I didn't know if Robert was as much a mystery to himself as he was to me. I had known him for years, now, but I wasn't sure what drove him, exactly; I found his life hard to understand. His Ivy League degree, coming from a family where almost everybody had one, meant much less than mine. It seemed as if Robert had learnt everything I learnt at university by the time he was ten, so his education didn't particularly impress me. I imagined going on holidays, as he had, with parents arguing about the attribution of paintings in Scottish castles. I could imagine the holidays, though I'd never been to Scotland, but I couldn't imagine how those holidays might have forged me. I remembered, instead, leaving my family on the beach and walking to local galleries to see whatever happened to be there. I knew precisely which exhibitions had shaped the direction of my life, had led me to study art history, because these had been the only exhibitions I'd seen as a teenager. They were rare and felt almost divine. I remembered these exhibitions like the sudden downpours that filled our water tanks during the drought, as both promise and release.

Hey Soph, Robert wrote. *Arrived at Fontana! Everyone calls this shelter the Hilton, and it's even got a shower. Packed, though, because the weather's been bad and everyone's holding off on going into the Smokies.*

Love, Robert.

P.S. Sorry about Mom. Will talk to her.

I clicked reply, planning to write back immediately, but instead opened up a private browser window and searched for *Cara Weathers*. She had a website, but it was sparse. I found her name on a university website and on some lists of artists participating in group shows at unfamiliar galleries in Brooklyn. I found one photograph, in a blog post reporting on an opening at a Bushwick art space, of Cara with her arm around another girl, slightly taller, who had brown hair pulled back into a tight bun, wearing a floral jumpsuit in shades of yellow that complemented her skin. Cara was wearing a black dress with a white lace collar and holding a red solo cup, smiling.

It was her Instagram account that gave me the material that I wanted. She posted images of sketches and the framed photographs I'd seen in the show, but she also posted images of everyday life. I didn't know if I was looking at the photographs because I was interested in her work or in her life. I didn't know if the images were work or life.

She had an eye for composition and an ease with displaying her own body that I imagined came from her youth, from growing up online. She had uploaded a picture of a blood orange, halved and flecked with juice and peeling pith, against a pink bedspread, looking almost pornographic, albeit in a clichéd way. She had uploaded a photograph of herself, in white underpants and a not-quite-opaque cotton singlet, reading a NYRB reprint entitled *The Murderess*.

She could get away with these images, I thought, because she was beautiful and her femininity was conventional; she was blonde and pale-skinned. She was able to celebrate her own vulnerability because she was powerful in an unassuming way. I wondered if her work was, beneath the attractive surface, a little dull, unexceptional. I wondered if I was objectifying Cara, if the work was calculated to create this sort of objectification, if my critique was, in fact, the point of the exercise. I didn't know if that was enough to make the work good.

I didn't know if her Instagram account was part of her artistic practice or just a casual means of communicating what was happening in her world. I was drawn in by it, though, and that had to mean something.

Hey, I replied to Robert, later. *That's exciting! I've just been working, really. Why do they call New York a concrete jungle and not a concrete forest? Do you know?*

I kept slowing and then quickening my pace outside the store each time I walked to the subway, considering going inside and then changing my mind. I supposed I wanted a friend in Cara, but the almost-nausea of my nerves was unfamiliar. I didn't remember it from the first days of my friendships with Lucy and Anthea. I was bewildered by the physicality of this state, of the way in which my desire to speak to Cara and my fear of approaching the shop registered in my wrists as a strange, slight pressure, a fizzing, almost stinging.

Forests are European and they're exoticising the city, replied Robert. *But I expect you know that and it wasn't a real question. Anyway, I don't think either phrase is apt.*

I wanted to tell Cara that I'd liked her work, but I couldn't return to the bridal shop to tell her this. I wanted to speak casually and that didn't seem possible in such a space, heavy with dust and lace, laden with expectations and assumptions. I tried not to look in the window as I scurried past and I sometimes went out of my way to avoid the shop, afraid of seeming overeager, too interested. At other times, I went out of my way to walk past it, hoping for some chance encounter.

I was nervous and glad, then, when I saw Cara locking the door as I walked home from the subway station later that week. She was wearing a heavy dress embroidered with blue and red hearts and Doc Martens in black patent leather. She must have recognised me, because, when she turned on the step, our eyes met and she smiled, tilting her head and narrowing her eyes.

'Hey,' she said.

'Hi,' I said. 'I saw your show. I liked your drawings.'

'Thanks,' she said, tucking the keys into her bag. 'Are you into art?'

'I work at MoMA.'

'That's cool,' she said, and seemed to examine me for a moment. 'Are you up to anything now? Do you want to get a drink?'

I was surprised, slightly taken aback. I had never encountered anybody who seemed so confident in approaching strangers. Coming to know another person was usually an awkward, gradual process. Cara hadn't told me her name and I hadn't told her mine, and yet five minutes later we were sitting in a non-descript bar with pink tiles on the floor, both twirling straws in water glasses, waiting for drinks.

'What's it like working in a bridal shop?' I asked.

'It's great.'

Cara spoke cautiously at first, as if she hadn't used her voice much in months and was not quite sure what it sounded like. But then, as if she hadn't used her voice in months and was amazed to discover that it was still there, she did not stop talking.

'It's perfect for me. It's kind of an empty shop. I'm allowed to draw whenever there aren't customers. And I'm surrounded by wedding dresses, which is – that's how I got the job, actually. I mean, you said . . . you saw my work. I went in to see if I could take some photographs and, well, it was just the owner, Maxine, then, and it turned out she liked the art I was making and we kind of became friends and then she was tired of working every day, so I've been working there for five months, now. Maxine designs a lot of the dresses that we sell.'

Her accent was sweet and sour, slightly Southern. She smelt a little bit like rain.

'Or, well, we don't *sell* many of them. I don't know how she pays me. But she designs them.'

I learnt that Cara was in her last semester of art school. The work I'd seen on Monroe Street was part of her final project. She wanted, afterward, to do something linking veils and ghosts, installing it in an old church somewhere in the countryside.

'It was nice chatting to you,' said Cara when we parted an hour later. 'You should stop by the store sometime. If you feel like it, I mean. Since you live nearby. It's always quiet. It's nice to have visitors.'

Robert hadn't replied to the last picture I'd sent, of long-eyelashed mannequins in a Fifth Avenue window, but I sent him a picture of an enormous crate in an empty gallery the following evening.

It was a strange shape, built to hold an architectural model with odd dimensions; tipped on its side and painted white, it looked like a cartoon iceberg. I was afraid of corresponding badly, of failing to write long, satisfying narratives, of not living up to Thoreau, but I would always be able to communicate with images.

I looked Cara up on Facebook, my cursor hovering over the *Add Friend* button. In her profile picture, her arms hung down beside her as if she were a rag doll or a broken puppet. She looked confident and awkward simultaneously, as she had been in the shop and in the street. It couldn't do any harm, I decided, to add her on Facebook. It wasn't necessarily forward, because she didn't know that I didn't add everybody I met. I clicked.

I was sitting on the floor of the living room, the page open in another tab, when she accepted my invitation of online friendship. I felt a strange rush and then I saw that she had sent me a message, too, and gladness ruffled with worry as I wondered how to reply.

Hey, she wrote.

Hey, I replied.

How's the museum today?

It was such an ordinary conversation and yet I felt so anxious, afraid of typing the wrong words. I clicked between tabs purposelessly, trying to fill seconds as I waited for her responses, though it was all small talk, inconsequential. I didn't know her and nothing she said could change anything in my life, really, but it felt already as if my mood might fluctuate with her response.

My phone rang.

'Soph,' said Robert. 'Hey.'

He was in a small town in North Carolina, borrowing somebody else's pyjamas to wear while he washed his clothes.

'You're done with the Smokies already?'

'The pass is for eight days, so you have to get through quickly. We'll be in North Carolina for a while longer, though. How are you?'

'Bit sad,' I said. 'It's strange being in the flat alone.'

'Have you been eating enough fruit?' he asked. 'It can affect your mood.'

As soon as the conversation finished, I returned to my chat with Cara, worried the interruption had ruined everything.

Sorry, I typed. *Phone rang.*

No prob, Cara replied. *Want to go to an opening on Thurs?*

7

I was still getting used to the spaces of the 1960s show, which I'd barely worked on. The exhibition was across ten galleries, one for each year, carrying visitors through the decade. I'd volunteered to do the gallery checks because I found it meditative to wander through the museum at the beginning of the day. It was an easy task; I just had to look at everything, then email Conservation, Registrar, the Director's Office and Sally if any of the artworks were damaged, or Housekeeping if I found clouds of dust gathered in the corners or scuffs on the walls.

OOF, said the Edward Ruscha painting in 1962.

If I timed my visit correctly, arriving after the AV equipment had been switched on yet before the museum filled with visitors, I could hear the music from Kenneth Anger's *Kustom Kar Kommandos* floating through the empty spaces from the 1965 gallery.

Dream lover, sang The Paris Sisters, against tinkling cymbals and a suite of instruments I couldn't identify, their voices cooing and whispering.

I felt, always, as if I rushed through the first half of the decade, past the E-Type Roadster that held all the tourists' attention, past Oldenberg's *Floor Cone*, which I actually really liked, simply to reach the video. *Kustom Kar Kommandos* was meant as a trailer, intended to arouse desire for an hour-long film that Kenneth Anger never raised enough money to make. I'd been hypnotised by it since the show had opened. I watched, again and again, as the words *Kustom Kar Kommandos* appeared against a bright pink background; the camera panned through a shining car to the opening piano notes, looking up at the glittering steering wheel, and down at the bright seats, their resemblance to red lips or vulvas impossible to deny. I wanted to be in the video, my hips in tight bright-blue jeans at the level of the carburettor. I wanted to gently polish the bonnet of the car with a marabou feather puff in pale pink.

Dream lover, called the video, stretching the words.

I watched the man climb inside the car, his legs bending to fill the screen, his body dappled with different tones of blue, his fingers twisting dials. I wished that I could desire any object as much as the young man in the video wanted this car, tenderly stroking it. I watched his reflection spin in a shiny surface and heard the high voices of the singers give way to the guttural growl of the car's engine. I felt almost as if I was the car, caressed by the motion of the camera, by the chords of the song.

Leaving the flat that morning, I'd found a postcard from Robert. The image was oriented vertically, and showed a waterfall tumbling down rocks. The sky, peeking through trees in the upper fifth of the image, was white like the water, which sprayed against dark-grey rocks framed by moist green leaves. I checked the date, which Robert always neatly inscribed when writing postcards, and saw that he'd sent it almost a month earlier, on his first day.

The highest waterfall east of the Mississippi! wrote Robert. *It's quite cold because of the altitude. Some people I've met are already feeling intimidated. This the hardest part because we know how much is ahead and there's so little behind us.*

I pinned the postcard up in my cubicle, placing the small vertical rectangle to the upper right of the larger horizontal rectangle of my computer monitor. I changed my desktop background to a detail from Florine Stettheimer's *Cathedrals of Art*, setting the pinks of the city against the greens and greys of the forest.

Anthea and I were sitting at a table in the sculpture garden. The willows spread across the space were bright green against the many shades of grey that composed the museum, and droopy and sinuous, countering all the straight lines. Coins glinted in the shallow pools crossed by thin bridges of marble. It wasn't a flexible space at all; it was designed for sculpture, it worked for sculpture, and it was everybody's favourite part of the museum, the area that nobody would dare to change. It worked for other things, too, like outdoor concerts and eating lunch.

Emma joined us, looking cheerful.

'Hope quit,' she said. 'Or I guess she got promoted? But she's leaving! She's going to PS1! This is the best day of my life.'

'Is she still not speaking to you?' Anthea asked.

'Oh, no, she's fine with me again, now. She even smiled at me this morning,' Emma said. 'You know who she's annoyed at now? Archives. She's mad that they're trying to archive the curators' emails. She keeps saying historians shouldn't need to know who she's meeting for lunch.'

I laughed. My own work would have been so different if there was no record of curators' lunches. Frank O'Hara's employment at the Museum of Modern Art would have been perplexing without his social scene for context; he knew all the modern painters because he drank at the Cedar and met gallerists for lunch. Grace's own artistic education had largely been a matter of sex, not lunches, but the principal was the same. 'You don't live a category,' she said, once, about her designation as an Abstract Expressionist. 'You were just hanging out with a lot of interesting people.'

Still, I'd heard the curators in my own department make the same complaints, claiming that you never knew who'd be looking at the emails, that it was an invasion of privacy. I never felt more like an art historian than when I hoped the archivists won the argument.

That afternoon, I gave a lecture for a university group, guiding them between Claude Monet's *Water Lilies* and Henri Matisse's *Swimming Pool*, both on the fifth floor, before taking them down to the Jackson Pollock show on the second floor. I explained that these artworks, even the paintings, operated as environments that the audience could enter, and so could be seen as forerunners of contemporary installation. I loved the Matisse room, which was composed of blue cardboard cut into shapes and pinned onto and around a thick frieze of cream cardboard atop raw canvas, as if figures were splashing around the room, and I wished that I could follow it with something more sensuous than Pollock. I'd led the session so many times that it now felt rote, but it meant that, technically, I'd been a guest lecturer at almost every university in New York – I kept a tidy list for future reference.

When I returned to my desk, Sally was perched on it, flicking through a magazine that had just arrived; I had to sort through the department's subscriptions and keep the shelf in the Study Centre current.

'It's going to be quiet for both of us, now,' she said. 'It's almost summer, so Antoine's going to be travelling, soon, and they won't want us to work on anything major since we're both leaving in fall.'

The curatorial assistants, too, were on fixed-term contracts. The rule was that after four years they had to secure a more senior position or leave. It was a system based on academia, on the idea of assistance as apprenticeship, of staying in place as tantamount to failure.

She held up the magazine.

'I'm reading everything,' she said. 'These journals are way too expensive.'

'I'm a bit scared about what comes next,' I said.

'Same,' said Sally. 'But it'll be fine. We'll always have MoMA on our resumes.'

She spoke as if we were on the same level, but she was a curatorial assistant and an American citizen. I was just a fellow, a foreigner, with a visa that was contingent on my job. If I tried to get a marriage visa through Robert, I wouldn't be allowed to work for six months. I wondered if HR knew this.

I wanted to apply for Sally's job when she left, but neither of us knew if it was going to be advertised. The department had just hired another Curatorial Assistant, Sam, several months earlier, plus the possibility of closing before the expansion made everything uncertain.

Sally wandered back to her own desk with the magazine, and I opened up my CV, adding the afternoon's institution to the set of names listed under the heading *Teaching Experience* and the subheading *Gallery Education*. I looked over the document, casually, as I often did, trying to see my life as a narrative rather than as fragments, trying to picture a logical progression. On the page, it looked so tidy and inevitable, so easy and organised, but each chapter of my life had felt like a surprise, utterly separate from that which preceded it.

I'd taken to trying on positions in my mind, imagining different lives, but I never got much further than imagining applications and interviews. The interns had visited Google Art Project and were given white t-shirts with *Google* printed in coloured sans-serifs across the chest. One morning soon after, Alana spilt her coffee, so she had to take the shirt out of the plastic packaging, slip it on and walk around the office as an embarrassed advertisement. I'd wondered if Google were hiring.

I scanned the job postings on the New York Foundation for the Arts website, pictured myself explaining that I could work in Marketing at Dia Beacon because my work on female modernists meant I understood and could respond to the misogynistic biases in Dia's history, pre-empting external critique.

I imagined these things, but didn't take any action to make them happen, as if ignoring reality might slow it down. I thought of my MoMA ID card, which gave me free entry to all the museums in the city, and of my reader's card for the libraries at Columbia, which I had secured through the museum. It was hard to desire a life that didn't provide this sort of access, even if another life might mean an escape from the postdoctoral decade of one- or two-year fellowships, endless applications and rejections. But I didn't know what another life might look like or if I'd be qualified for it. The privileges of museum life glowed with a sharp heat, at once reassuring and dangerous in its seductions.

At the end of the day, I had a headache, so I stopped at Walgreen's on the way to the subway. I wanted to google Kenneth Anger when I got home, and use up the basil on the kitchen bench before it began to brown, but I feared I'd order takeout and fall asleep.

ITEM OF THE MONTH, read a large sign floating above a display of Deep Woods Insect Repellent. *Reduce your risk of Zika Virus*, said an A4 printout pasted beside it. I took a photograph and emailed it to Robert and wondered, turning back onto Sixth Avenue, if there were any trees in midtown that weren't privately owned.

8

I met Cara at the shop just before closing time. She didn't look particularly happy to see me. She seemed to frown slightly as I opened the door.

'Want to get a beer before we head over?' she said.

We went to a bar around the corner. Our drinks arrived and Cara frowned again.

'Do you really want to go to this opening?' she asked. 'I actually don't. Is it okay if we just stay here?'

I'd looked up the opening that Cara had mentioned earlier. It was at a small photography gallery in Chelsea, on the sixth floor of a building stacked with galleries on a street lined with galleries. She'd told me this gallery represented a lot of younger artists, including some people she knew, and that she liked to keep an eye on them 'for the future'. I knew the way that openings worked; we'd go to one and then another, strolling from place to place for a few hours. I'd checked the listings to see if there was anything in particular that I wanted to see, but nothing had stood out. The more exciting shows – Cindy Sherman's latest photographs at

Metro Pictures; Carmen Herrera's bright, flat paintings in Lisson Gallery's new space; and Felix Gonzalez-Torres, always a favourite, at Andrea Rosen – wouldn't open until the first week of May.

'It's fine,' I said. 'I don't mind at all. I see enough art at the museum.'

I was tired of art openings, which were always work events and felt like tests to me. They were for networking, which basically meant being dressed expensively enough to imply success and being greeted by enough older people that younger people started to wonder who you were.

'I'm sorry,' she said. 'I just can't be bothered dealing with people today.'

I didn't know what to say. Cara didn't seem as if she wanted company at all, and yet she had suggested that we order drinks; she hadn't said that she wanted to go home. I felt small talk would infringe upon Cara's exhaustion, but I did not know her well enough to ask about her mood or sit comfortably in silence. I wondered if I should ask about rescheduling, but feared if I did so I'd never see her again.

'How did you come to be interested in weddings?' I asked, instead, and then flinched, realising that I sounded as if I were interviewing her.

'I don't know,' she said, sounding bored. 'I mean, lots of reasons. They're like huge installations with a performance element. I think they're the closest that a lot of people get to making art.'

'Do you ever think about their history when it comes to women? Isn't it kind of awful?'

'Maybe,' she said. 'Everything's bad if you analyse it. But I do think love can transcend all that. I'm so bored by *the darkness of patriarchy*, and all that. I just want beauty.'

Cara did not sound happy about this.

'Do you want to get married?' I asked, awkwardly, though Cara seemed much too young to be considering the question.

'Someday,' she said. 'Yeah. Once I meet the right girl.'

She leaned back, as if her mind was elsewhere. I wondered if I was boring her. I felt sure I was asking more interesting questions than the last time we'd met, when I'd been nervous and ill-prepared, caught off-guard by her company. I wondered if Cara was a little more awkward than I'd initially realised, more like me than I'd imagined, which was comforting. I took another sip of my drink and held it on my tongue before swallowing, let it fill the front of my mouth.

'Can I be honest?' she asked, suddenly.

'Yes,' I said, startled.

'I got some bad news last week and I'm a bit distracted,' she said. 'I almost cancelled, but . . . I wanted to see you.'

I felt surprised and comfortable. She'd wanted to see me.

She barely knew me, but she'd wanted to see me.

'I'm sorry,' she said.

'I'm an awkward person anyway,' I said. 'You don't need to apologise.'

'I can be awkward, too,' she said. 'I find socialising pretty easy, though. Maybe it's because my job involves standing around in a shop all day.'

Cara told me that she was not herself, which I found intriguing as it suggested that Cara had a self, fixed and identifiable, unknown to me.

'One part of me wants to just go home and another part of me wants to stay out,' she said, leaning across the table. 'I'd invite you back to my place, but I live in Ridgewood.'

'You can come to mine, if you'd like.'

'I think I just want to go home,' she said.

I hadn't had dinner, but I didn't feel like eating. It was raining lightly as I walked home, but I didn't especially mind. I kept thinking about Cara's large eyes, her lovely way of leaning in toward the table, the softness when she'd kissed my cheek before disappearing into the subway. She had seemed so small against the darkness, her frame slender to the point of being absent, ungraspable. My feelings about Cara had begun in my head, with my curiosity about the store and appreciation of her work, but were migrating downward, filling my stomach. The drops of rain felt warm as they fell upon my cheeks and hands, nestled amongst my hair.

I looked up Cara's Instagram again that night, scrolling back further and finding fewer images of her bedroom and more images of parties. The crumbled sheets and dried flowers in speckled daylight gave way to dancing bodies against red and green lights, steam rising from manholes in the Meatpacking District, and the occasional image of the same girl I'd seen on the blog, smiling at the lens from a bed in a different room, one that didn't appear in the recent pictures. There were photographs of large paintings of women in pastel tones, with sugared blue limbs and lilac cheeks, and one image, taken in a studio, of the girl in dungarees covered with paint, pointing the paintbrush at the lens teasingly, the bristles in the foreground heavy with a saltwater-taffy green. I clicked on an image of this girl, in tapered trousers, white shirt and bow tie, against the bright shelves of a bodega. The caption read: *she shines at the grocer's store at Sevenoaks.* I didn't know what this meant.

I supposed that this girl was, or had been, Cara's girlfriend. She hadn't appeared in any images for over a month. She wasn't tagged in anything, which probably meant she didn't have Instagram herself. I tried to remember her name from the photograph I'd seen on the blog; it felt as if looking it up to find out would be crossing some sort of boundary. I wanted to see more of her paintings, which I liked, but decided to wait until I knew Cara better.

I couldn't concentrate on my work that week. I kept wondering how to start another conversation with Cara, imagining dropping into the shop, trying to think of events to which I could invite her without coming across as too intense, too eager. I kept wondering if I would hear from her, when I would hear from her, what a lack of messages for three days meant in 2016, what she would think if I sent a message, how I might phrase it, telling myself that the syntax of my sentences wouldn't change anything and then telling myself, five minutes later, that the syntax of my sentences could change everything. I kept going back to our earlier conversation on Facebook messenger, reading over my last messages and wondering if I'd been too eager or not eager enough. Should I have used an emoji? I was filled with too much adrenalin for data entry, though I managed it, somehow, and the days passed.

I checked my email.

Could you please stop sending these photos? Robert had written. *They don't make a lot of sense to me and downloading them uses too much battery out here. I'd like to hear more about what you're doing! Can you tell me what's going on in your life?*

I googled *how to stop thinking about someone.* The articles that appeared were for teenagers with crushes. I tried, anyway, some Cognitive Behaviour Therapy trick that involved saying *STOP* to myself repeatedly. It didn't work.

Try picking up a hobby, suggested the internet. *Try going for a walk.*

There didn't seem to be any advice on what to do at work, when it wasn't possible to go outside or read a novel. I was supposed to be writing object labels, describing paintings, but I felt as if I were working in a foreign language, with some sort of gulf between my mind and the page. It was difficult to concentrate. I hadn't felt like this in years. I had thought about Sally, constantly, when I arrived at the Museum, but I could throw myself into my work, then, because work was proximate to Sally, because finishing a task meant I could email it to her.

I gave into myself after a few days, noting that Cara had told me to drop into the shop. She looked up when I opened the door, smiled. She seemed pleased to see me. She'd been leaning on the counter, examining her sketchbook, and flipped it closed.

'I'm sorry about the other day,' she said. 'It's a strange time for me. My girlfriend broke up with me and I'd just heard . . . well, something. It doesn't matter. I didn't want to go to the opening because she would've been there, probably with somebody else, and all her friends would've been there even if she wasn't.'

'Are you feeling better?' I asked, and she shrugged. 'Had you been together a long time?'

'Since I moved to the city, basically,' she said. 'All through art school. I didn't make any friends because I had her friends, so, and now it's like the city's suddenly emptied, except I can't go anywhere because it isn't empty at all, because she's at every fucking event. If she's not there, some famous curator is talking about how she's the next big thing.'

This explained Cara's friendliness toward me, her eagerness to talk; it emerged from loneliness. I wondered if my own eagerness for a friend, my receptivity to Cara's invitations, my preoccupation with her, was born of the same thing – of Robert's departure, of a loneliness that I hadn't really registered.

I loved midtown in spring. There was a woman who had set up a business on the sidewalk outside Linklaters, arranging two small blue picnic chairs, a folding table and a sign reading *PSYCHIC* beneath the skyscraper that had dropped icicles after January's blizzard. She wore a pink tank top and sat in one of the picnic chairs, legs crossed, leaning back, waiting. I saw balloons tangled on a flagpole; *30*, they said, and *happy birthday*, above a dirty piece of fabric printed with stars and stripes. I wondered if somebody would buy balloons like this for me in August and if they, too, would float away. I saw a group of men in naval uniforms crowding around red letters reading *LOVE*, posing for a photo, and as I waited at the crosswalk a man on a motorcycle tore past, a plastic bag reading *I ♥ NY* dangling from the handlebars. I shared an elevator, at the museum, with film canisters piled on a cart. *LOVE BIRDS*, read the piece of paper taped to the cart. *TWO REELS*. I loved this season for its immediacy, its superficial intimacies, their lack of meaning.

9

I arrived at work to find the sculpture garden closed, with strange boxes placed around the base of each sculpture on display. Isa Genzken's thirty-six-foot-tall rose was wrapped up, as if in bandages, red petals peeping out the top. The museum's main fundraiser, called Party in the Garden, involved transforming the garden from a masterpiece of mid-century design into a non-place, all Styrofoam and plexiglass. I remembered this from last year, but still found it jarring. The party was intended, this year, to honour three rich people I kept forgetting to google.

I commented on my frustration to Mark, who stood staring out the window.

'You're preaching to the choir,' he said.

In the Gund Lobby, the Events Department had draped leaves around the pillars and everything smelt like fresh dirt. It seemed strange that they would hide the garden outside, erecting a roof over it, rolling out a white carpet and placing railings around the trees, only to create an artificial garden indoors.

'Why would anyone ever use white for a floor?' said Anthea, at lunch. 'It gets dirty so fast.'

I understood, with the constant hum of preparation for the party, the desire to leave the city. Robert had sent me a postcard, addressed to the museum, from Tennessee, and I'd pinned it to my cubicle wall, below the postcard of the waterfall. This postcard showed a set of three mountain ridges, layered against one another, in shades of distant blue, framed by the silhouettes of fir trees wreathed with mist in the foreground. *GREAT SMOKY MOUNTAINS* read the words superimposed over the trees, at the base of the image, and then, in smaller letters, *America's Most Visited National Park.*

I googled the Smoky Mountains and found other images like this alongside images of riverbends, caves, black bears beside trees and fields of rhododendron. I learnt that bears liked to nibble at cherry trees. I learnt that the national park's name came from the fog that hung, as in the postcard, looking like plumes of smoke from a distance, and that it rained, often, because the air was humid and somehow subtropical. I learnt that Dolly Parton performed there, in 2009, and wrote a song that was never released through a major label, was available only at Dollywood.

It's possible to escape the crowds if you really try, read a travel article. It was odd, I thought, to advertise the fact of being America's most visited national park. It made the mountains sound crowded, which surely wasn't what most people wanted in nature. It had opened in 1934, though, and all the early pictures I found online celebrated the automobile, with lavish roads instead of fir trees framing vistas.

Robert had written on the postcard, but he'd sent a letter with it, too, because Robert liked to write long letters. He knew that I liked the images on postcards, but he was frustrated by the constraint of their small size. I liked language that was tight, like text on gallery walls, while Robert liked language to relax, stay languid.

I couldn't concentrate on work, with the soundchecks and drilling noises continuing, Mark watching and occasionally yelling out an aggravated comment, and so I took Robert's letter out from my desk drawer.

I wish you were here, he wrote. *That's a cliché, especially with a postcard, but I do mean it. I guess that's what it's like hiking, too. America's beauty, and the scale of that beauty, might be a cliché, but it's still real. There's a sense of place here that's physical rather than intellectual. You know, most of my work's been in the north, and I grew up in the north, and in the south I feel like I'm coming to know what America really is, and a lot of it's pretty dark. I have a real sense of my own privilege here and I do wonder what it means to walk so easily through landscapes that aren't my own. I don't know much of the history and I'd like to know more. We've got a responsibility to learn more, I think. I can't talk about this side of stuff with the other hikers. They're great, but most of our conversations are about mileage and food, the kind of stuff you'd roll your eyes at. I do think you'd be interested, Soph, in these thoughts I'm having about America. I know you like to act as if you're a city girl, that you hated growing up in the countryside, but the mountains aren't exactly the countryside. I've been thinking a lot about the fact that we can't see or know everything, and about that whole enlightenment desire to classify everything, which we've talked about before . . . Being here, walking along this path, hitching to the nearest towns, really shows me how much I'm not seeing (like those mountains on the postcard, all these ridges I just glimpse in the distance), how big America is, and I'm thinking of you in the city. It's the same thing, really, because you can never totally know New York. It would probably take as long or longer to walk down every street in the five boroughs as it does to hike the Appalachian Trail and even then there's all those buildings that you're not stepping inside which have their secrets.*

Robert had written that he didn't know the history of the Smoky Mountains. I turned back to my computer and kept reading. I read that these mountains were part of the Cherokee homeland. I read about the Treaty of Calhoun, in 1819, which pushed the Cherokee from their settlement at Tsiya'hi.

I read about the Indian Removal Act of 1830, about the forced westward migration of thousands of people along the Trail of Tears and the small group that escaped by hiding in these mountains, led by Tsali. I read about the loggers that arrived later in the nineteenth century and about the clearcutting that started to destroy the area. The national park was proposed as a solution. I read about the Works Progress Administration, during the Great Depression, building elegant stone bridges and rustic shelters so visitors could picnic even in the rain.

I read about Horace Kephart, who looked for the least detailed part of his map, convinced that there lay wilderness, and went to the Smokies and stayed until his death, in an automobile accident on a mountain road. Kephart was involved in plotting the route of the Appalachian Trail through the Smoky Mountains and the trail went, now, across the southern slope of Mount Kephart, named for him in another unnecessary flourish.

I kept forgetting that I was at my desk, that I was supposed to be working, that the sculpture garden was being transformed into something bland beyond the window. I was sickened by all of it, kept thinking of the Cherokee trails that long preceded the

Appalachian Trail, kept thinking of all the blood that had been shed in the name of westward expansion, imagined rhododendrons fertilised by loss.

I knew that Massachusetts and New York were haunted, too, but the expanse of the Smokies, the idea of looking up at the stars and thinking of everybody that had looked up at them before, reminded me of how I'd felt as a teenager when we were out in the fields looking for the Southern Cross. Our teachers told us that settlers used the stars to navigate, and never mentioned everybody else, before that, who knew the same stars by different names. It was a type of grief that I found hard to bear, and so I flinched when I was forced to face it, embarrassed at my second-hand sadness and at history's gaping chasms, unsure of how to take responsibility and afraid to commune with ancestors I didn't want to know.

We didn't do much work that week, distracted by the scenes outside the window. Mark, standing near my desk, talked about the many different ways in which museums prioritised money over art. He told me about another museum with a fundraiser entitled One Great Night at which men, and only men, smoked cigars in galleries, using a Louis Comfort Tiffany humidor. He told me about an eighteenth-century drawing, at another museum with another smoking fundraiser, that had caught fire as a trustee showed it to a friend.

———

I knew that Robert wasn't in the Smokies, anymore, but I felt a sort of responsibility to read Wikipedia pages for places that he'd been. I skimmed them, mostly, and wasn't as absorbed as I'd been when reading about the Smokies. Hot Springs, North Carolina, had been home to one of the most famous resorts in the south, with sixteen marble pools alongside croquet and tennis courts; it became an internment camp, in World War I, and subsequently burnt down. Waynesboro, Virginia, was a factory town, surrounded by Civil War battlefields, where Spandex had been invented in 1958. It was interesting, but the buzz outside the windows was a lighter, easier distraction.

I lay on my bed, the night of the party, wondering how it was going. I looked up Party in the Garden on Instagram and discovered a whole class of young people who attended museum fundraisers, paying hundreds of dollars for tickets and hundreds of dollars for clothes to wear and posting pictures on Instagram, gathered under *#foragoodcause*. There was little sign that they actually cared about the cause; they did not look like the type to step inside the museum during opening hours. I looked at their Instagram biographies, trying to figure out their lines of work; I found they often self-described with words like 'writer', posted images labelled *#adjunctlife* or photographs of their NYU graduation ceremonies. I knew that it must be family money, but I found it hard to imagine a world in which people routinely spent hundreds of dollars on party tickets and even harder to imagine a world in which parents or trust funds paid for graduate students or writers. Robert's family were wealthy, but not like this.

I knew that New York was not like Australia. I walked, every morning, along 54th Street, past the Manolo Blahnik store and mysterious spas. I had visited the apartments of trustees; I had patted Agnes Gund's dog under the gaze of a William Wegman photograph, laughed with her butler about the secret service dogs that pushed around Wolfgang Laib's piles of rice before a fund-raiser she'd hosted for Hillary Clinton. I'd been given a set of nine chocolates, which I'd seen priced at sixty dollars at Chelsea Market, as a courtesy gift for attending a Harvard alumnae lunch. I found it hard, in such proximity, to hate the rich. If I'd been born with money, I would have used it in the same way that Agnes Gund did, setting up artists and edible gardens in public schools, inviting MoMA's interns and fellows for lavish afternoon teas. I wasn't so sure about the heiresses who were my own age, though. They seemed to lack awareness.

This was the longest part, I reminded myself. The Appalachian Trail went through fourteen states, but almost all thru-hikers spent over a month in Virginia. Robert would fly back to New York in a couple of weeks for a conference, and then I'd see much more of him when he was hiking in the north and I could take weekend trips.

I was hoping for another postcard. I knew, from his brief emails and his hopeless attempt at an Instagram account, that Robert was almost at Harpers Ferry, West Virginia, which was known as the psychological halfway point for the Appalachian Trail. The technical one came later, in Pennsylvania.

I'd reminded myself, that week, that I needed to engage more with what Robert was doing. I hadn't been paying enough attention to him. I'd used distance as an excuse. Was I resisting the Appalachian Trail because I felt that he'd abandoned me for it? I supposed that I'd feel more connected to Robert when he was close again, that the engagement would feel real when he was back and we were able to talk about it.

I met Lucy, that Friday, on the roof of the Met, open for summer. There was a house there, too, though it was only a house from certain angles. It was Midwest red against the fading blue sky and the neat green hedge and the tops of the trees in the park, bright against the grey and beige skyline. There were steps up to a porch, the entrance surrounded by wooden lace, though all of this was roped off. It was about thirty feet high, I estimated, and it felt relentlessly vertical despite the horizontal slats of wood. I wondered if this was because of the roof's steep incline, the tall, narrow windows. It wasn't a comforting house, but a haunted one, made in the image of the house from Hitchcock's *Psycho*, which was itself born of an Edward Hopper painting that hung near the escalators on the fifth floor at MoMA.

It was a house from where Lucy and I stood. Cornelia Parker had labelled it *Transitional Object*, borrowing the term from psychology. It was a substitute for the parent, a means of detaching, of increasing distance, like a beloved stuffed toy. It would soon be the most Instagrammed house in America.

'I have to tell you something,' I said. 'But please don't get too excited.'

She already looked excited.

'I guess I'm engaged?'

She looked confused, now.

'You *guess* you're engaged? What do you mean?'

'I am engaged, then?'

I looked at the boxes filled with plants at the edge of the roof, as if ashamed to meet Lucy's eyes, and then cautiously back at her.

'Congratulations, firstly,' she said. 'But when did this happen? Are *you* excited?'

'Before Robert left.'

I swallowed the last bit of wine in my glass.

'I am excited,' I said.

'Before he left?'

'You're the first person I've told, actually.'

'The first?'

'Robert told his parents, so they know, but you're the first person that I've told.'

Lucy looked uncertain, still, but smiled. I wasn't sure if it was feigned.

'We should get another drink, then,' she said. 'I'll buy you a glass of champagne.'

She darted away before I could say anything. I wandered to the rooftop's southern edge, past the point where the house was revealed as an elaborate façade supported by a scaffold. I looked back at midtown, framed by the park and the encroaching twilight, and pulled my phone out of my pocket.

It was hard to take a good photograph of New York City. It felt naïve to call it beautiful. There were whole sets of photographs, infinite on Instagram, increasing as one scrolled, that didn't make the skyline seem any more magical than it was. The spire of the Empire State Building, which I couldn't see from here, was always a little grainy in those pictures, zoomed digitally rather than optically. If the image was clear, it looked like a stock photograph, not at all like New York's messy reality. I wondered why it was that we kept wanting sunsets and skylines, anyway. I'd seen enough images taken from the rooftop of the Met, skyscrapers framed by the park and the encroaching twilight, to be bored by them, and yet I always pulled my phone out to take another, feeling my tongue pause against the sandpaper finish of my front teeth and my eyes smart as I focused. The process of taking the photograph reminded me that whatever happiness I found in midtown Manhattan was temporary; it could not be preserved through a picture on my phone.

Nonetheless, I uploaded it to Instagram.

'It's not actually champagne,' said Lucy, returning. 'It's Californian. But it's still sparkling! Congratulations! You've got to tell me about it, now, about how it happened!'

10

In the evenings, I kept thinking of Cara. I found myself unable to read, to watch television; my thoughts wandered. I turned to my work, writing about Grace. Her paintings, with their messy brides and bright colours, seemed to offer a way of thinking about Cara, finding a way into her life. I felt that I was waiting for something, but I didn't know what it was; I was in a state of readiness, anticipating something unknown that might never come. I was preoccupied with past and future but had a limited vision of both. I reread the last message Cara had sent me, touching my phone gingerly in fear that I might accidentally click or type something that revealed this rereading.

We spoke on Facebook messenger, sometimes, and then began to talk on the phone. Cara told me that she didn't like tragic stories. She was tired of hearing them, felt that women were always exchanging their trauma with one another to create intimacy.

'I'm sick of being asked to understand people because they're traumatised,' she said. 'It's dull. I'd rather hear about beautiful things.'

Instead of secrets, I told her about the wattles that turned the Australian countryside golden at the end of winter, of how we'd played audiobooks overnight in the barn to deter foxes from the hens, about trips to the women's baths in Sydney. She told me about the kombucha bar and weekly drum circle in her hometown surrounded by mountains, about watching *Broadway Melody* films as a teenager and dreaming of New York, of the occasional visitors to the bridal shop and her assignments at Pratt.

I didn't know if Cara called me because she wanted to tell me things or because she just wanted to speak to somebody, anybody. I saw Lucy fairly often and had lunch with Anthea almost daily. I could have emailed Robert more often, or scheduled more calls when he had cell phone reception. I had known myself for long enough to know that I wasn't lonely and yet I kept talking to Cara, wandering down to her shop on Saturday mornings, going for drinks with her after work, and it felt necessary.

Cara had been surprised when I'd told her I'd lived on the Lower East Side for eighteen months and hadn't had my aura photographed at Magic Jewelry. I'd always been intimidated but intrigued by things like that. I'd taken photographs of the purple neon PSYCHIC signs hanging in West Village windows yet never dared to step inside. I'd glanced at the tarot reader who sometimes had a booth in street festivals around Cambridge but moved my gaze if she looked up. Even in childhood, I'd been slightly afraid when other children read my palms. I felt the same way about having my aura read, as if I had to do secondary reading first so that I might evaluate things accurately.

'It's fun even if you don't believe in it,' Cara said. 'I did it for Instagram, the first time. The pictures are cute.'

Cara pulled out her phone and scrolled for a minute.

'See,' she said, showing me an image on her own feed, a picture of two photographs, the reflection of the phone's camera glancing off one of them. 'I love the colours.'

Cara was wearing a pale shirt in her photograph. Her bright cheeks and blonde hair, dulled by the dark setting, were framed by clouds of yellow, red and lime green. In the other photograph, the darker face of the girl I'd often seen in Cara's pictures was surrounded by pink, purple and blue.

'Stacey's aura was always like that,' Cara said, sighing slightly. 'So much better than mine. I kept dragging her back, every few months, hoping that my aura would show up like that, but I kept getting yellow and green.'

She pushed her phone back into her pocket.

'I guess she was bisexual, so it's only fair.'

I laughed. I wondered if my aura would look like Stacey's, vivid clouds of blue and pink, sometimes blending together into purple. Cara was right; it was a nicer set of colours than her own.

'Let's go now,' I said.

Cara shook her head.

'I don't really want to go back for a while. It's better to go in the morning, anyway, so the queue isn't too long.'

I was following Cara on Instagram, now, rather than stealing surreptitious glances, and she was following me, too. I mostly uploaded pictures of the museum when it was empty, focusing more on the spaces themselves than specific artworks. I tried to see how many different shades of white I could include in a single image, using shaded corners and patches of sunlight for tonal contrast. I rarely included photographs of myself.

Cara's images were almost all of herself. I still didn't know if her Instagram account was an experiment in self-portraiture or just the way in which those in their early twenties communicated visually. I'd read about the 'Selfie Generation', admired the confidence of their praxis. I felt guilty for looking at Cara, though she was offering herself up to everybody's gaze; I didn't tap the heart symbol.

Cara seemed comfortable with her own body in a way that wasn't surprising, given her beauty, but which still seemed alien to me. It was as if she was insisting that she existed as a physical entity, whereas my own images were cerebral, refusing to admit the messiness of life. I had to remind myself to check Robert's Instagram account, which I'd made him set up before leaving, where he posted images of mountains without filters and grainy, blurred photographs of new friends smiling about the junk food they'd purchased in towns.

It was sweet, I thought, that Robert continued to post on Instagram. It provoked a strange sort of tenderness in me, perhaps due to my suspicion that he posted simply because I'd asked. He only had ten followers and one of them was Poughkeepsie Footwear. I played our Fleet Foxes record, sometimes, as I looked at Robert's pictures, trying to conjure the atmosphere of the Blue Ridge Mountains. I clicked the heart beneath the images to encourage him rather than because I admired their composition. I wished that I was there to take photographs for Robert, to select the details that would best communicate his experiences to those left in cities, like me.

Instagram was something that offered snippets of proximity to my friends' daily lives, but in Robert's pictures, I saw a set of strangers and unfamiliar forests. He didn't appear in the pictures and he left the captions empty, save the occasional *#ATclassof2016*. It was hard, studying these squares, to imagine what it felt like to climb mountains and pitch a tent. I didn't know what Robert and his new friends talked about around campfires at night. I didn't know if they were allowed to light fires in Virginia.

Lucy and I arranged to meet on Saturday outside Magic Jewelry. I arrived early and walked back and forth across Centre Street, until a group of three confidently arranged themselves beside the doorway and I thought I'd better stand there lest the line extend quickly. The store had such a small, unassuming façade, with large amethyst gourds and dusty beads arranged on shelves beneath two small neon signs. There was an A4 printout in a corner of the window advertising AURA PICTURE ANALYSIS $20 and the slim door was crowned with an air-conditioner.

Inside, I sat on the wooden stool, placed my hands on the silver plates to either side of me and stared straight ahead, unsmiling. Grey cords, tangled on the worn blue carpet, led to a large box held together by yellow tape, and the man standing behind this contraption, the camera, took the picture immediately, waving me up and away from the black velvet curtain. I didn't photograph well, usually, and I was afraid that I'd have an odd expression on my face, but when the woman behind the counter laid out the print I found I was barely visible.

In the photograph, I receded into the darkness, overtaken rather than framed by my aura. I loved it. Lucy's picture lay beside mine on the glass counter, above boxes of citrine and jade. She'd worn a cream-coloured blouse that glimmered in the dusky light, edged by a cloud of white light tinged with yellow.

'Would you like an explanation?' asked the woman.

She explained Lucy's aura first. She said that Lucy was exhausted, that that was why her aura was largely colourless. She told her that she wanted to be a leader, and that she was intellectually sharp, but that she lacked balance, that she'd been neglecting other areas of her life. Lucy didn't say much in response, but looked displeased.

The woman turned to my photograph.

'You're ambitious,' she said. 'That's what the red colour represents. There's a lot of colour on the right-hand side, especially. You're working hard and you're going to have a productive month. But you're in your head too much. Make sure to take action.'

I nodded.

'You're uncertain about a romance,' she continued, moving the back of her lidded pen above the image. 'It could be that you've just met somebody and you don't know what will develop, or it could be that you've been with someone for a long time and it's not going where you wanted. It might be on the rocks, but you haven't talked about it. There's a lot of confusion.'

The tiny store was tightly packed and the line was extending down the street. I was glad we'd arrived early. As we left, the people standing in line looked toward our photographs with envy, curiosity.

'You've just met someone?' Lucy said, outside, shifting from neutrality to laughter. 'That was wild. It's hilarious how she just said all that stuff. It was so far off. And you just kept a straight face. Well done. I was so close to losing it.'

'She did say that I might have been with someone for a long time,' I replied.

'You just got engaged,' said Lucy. 'It's hardly on the rocks.'

I wondered if what the woman had said was true. I couldn't admit it, really, but I had felt uncertain about Robert since he'd left. I was sure it was a combination of distance and anxiety around the idea of marriage, that it wasn't about Robert at all. I could project things onto Robert when he wasn't around, and I'd been projecting the wrong things, letting him represent a certain sort of future rather than seeing him as he really was, as a person, in the present. It was meaningless, I knew, but I didn't like that I had to reassure myself of that.

We stopped at a new pencil shop that Lucy had been following on Instagram and she bought some Palomino Blackwings, an eraser and a pencil sharpener with a special technology I didn't understand. I wanted to walk to Gem Spa, then, to get an egg cream in an Anthora cup, because I was feeling a bit nostalgic, because if we were being tourists on the Lower East Side we had to do it properly, but Lucy wanted to sit down somewhere, to lay our pictures out on the table and look at them again, to take a photograph of the pictures together before we went in separate directions.

'Have you started planning the wedding yet?' she asked.

'I went to a few bridal shops with Robert's mother.'

'How was it?'

'Awkward, mostly. Her taste's so different to mine. We went into one store that I suggested, near here, and she didn't even touch the dresses, just stood near the door looking appalled.'

'I can imagine.'

'I made friends with the shop assistant there, though. She's an art student at Pratt,' I said. 'Her name's Cara. She's doing her thesis project on wedding imagery. So maybe that'll help me find a way to get into the whole thing.'

'I'd rather be planning a wedding than applying for jobs,' said Lucy. 'I'd trade any time. This is, like, the first time I've taken Saturday off in ages, and I've still got a journal article to work on tonight.'

'I have to apply for jobs, too,' I reminded her. 'I finish at MoMA in September.'

Our iced coffees arrived and I picked up my aura photograph from the blue table and tucked it into my bag, afraid it might damage easily. Lucy picked her own up and studied it again, more closely than before.

'I look like a ghost in this picture.'

'Cara says every wedding needs a ghost,' I said.

'I'm not wearing white to your wedding,' she replied. 'If you want a ghost, you can just invite one of your exes.'

I laughed, but also wondered how Lucy envisaged my exes. I didn't have any exes that were significant, unless Emily counted, and I'd never talked about her with Lucy. I wondered, sometimes, if I used my attraction to men to bond with straight women and my attraction to women to bond with straight men. It helped, initially, to reduce the threat; nobody feared that I was flirting. Now, though, engaged and talking to Lucy, I felt as if I really were a straight girl, and I hated it.

It didn't make much sense to me that so many art historians appeared to be heterosexual. If queer female desire pivoted on yearning, museums offered the perfect career. They were filled with paintings of naked women. We'd chosen to study them, often starting out as teenagers, spending our formative years developing intimacy with these images, writing essays on the female form or, if we were working on postmodern or contemporary art, the deconstruction of gender. Our voyeurism was obscured, sometimes even to ourselves, by academic language.

I had heard, by now, about Cara's last relationship. I did not want to think that she was still drawn backward into her past by the giddy emotions that she had described. I was not sure why she'd told me about Stacey, if I should take it as an indication that she felt close to me, trusting me with the truth of how hurt she'd been, or if it meant instead that she was preoccupied, taking any excuse to speak of Stacey to an audience.

I lay awake, one night, running through the story that Cara had told me about their meeting. Stacey, a year ahead at Pratt, had been on the committee of a student society and Cara had attended an outdoor event one evening around the start of her first semester, when it was raining, the flash floods of summer coupling with the fall chill. Everybody else had stayed home. Stacey, organising the event, couldn't. They stood there, making small talk under an umbrella, and when it became clear that nobody else was coming, they went into the first bar that didn't ask for ID and tried to dry their clothing with the hand dryer in the bathroom. I wondered what Cara had been wearing. I wondered about Stacey's sense of style.

'That was it, really,' Cara had said. 'I didn't bother making friends. She already had so many and I had her. I didn't need anybody else. I really loved her.'

I didn't ask Cara any questions, but I kept thinking about it. Cara seemed to believe in love's potential to be a universe, wanted to be overwhelmed by it. I had always been cautious, in my relationships, eager to ensure love didn't total me; I kept my emotions at arm's length and made friends who might support me when things crumbled. I forgot that I hadn't always been like this – my caution had come from being hurt when I was younger. It was easy for me to imagine what Cara described, to feel the freshness of pain that had overwritten her memories.

It was easy, too, to imagine the thrill of that meeting, to feel the flush of desire with which it had been coloured. I recognised, in the girl who had gone out into the rain alone while everybody else stayed indoors, the same person who had asked me to have a drink on the strength of a five-minute conversation. She was brave about these things. It was disarming. I imagined that she would have been brave, too, about falling in love, would have done so quickly, stayed vulnerable and open.

I felt a little guilty dwelling upon these things, as if I were transforming Cara's stories into something pornographic. I imagined the wet fabric as almost translucent, clinging. I imagined a tiny student room with only a single bed, a desk, and some drawers, imagined drinking cheap whisky from teacups, laughing at the rain, cautiously wanting one another, identifying these feelings, testing glances, recognising desires as mutual. I imagined hands grasping one another, fingers enmeshed, knees turning inward toward one another.

This fantasy was interrupted by the realisation that I was not picturing New York but Sydney, remembering Emily's bedroom.

11

I tried to organise my thoughts about weddings in exhibition form, thought about artworks that I might include. Grace's *Grand Street Brides* was the centrepiece, of course, and I also thought of *Bride and Owl. It seems ludicrous to me to go through that fuss*, she'd said about weddings, and yet she went to so much trouble for these paintings. She had said, in an interview, that her subjects were loneliness, alienation and anxiety. It seemed, for Grace, these emotions were closest to the surface in a wedding dress. It was the drama, perhaps, that had attracted her to the subject, rather than the institution itself; she was interested in weddings as bull fights and masquerades.

I remembered Marisol's *The Wedding*, made almost a decade later, in 1962. It was a playful sculpture, in which both bride and groom had the artist's face. The two figures were delineated by their outfits, with a triangle of white and gold slipping a hand through the arm of a tuxedoed rectangle.

Marisol had arrived in New York in the late 1950s, moving from Los Angeles via Paris, and dropped her surname along the way.

She'd briefly dated Mike Goldberg, one of Grace's exes, and he had brought her to a dinner, once, on the roof of Grace's Essex Street studio. Marisol later noted that she felt that Grace, along with Elaine de Kooning, had made many things possible for her as an artist. I didn't know Grace's thoughts on Marisol, but I found Marisol attractive, and I liked to imagine a certain frisson between them. Marisol was famously elusive, referred to as 'the Latin Garbo'; I liked to assume this meant she slept with women.

This was gossip, though, not art history. There were so many different ways to represent marriage, a ceremony that sat, awkwardly, between the libidinal and the legal. I couldn't always make sense of my own life through other people's images.

Cara came to the museum. I set aside a ticket for her at the information desk and met her at the bookshop on the second floor in my lunchbreak.

'Last time I was here was for a talk about the rainbow flag,' she said. 'In January.'

'I was at that talk,' I said.

It had been a crowded event; I'd loitered in a corner. The flag had been displayed on the fourth floor, close to the window overlooking the sculpture garden. I'd seen it from my office over the months during which the exhibition, *This Is for Everyone: Design Experiments for the Common Good*, took place. It had been replaced, in February, with a gauzy curtain that regulated light levels for an exhibition on Japanese architecture, and I missed glancing at the rainbow flag as I waited for the lift, thinking of Gilbert Baker and his friends sewing colours together in San Francisco.

Cara and I went to see *Perth Amboy*, a small exhibition of work by Rachel Harrison. The gallery was filled with cardboard boxes, which were forest-like and meditative in the morning, before the museum opened. It was a little harder to navigate at lunchtime, full of visitors.

'The boxes are intended to block the objects on display,' I told Cara. 'So that when you step into the gallery spaces you just see the boxes and some of the pictures on the wall, hinting at what's hidden.'

'I like that,' said Cara. 'It's so suburban. Everything happening behind bland, flimsy shapes.'

'I've never lived in the suburbs,' I said.

'Neither,' said Cara. 'Asheville's not like that.'

The photographs were beautiful. Harrison had gone to Perth Amboy, in New Jersey, where people claimed to see the Virgin Mary in a window of an abandoned house. The house had consequently been opened to the public, and crowds climbed the stairs to the second floor in order to touch the window where the Virgin Mary had appeared. Harrison, outside, took photographs of this practice. In the images, devotion seemed a careful and mysterious practice, in which figures were caught, like windows, between the indoor and the outdoor. The landscape entered the interior through its reflection, layered on curtains and faces and hands pressed against the glass.

'Do you think it was all staged by a real estate developer?' I asked Cara.

'God. No?'

'I mean the Virgin Mary sightings,' I said. 'Not the photos.'

'Still,' said Cara. 'That'd be a weird strategy.'

'Are you religious?' I asked.

'No,' she said. 'But you know . . .'

In these images, religion seemed linked to the desire to escape domesticity. The figures were trying to push through the limits of the home, the walls and windows, reaching out in hope of transcending suburban New Jersey.

We wandered through the cardboard boxes, past the objects, which all dealt with American suburbia, pulling back from the beauty of the photographs, contextualising them in kitsch. There were plastic Dalmatians arranged, on a plinth, looking at a white bag. There was a Barbie-like doll on another plinth, in a wheelchair.

'She's a photographer,' Cara commented, pointing at the toy camera that hung around the doll's neck. The doll was positioned to look at a photograph, hanging on one of the cardboard boxes close to her plinth, of something green.

'I didn't know that Barbie had a friend in a wheelchair,' I said.

'Her name's Becky,' said Cara. 'She can't visit Barbie in the Dream House because her wheelchair is too wide for the door! I can't believe you've never heard about her.'

I laughed at how sad it was and then felt guilty for laughing. I thought of children grappling with the limitations of infrastructure and the way in which this toy introduced reality into their daydreams. I could see why Becky, a photographer, would be interested in Perth Amboy, but I also wondered if she was outside, taking pictures, because she couldn't make it to the top floor to touch the window.

'I love the idea that everyone comes to the city to forget their past,' I said, as we sat in the sculpture garden afterwards. I was still thinking of *Perth Amboy*, of that suburban longing.

Cara scrunched her face in disagreement.

'We don't forget our pasts,' she said. 'We just don't talk about them. But they're there, in every interaction. Like, you romanticise the idea of forgetting the past, but that definitely says something about your past.'

She paused. I was about to speak, I think.

'I'm not interested in knowing what you're trying to forget, Soph,' she said. 'I'm tired of that. Art school's like group therapy, sometimes. I'm not into it. I'd rather talk about, like, actually making art. Or looking at it.'

I laughed.

'I have to get back to work,' I said. 'It's never group therapy here.'

We'd agreed that Cara would spend the afternoon at the museum, that I'd meet her at five thirty and we'd go to her flat. I'd invited myself over, essentially, by telling her that I'd never been to Ridgewood, which was true, and asking her to show me around.

'There's not much to see,' she'd said.

'I can see your work,' I'd said. 'We can call it a studio visit.'

I thought, that afternoon, as I worked, of Cara in the galleries. I wondered which pieces she'd gravitate to. I imagined her looking at Matisse's *Dance (I)*, captivated by the loose circle made by the arms of the five women.

'Can I see your office?' she asked when we met in the lobby at the end of the day.

She was astonished by the view over the sculpture garden and by the silence. Mark was leaving, waiting for the elevator as we alighted, and I smiled at him in acknowledgement, but most people were quietly typing or reading emails at their desks.

'I feel as if I have to whisper,' Cara said.

'You don't,' I assured her, but knew, as I said it, that everybody could hear us.

I showed her my cubicle and the first thing that she noticed was Robert's postcards, still pinned beside my computer.

'Hey, I'm from near there,' said Cara, pointing at the postcard of the Smoky Mountains.

'You're from Appalachia?'

I'd known Cara was from North Carolina, and she'd told me about her summer job at Biltmore, but I'd never thought to connect that to the landscapes that Robert was passing through. She'd said that her hometown was surrounded by mountains, but I hadn't realised that they were these particular mountains.

'Yeah,' she said. 'And it's App-el-at-cha, not Appal-ay-cha. Like, if you wanted to warn somebody that you were throwing some fruit at them, you might say "I'm gonna throw an apple atcha."'

'Appal-at-ya,' I repeated.

'Appal-at-cha,' she corrected.

Cara's apartment was quiet. It was on a residential street in a part of Queens that felt like Brooklyn; I'd lost count of the stops on the L Train from Manhattan. I didn't see Cara's flatmates, though unwashed dishes in the kitchen and occasional shuffling sounds hinted at their presence.

I sat on Cara's bed and leaned against the wall as she took drawings and collages from a chest of drawers pushed close to the window. It was a small room, most of which was filled by the bed, with a small wardrobe by the door.

Cara had taken the idea of a studio visit seriously and kept showing me things. I'd expected that her work would mostly be drawings and photographs of weddings and saints, like the work I'd seen in the show on Monroe Street, but I'd forgotten that she was young and still developing as an artist.

I could see, now, that Cara had gone through different phases. She'd taken photographs of the forest, of animals and birds, and sewn sequins onto the images so that the creatures slipped between the natural world and the world of fashion. She'd designed anachronistic costumes and taken photographs of her friends wearing them in Midtown. She'd done projects with food, with television, with nail polish. Some of these worked well, or at least didn't fall completely flat, and I liked that they showed me more of Cara's past, but nothing had the tender, spectral pull of the first drawings that I'd seen.

Cara's room, though, had the allure of those drawings. It was decorated with dead flowers, dried and crushable. There was a bucket in a corner filled with hollow orange bulbs and tight purple blossoms like knots at the end of stems; a wine bottle on the desk held two roses haunted by dust. I asked if I could charge my phone and as I leaned over from the bed, pushing some flowers aside to find a plug, I felt petals crack and fall.

I felt monstrous amidst these delicate flowers. I felt as if the world were sorted into two categories; everyone and everything was either vulnerable or powerful. I was strung between the two categories: an entry-level employee with the approval of a powerful institution, an immigrant with white skin and a visa. I felt precious and easily crushable. My emotions were muscling forward, threatening something.

I had more power than Cara, who was still a student in a shared apartment, and yet I felt as if everything hinged upon her judgement. Cara's room was messy and organic, layered like a forest with dappled light filtering through lace curtains. I thought of it, on the subway home, as an art installation in which I felt forbidden from touching anything. Later, I found strands of Cara's blonde hair clinging to my skin as I undressed.

I wondered what Robert would think of Cara. I couldn't imagine them interacting. I was never sure what was in Robert's mind; when he told me, it was often much more banal than I had expected. I remembered asking him, earlier that year, what he was thinking as he gazed out the window of the apartment.

'I'm not sure if I should take an umbrella or wear a raincoat,' he'd replied.

I was, sometimes, drawn into Instagram's chains, jumping between hashtags and locations until I found myself unsure of how I'd reached the image I was looking at or the link I'd clicked. Today, I remembered certain points along the route I'd taken – the girls paused as they leapt into the air, the water beneath them still unbroken; the giant inflatable unicorn alongside the giant inflatable swan – but I was embarrassed to find myself on Amazon, looking at a product entitled *Giant Bling Ring Inflatable Pool Float*. On the box, a woman was shown clinging to the enormous ring, buoyant and boring, as if she were happy to drift wherever this ring might take her, whether that was toward a familiar shore or out into the shipping channels. *THIS IS NOT AND SHOULD NOT BE USED AS A LIFESAVING DEVICE*, read a warning at the bottom of the page.

12

Robert was back, temporarily, for a conference. It felt strange and luxurious to have him there, in the apartment, eager to talk to and touch me. On the afternoon that he came home, we closed the blinds but left the windows open. Our neighbours were having a small party, with guitars and out-of-tune voices. They were singing *you've got to hide your love away* as Robert ejaculated and when I returned from washing my hands an oddly cheerful chorus of *only love can break your heart* floated up as the day's last rays of sunlight fell in lines across Robert's body. I looked at his dark eyes, with pupils like boiled sweets, round and glossy, offset by the messy curls that surrounded his face. It felt, when I said Robert's name, as if my mouth was filled with honeysuckle.

I did love him, I thought. I was surprised to find myself noticing this, registering it as an answer to something I'd never realised was a question.

'There's a strawberry moon tonight,' said Robert, opening the blinds. 'I don't think we can see it, though. Oh, maybe.'

He opened the window and leaned out onto the fire escape, reaching back for my hand.

'Look,' he said, guiding my shoulders through the window frame. 'It's called a strawberry moon because it comes at the peak of strawberry season. It happens once in a generation. The last one was in 1967.'

It looked like any other moon, but it was sweeter because of the name, and because Robert was beside me.

I asked, lying in bed, later, when the next strawberry moon would appear.

'2062,' said Robert.

'We'll probably be dead by then.'

'No,' said Robert. 'We'll be about eighty, or just under. That's not so old.'

'Maybe we'll be famous.'

'And we can publish a book about how we were down and out in the East Village, lying on a bed with flannel sheets, last time there was a Strawberry Moon.'

I laughed but felt the beauty of our life acutely. He had job interviews for Ivy League schools; I worked at the Museum of Modern Art. We had a lovely apartment in Manhattan. We had been out to dinner at Lucien, consumed both wine and dessert. This was, to me, a dream; it wasn't *down and out*.

Robert's conference paper looked at Benton MacKaye's early presentations of the Appalachian Trail in relation to Robert Frost's poetry. He practiced it in front of me, telling me that

MacKaye had first published his idea for the trail in the *New York Times*. MacKaye had loathed growing up in the suburbs of Washington D.C. and then, living in Manhattan as an adult, longed to move his wife to the Hudson Valley.

'I want to know more about his wife,' I said when Robert asked if I had questions.

'The suffragette?'

'Yes. It seems interesting, to me, that she didn't want to leave the city.'

Jessie Hardy Stubbs had thrown herself from the Brooklyn Bridge when Benton MacKaye tried to take her upstate. MacKaye told his wife that her mental illness had been brought on by New York, a city in which women were dedicated to their work, against their natures.

'That's more history than literature,' said Robert. 'It's interesting, but . . .'

'Beyond the scope of the paper,' I said, teasing him.

I didn't think, really, that the city was so far removed from the forest. I wondered if, in both places, people were just looking to be overwhelmed, placing themselves somewhere large so they could struggle through it, conquer it and claim ownership, redeem themselves through that success. I knew that Robert would dismiss this as cynical, but he'd always been the romantic while I'd been the cynic, and both ways of seeing were post-industrial. I wondered if the forest and the city were two sides of one coin, waiting to be flipped. This coin, I thought, was modernity.

The next day, I asked Robert if he thought that the internet was like wilderness – a human construct, messy and unending. I'd read something like this on my lunchbreak at work, when I'd googled Jessie Hardy Stubbs and ended up on a book about making tracks through the forest.

'It's a common argument, but no, Soph, I really don't agree,' he said. 'Wilderness is a word that represents something important.'

'Isn't it just a way of making sense of nature?'

'No,' he said. 'It has practical consequences. Like, in Vermont. Near where Robert Frost lived. There are old growth forests that would have been destroyed if they hadn't been categorised as wilderness. Those trees are protected by the word, even if they weren't created by it.'

He paused for a moment, thinking.

'I'm sure that somebody's written about this. Look up the Wilderness Act of 1964.'

I opened up the Notes app on my phone and typed in the phrase for later reference. I was disappointed that my observation had fallen flat. I'd hoped to sound smart, but I sensed that Robert was hurt that something so precious to him could seem meaningless to me. I wondered if he realised that I'd never set foot in one of New England's old growth forests.

'Words do matter, Soph,' he said. 'You can't deconstruct everything.'

I wanted something in which I could believe as Robert believed in, and was comforted by, wilderness. I didn't know anybody who related to modern art in that way; we appreciated it, were obsessed with it, even, but couldn't cast aside our subjectivity.

We'd met too many people who told us that their kids could do it, read too many texts about propaganda to wholly trust our own judgement. We were jaded, too aware of how canons were formed. This self-consciousness, I thought, was key to modernity. I loved Grace, but I couldn't give myself over to her. I couldn't believe that painting might save the world.

The summer interns had arrived; everybody referred to them as 'the interns' rather than as Trevor and Kelly. They were given a desk, to share, near mine. I hated the way in which the intern system was a revolving door; Georgia and Emma had been here, when I arrived, then Tessie and Joseph, Alana and Lou, and now Trevor and Kelly. With each rotation, their individual personalities and my relationships with them seemed less and less important. It felt as if the interns provided novelty and additional labour rather than really integrating into the department, and yet I found the interns, who were rarely too busy for lunch or a conversation, easier to befriend than those on longer contracts. I smiled at Trevor and Kelly, when we were introduced, and wondered if I would miss them when they left, in four months, before realising that I would be leaving then, too.

I wanted to know if the Appalachian Trail was changing Robert. It was so hard to tell. He had always been quiet, processing through silence rather than speech. I wondered if he had been thinking about marriage in literature, while walking, as I'd been thinking about marriage in art. I suspected, though, that he was probably thinking of birds, of nature, of passages from Annie Dillard about strange insects.

There was, just after midnight on the day after Robert left again, a sound like a car backfiring, but louder, a huge bang, and then a colossal chattering of seagulls, flying and squawking and coming closer. I thought of the previous summer, when there had been construction work in the street outside and of the way in which I'd discovered that the city was full of birdsong, suddenly audible when the hammering and whirring stopped. I imagined the birds, lifting from the fire escapes on which they perched, fluttering upward, and I listened to the sigh of FDR Drive, imagining that it was rushing water rather than cars fuming into the wind. I thought of Robert, not yet back on the trail; I imagined him fording streams in gumboots. Hikers didn't wear gumboots, though. Too heavy. Not good for walking. I felt guilty for having said goodbye while only half-conscious, and to have been wrapped up in beige sheets clutching a cellphone, for spending most of the day in bed. I thought I was becoming ill, though I might just have been sad.

13

I didn't realise, at first, that it had been a queer space. *NIGHT-CLUB SHOOTING*, I'd read, and felt a bolt of exhaustion and gloom, queasiness. *49 Dead; 53 Wounded.* I didn't click on headlines like this, fearing the details, and so it wasn't until later, on the train home, when the attention had shifted away from the shooter's identity and toward the victims' lives, that the rainbow flags illustrating the articles struck me. The headline had been updated: *Gunman Attacks Gay Nightclub*.

I realised, then, that it had been people like me, like my friends in Australia, who had been targeted. I opened the article, but I couldn't piece together the sentences. *Crowded*, I read. *Blood.* I couldn't look at the screen long enough to take in all the details. *Flashing red lights.* It felt as if to look at the words, somehow, was to re-enact the attack. *Trapped inside.* I couldn't keep scrolling; it felt too violent.

The fragments kept circling inside my head as I walked home from the subway. Unlocking my front door, with the image of a parking lot bright with the lights of ambulances in my mind, it occurred to me that it wasn't really people like me, like us, at all, and that to presume a kinship based on queerness was to flatten identity. I felt guilt alongside the nausea. I'd premised my initial empathy on the idea that this was my community, which was a weak form of feeling, sentimental and selfish. *Orlando's Latin Hotspot*, I'd read. I'd never even been to Orlando and I wasn't Latinx. I didn't know the names of these people; I couldn't picture the inside of that nightclub or any like it. I just kept picturing blood under strobe lights and trying to blink it away.

I warmed canned soup on the stove. I felt guilty for my laziness in finding queer friends in New York, guilty for passing, so often, as straight, guilty for being disengaged, for running away, for staying silent.

This was the main reason, I supposed, that people didn't want to move to the United States, didn't think the country's possibilities worth testing. Each time another shooting appeared on the newspaper's front page I felt jolted from complacency. I'd felt shaky for weeks, at the beginning of my fellowship, when the museum had organised an obligatory training session in which a former police officer asked us to look around our offices and consider where we might barricade ourselves, which pieces of furniture might have sufficient weight to hold a door. I'd mostly forgotten that fear, now, but the shooting brought it back and the news made me wonder, however briefly, if I'd been wrong to try to commit to this country.

———

I didn't talk about Australia much, though I thought of Australia sometimes. I remembered the flatness of the landscape, the softness of the greens and pinks scorched pastel by the sun. I associated the colours with boredom, with an adolescence spent waiting to be elsewhere, though there was a nostalgic beauty to the tones when I encountered them as saltwater taffy in America. I remembered the chlorinated blue of the Olympic Pool in Wangaratta, a gesture to outsized ambition that was only acceptable when linked with sport. I thought of the landscape in which I'd grown up as a landscape of yearning, a topography that offered space that could be filled with dreams but usually wasn't. I remembered the sheep, slightly orange from the iron-rich dust that lay beneath the grass they ate, and remembered that that place had felt impossible to escape. The rivers, coloured with mud, were stagnant and looked thirsty even before the drought began. There was no sign of the world beyond Australia; the only sign of Sydney, even, was on the highway just out of town, reading *512 kilometres*.

I thought of Sydney, now, as a stopping point on my journey to New York. I'd idealised the city and then, once there, I'd idealised the United States. I'd seen the East Coast as a place where it might be easy to be queer, though I wasn't quite ready for New York when it came time to apply for graduate school and picked Massachusetts instead.

I remembered the years in Sydney, where I'd actually been to queer nights at clubs, remembered drinking vodka from a flask with a person I'd just met, in a bathroom queue, who had driven from New York to Los Angeles, sleeping at campgrounds and cheap hostels.

'America's amazing,' they had yelled into my ear. 'I really want to go back.'

It was odd, I supposed, the ways in which we talked, then, about our desire for other places, looking sideways toward freedoms that we believed were only available somewhere else. I looked back, now, and wondered if those undergraduate nights, that belated adolescence, was the closest thing to freedom that I'd ever experience. It wasn't easy to be queer anywhere. If it had looked easy in America, to me, that was because of my privileges; my problem was a lack of confidence and a small-town fear of gossip, not the constant threat of violence that seethed through the air for so many others. It felt pathetic that I struggled with my own invisibility when so many people were dying from being visible, when the only thing that was extraordinary about today's queer deaths was that they were, for once, on the front page of the *Times*.

We didn't talk about it much at work on Monday. I didn't say anything, because it wasn't my tragedy. I felt grief, but it was a voyeuristic, second-hand grief, and it felt as if to speak would be inappropriate. I supposed that others felt this way, too. We were just sad and silent, and Gilbert Baker's Rainbow Flag was put on display, again, this time in the lobby. Trevor, the intern who sat beside me, was asked if he wanted to come in early on Wednesday morning to witness the flag being raised.

49 dead, I thought. I kept trying not to picture it.

I didn't want a term like bisexual, that trailed a disclaimer, a need for clarification, behind it. But who was asking me to clarify? I rarely said it aloud. I didn't want a term at all; I just wanted to exist in all my dimensions. Sexuality, to me, was something smudging and subtle, almost liquid, and labels hardened things, made them rigid, gave credence to categorisation as an idea.

On my way to work, I'd seen a purple cue card lying on the grey sidewalk with black letters reading *MYTH.* I'd seen a crowd of five people with a ladder in the sculpture garden, staring up at letters spelling *The Kenneth C. Griffin Building*, making some sort of decision. On my lunchbreak, I saw a protest outside Trump Tower, with signs reading *TRUMP WILL NOT DESTROY WORKING CLASS UNITY* and *WE ARE ONE! DUMP TRUMP!* and *Hunan House Restaurant, contemporary Hunan cuisine, West 56th Street.* Walking home, I noticed the usual queue to pose by Robert Indiana's *LOVE* sculpture. I took pictures of all these things, trying to preserve Midtown's small details. I hoped these photographs might tether me, somehow, to my own life.

14

It wasn't all about the wedding, Barbara told me, when she invited me to the Met Breuer. She just wanted to spend some time with me and thought a trip to the museum might be fun. I didn't know if Barbara was taking more of an interest in me because Robert and I were now engaged, or if it was that she worried I might be lonely while he was out of town.

I'd messaged Robert, nervous, as soon as I agreed on the plan.

She'll just want to talk about art, Soph, he replied, the next day. *You'll be fine. She thinks you're an expert. (You are an expert.)*

She doesn't expect you to speak French, he added, five minutes later, which made me wonder if she did.

I waited outside the Met Breuer, idly looking at a stall that sold hot dogs and ice-cream. The stacks of cones were each in an individual paper wrapper printed with the American flag; I was considering the way I might frame a photograph of them when Barbara appeared.

'Oh, Sophia, you could have waited in the foyer,' she said. 'I would have found you.'

I told her I liked watching the people outside. It was more than the people, though; it was the details, like the ice-cream cones, and the monumental properties of Marcel Breuer's building, which was heavy and sculptural, a grey ziggurat that stepped outward toward the sidewalk, hanging over pedestrians rather than tapering away. I liked framing these things through my phone, trying to preserve the moments that kept slipping away.

REAL NEW YORKERS RIDE YELLOW, read a sign atop a cab pulling up beside us, emptying another museumgoer onto the sidewalk.

I hadn't visited the building since it had reopened in March; the Met had taken it on a lease from the Whitney Museum, for whom it had been constructed in the 1960s, and were planning to use it for their modern and contemporary shows. We entered via a small footbridge from Madison Avenue that exacerbated the feeling of the building as a fortress.

Barbara and I caught the elevator up to *Unfinished: Thoughts Left Visible*, the show intended to launch the Met Breuer, a declaration of the institution's approach to modern art. It was an odd declaration, given it began with Renaissance paintings. We looked at Titian's *The Flaying of Marsyas* at the entrance of the show, and I wondered if I would recognise the painting as a masterpiece if I hadn't read it described this way in almost all the reviews.

Inside, the curatorial conceit seemed heavy-handed. The wall text constantly asked visitors to consider whether a work could be seen as 'finished', turning the exhibition into a party game. The object labels for each piece operated as a set of puzzle solutions, explaining the point at which the artist ceased work, resolving the question in a sentence or two. It was didactic and repetitive, without depth and dimension.

'Oh, Sophia,' said Barbara. 'Here's Saint Barbara. My namesake. She was stylishly dressed and spent her time reading and thinking, living in a tower. I never quite managed. I think you're closer to her, really – well-dressed and intelligent.'

I looked at the drawing, by Jan van Eyck, but didn't know what to say. It was incredibly detailed, showing a young woman sitting with a book in front of a gothic tower with intricate stone tracery around the windows; behind her, on either side of the tower, a crowd of people moved across a landscape that receded to the horizon. The skies were filled with stars and, unlike the rest of the drawing, painted in a pale blue. I didn't think I'd ever received a compliment from Barbara before and this one felt uncomfortably intimate.

'It's a beautiful drawing,' I said, uncertainly, and trailed Barbara into the next room.

It was odd to follow pieces like this, seemingly neglected unintentionally, with the modern objects in the second half of the show. In the twentieth century, artists had been actively considering the question of completion and the viewer's role in activating an artwork. The curatorial binary set up by the wall text, which asked simply if something was 'finished' or 'unfinished', reduced these concepts and constrained the modern work.

I was frustrated by something more tedious. It felt childish to be annoyed that most of the mid-century work was by famous white men, given this was almost always the case, but I'd written my dissertation on Grace Hartigan in large part because I'd distrusted the narrative of Abstract Expressionism presented to me as an undergraduate, one in which painting with loose brushstrokes on a large canvas was repeatedly theorised as masculine. It felt essentialist, and just wrong, to say that strength and energy belonged to men, and I hated the idea that the only way to respond, if you were a feminist, was to reject the movement wholesale. I'd been delighted when I found evidence, in Lee Krasner, Joan Mitchell and, finally, Grace Hartigan, that my conviction was correct. This show, though, reinforced the older narrative; there were a couple of Mondrians, one of Robert Rauschenberg's white paintings, a set of Cy Twombly paintings that I adored, a Willem de Kooning and a Jackson Pollock. I hated that most people probably wouldn't see this as misrepresentation.

I resented Frank O'Hara, sometimes, for having written a monograph on Jackson Pollock instead of Grace Hartigan or Joan Mitchell. He wrote poems for them, but he gave Pollock a survey show.

'So,' Barbara said, once we were back outside. 'What did you think?'

I felt nervous. Barbara saw me as an expert, but my thoughts on the exhibition weren't particularly sophisticated. I thought, mostly, that the show was too big, but I wanted to impress Barbara and worried that that response might suggest I had a short attention span.

'I'm not quite sure it worked,' I said. 'It felt like the museum was asking one question for a whole crowd of different works that had more to say about many other things, really. There were some impressive loans, though. What did you think?'

'It was too big,' said Barbara. 'We need a drink.'

The Bemelmans Bar, just up Madison Avenue in the Carlyle Hotel, felt surprisingly like an upscale cave on a summer afternoon. The lighting was dim, but bounced off the ceiling, which was lined with gold leaf, onto brown leather banquettes and wooden tables. I wanted to examine every inch of the murals, which had been painted by Ludwig Bemelmans, author of *Madeline*, in exchange for eighteen months rent-free in the hotel. The glamour was disrupted only by the carpet.

'It's such a drag that the Whitney's moved downtown,' said Barbara. 'I wanted us to go there, Sophia, since I know you study American art, but I also wanted to take you to the Carlyle for a drink.'

I'd always wanted to visit the Bemelmans Bar and had been delighted when Barbara suggested it; on my own, I would have feared seeming too much like a tourist in a hotel bar. By contrast, I went to the Whitney every time an exhibition opened.

'The conservation of all these murals must be difficult,' I said. 'With all the drinks and food around.'

'And smoke, for decades, too,' said Barbara.

'We have a team who take care of it,' said the bartender. 'They used to use wet Wonder Bread to sponge off the nicotine stains.'

Barbara ordered something called a Vesper, which seemed a variation on a martini, and I ordered a Manhattan. I had expected the drinks would be bad, because the setting was so compelling, but mine was actually very good.

'This was all I wanted, as a child,' Barbara said.

'A martini?' I quipped, and she laughed.

'New York, really,' she said. 'I love this bar because it's so nostalgic, and I thought you might like it, too. I think there's something that attracts everybody who moves to New York, and for me it was the children's books. *Eloise* at the Plaza, *From the Mixed-Up Files of Mrs. Basil E. Frankweiler*, all of those. The thing that I *really* wanted was to be inside the Met when it wasn't open, when the museum was just waking up and empty of people, and now I'm a member of the Met and they do have those early mornings for members. I don't get to them very often, because of the trains, but I feel like a child at Christmas every time.'

I hadn't really thought of Barbara as being young, as moving to New York. I'd thought only of the point at which she'd moved away, gravitating to the suburbs to raise children. She seemed as if she'd been formed by the Upper East Side and trips across the park to the opera at Lincoln Centre.

'Had you visited much?' I asked. 'Before you moved here?'

'We would come from Cleveland once every few years and see the Christmas windows, go skating in Central Park, pick out presents at FAO Schwarz. We'd drink hot chocolate here, at the Carlyle, or at the Plaza's Palm Court, and I felt so grown-up, because they put whipped cream on top. We'd catch the double-decker bus up and down Fifth Avenue. I just stared out at all the real New Yorkers and thought they were so glamorous! I know now, of course, that they probably weren't real New Yorkers. They were probably tourists, too.

'And then,' she said. 'I went to Smith and met Robert's father. When we first got married, we wanted to live in that little flat that you and Robert live in now, which belonged to Jack's parents, but everybody thought it was too dangerous so we lived up here instead. New York was different, then. I would have liked to have lived downtown though.'

I couldn't imagine Robert's parents living in the East Village in the 1980s. I couldn't imagine Barbara and Jack choosing something other than safety, respectability. I had created a picture of Robert's parents based on their house, their enunciation and their knowledge of opera, and I reminded myself that this was reductive.

'Of course,' she said. 'It's hard to stay in the city when you have children.'

She looked at me expectantly, and I bit the lip of my glass.

15

I wondered if they'd scheduled the Nan Goldin show for June because it was Pride Month. *The Ballad of Sexual Dependency* screened in a dark room, the photographs set to music and repeating every forty-five minutes. There was a gallery, preceding the slideshow, in which stills and publicity materials from early screenings were displayed.

I sat in the darkness and imagined that the people in the slideshow were my friends. It wasn't easy to communicate bisexuality in a single image, I thought, but it was easier with a slideshow. I admired Goldin's ability to articulate her sexuality, both visually and in interviews. I'd read, in the daily roundup of press clippings, that Goldin refused the description of her work as focused on 'marginalised' people, arguing that her friends couldn't be marginalised because they were an entire world to one another, because they didn't care what straight people thought of them, because they were only on the margins when seen from a particular position.

I wanted to learn, from Nan Goldin, how to live a queer life whilst remaining with Robert. *The Ballad of Sexual Dependency* represented plenty of relationships between men and women, including Goldin's own, and yet it was routinely discussed as a masterpiece of queer representation. I watched the slides change, flickering past a heart-shaped bruise on somebody's thigh, somebody else preparing heroin above a patchwork quilt, two people kissing in a chair, their arms and legs wrapped tightly around one another. It had an immediacy and glamour, but it wasn't aspirational. The flash exposed pain alongside intimacy. I looked at Nan Goldin's bruised eyes, in a self-portrait, at the cut beneath her right eye and the bright blood that pooled in her left sclera. The slideshow moved, eventually, to images of graveyards, of her friends' funerals, and ended with a photograph of graffiti, a white stencil of two skeletons locked in an embrace.

It felt like everything was happening at once. I blinked from email to newspaper and saw that Britain had voted to leave the European Union. I felt as if I were looking out through a small window while the museum, self-contained as an aeroplane, held me aloft, apart from the world.

At the end of the day, I walked past the Nouvel Tower construction site, buzzing with power tools. On Facebook, I had seen many different expressions of sadness, mostly from acquaintances who were from or had moved to London. I thought about the different forms that reactions took, considered how to remain angry and active in the face of such large-scale disappointments. I wondered if 'remain' was the right word, here, if I'd been angry and active or if I'd just been complacent. I wondered why I cared so much; I'd never visited Europe. I thought of the artworks in the museum, often criticised as Eurocentric. I felt as if I knew Europe.

'It's like 1915,' Trevor had said, that afternoon. 'It feels like things are sealing up everywhere.'

On the subway, I looked up at the advertisements. *It's scary how well @spotify discover weekly playlists know me*, one read. *Like former-lover-who-lived-through-a-near-death-experience-with-me well.* Beside me, a man took and edited selfies on his phone. I wondered about the bubbles that I inhabited. I didn't know anybody who was pleased about the news today, though statistically I knew that many people must have been happy. I wondered if this was the reason that I loved the museum so much; we all shared a common politics, a common purpose, or at least it felt that way. I thought of the cart filled with white paint that I saw most mornings, blotting out stains or signs of the world beyond the walls.

I queued, on a Saturday, for a sale held by Dover Street Market. I stood, alone with Grace Hartigan's journals in my hand, for three hours near the West Side Highway, edging my way toward a warehouse entrance, watching as women clambered out of black cars and exclaimed at the length of the line. I took photos of artificial flowers lying in the gutter with my iPhone, and nodded my head at the guy who walked down the line, after leaving, to warn everybody else.

'There's no Supreme in there,' he said. 'Just so you know. It's not worth it.'

I felt, reaching the front of the queue and checking my bag

into the cloakroom, a surge of adrenalin at the thought of cheap Comme des Garçons.

Inside, everything was still expensive.

I was thrilled to be there anyway. Dover Street Market was known for its visual merchandising, which bordered on art installation, even at the sale. I took photographs of the enormous ice-cream cones that stood amongst the wreckage of racks that were picked over as quickly as the sales assistants could restock them, of the remaining pairs of shoes balanced atop Aalto stools painted green. In the background, young men in baseball caps rifled through the racks quickly, eager for streetwear, carrying the large, madras-plaid plastic bags we'd all been given at the door beneath their arms.

I was here, mostly, because I didn't want to stay at home. Cara was at work. Lucy was polishing job applications and I didn't want to call her, to remind myself that I, too, should be doing the same thing. I didn't plan to spend much money. I could only justify practical clothes, affordable black skirts and shoes in which I could walk and work. I expected all of this had sold out on Friday morning, after people had queued overnight or paid line-sitters thirty dollars an hour to hold their places.

The racks of elaborate dresses, though, were largely untouched. I walked over to one of them, pulling out a confusing garment composed of geometric panels that seemed to be made out of pink plastic and then a plain black dress with an embroidered collar that would have been sensible if it hadn't been, even at seventy percent off, six hundred dollars.

I saw a white dress at the end of the rack. It was made of so much tulle that it seemed almost a cloud, shifting and shadowing, ready to burst, unleashing rain. It was beautiful. I took it down and carried it to the corner, tried it on and was surprised to find the lining was cool and silky, surprisingly comfortable. The tulle flared out, obscuring the contours of my torso; I appeared lighter, all limbs. The dress stopped just above my knees and seemed too comic and playful to be a wedding dress, though too extravagant to be worn anywhere else.

It was expensive, despite the sale, but I thought that Barbara would be pleased if I bought a wedding dress, even if it wasn't a traditional one. It finished at the knee; it didn't have to be a wedding dress, really. If necessary, I could dye it. It could probably be sold on eBay, given the provenance. There was, I thought, no reason not to buy this dress and so, suddenly, I spent five hundred dollars, more than I'd ever spent on a single item of clothing, on a pile of tulle at a sample sale.

I was going to hang the dress in my closet, but then I remembered that Grace Hartigan had hung a wedding dress on her wall as she considered painting *Grand Street Brides* and *Bride and Owl*. I remembered, as I removed a framed photograph of Walden Pond and looped the coat hanger onto the picture hook, that I'd asked Cara, in her bedroom, what she would wear if she were getting married.

'Probably an old nightgown,' she'd said. 'But if I had more money . . .'

Cara had climbed onto the bed beside me, opening her laptop. She'd pulled up a website and shown me a lace dress, worn by an unsmiling model with black lipstick, which hung on thin silk straps, jutting out from the body. The photograph was cropped at the nose and hips, with just a few strands of blonde hair visible at the top of the frame, and the image was grainy, as if taken in dense fog or smoke, with the detail of the lace dissolving as the dress receded with the body.

'Anyway,' she'd said. 'It's like a million dollars. I'd learn to sew and make my own dress. And I'd kind of like to wear a black dress, really.'

She'd closed the tab, quickly, and I'd tried to find the dress again, later, at home, wading through wedding websites with names like *One Fab Day* and *Bridal Musings*.

It seemed like there were two ways in which most bridal shoots were styled. I didn't like sculpted eyebrows and fake tan, which reminded me of high school. I preferred brides who were gaunt, gothic, without breasts and hips, and yet when I saw models like this, with heavy eyeliner, I wanted to cry out to stop them from marrying, to tell them that they were much too young, that both the modelling and wedding industries needed reform.

I didn't hate the dresses, though. I'd found many of them beautiful, with underlayers that matched the models' skin tones, with pearls and false flowers sewn into thin lace. I imagined that if the photographs had been styled differently, or perhaps if I hadn't been imagining myself in the place of each of the women, airbrushed and filtered, freed from personality, I might have been charmed.

I found the label that made the dress that Cara had shown me, eventually. I liked the dress she'd shown me more than the others, because when I looked I thought of Cara, rather than myself, in it. I could imagine her melting into air as the girl in the picture did.

I'd wondered, at the time, if the fact that I was considering these dresses meant that I was moving toward marriage, tacitly accepting it, or if marriage exerted the same fascination as a mysterious medical symptom, inspiring internet searches that fed rather than placated an outsized dread.

I'd bought a dress, now, though.

One of the framed stills in the Nan Goldin exhibition was *The Parents' Wedding Photo, Swampscott, Massachusetts*, taken in 1985. It was a rare image of an empty room, with yellow wallpaper patterned with flowers, a bureau at the centre, atop which was a small mirror and a framed photograph. The photograph was a formal portrait of a couple, with a man in a suit standing behind a woman in a white dress, their heads tilted together. It was framed by a white mat and I noticed a sort of echo in the open window, to the left, where the window frame, painted white, gave way to a lawn, a caravan and a shed beneath a tree.

It was intended as a haunting image, perhaps, but I found it comforting. I wondered if it was a photograph of Goldin's family home. I knew that she'd run away from her middle-class upbringing at fourteen, traumatised by her older sister's suicide and her parents' refusal to acknowledge it. Each time *I'll Be Your Mirror* played on the slideshow's soundtrack, I thought of the way in which Goldin's whole photographic project seemed informed by these events. She'd chosen a life that refused or inverted the bourgeois norms with which she'd grown up and she'd made this life public by transforming it into art, offering everything to an audience rather than adhering to an aesthetic of respectability that demanded sexuality stay private.

I wondered if I'd done the reverse, if I sought the trappings of upper-middle-class life because I'd grown up outside it. I felt uncomfortable in the world of hereditary privilege, of nuclear families in the suburbs and wedding photographs atop bedroom bureaus, but I was embarrassed, sometimes, by my attraction to it. I'd known many art historians who dismissed white wedding dresses as retrograde, but they'd been the graduate students who wore torn jeans to deliver lectures while I kept an iron in the corner of my bedroom. I lived on the Lower East Side, like Nan Goldin, but I lived on a Lower East Side that had gentrified. I wondered if I was a little like the museum itself, co-opting the aesthetics of the radical whilst living a bourgeois life, displaying posters for grungy, dive-bar screenings of *The Ballad of Sexual Dependency* on white walls that were touched up daily. I kept looking at *The Parents' Wedding Photo*, wondering if my desires and my values coalesced.

I felt too nervous to go to the Pride March alone. I lay in bed looking at photographs of women in t-shirts that read *BISEXUALS ARE NOT CONFUSED*. I was confused, though, and I didn't really know why I should rally against confusion. It seemed like a natural response to the world in which we lived, to a society that assumed desire was binary. I wanted to embrace confusion, to use it as a means of reconfiguring identity, though I didn't know how to put theory into practice.

I stayed at home and worked on an academic article focused on some Joe Brainard drawings that I knew would help with fellowship applications. I'd had an idea for the article, about friendship economies as a reaction to Clement Greenberg's *Avant-Garde and Kitsch*, a few months ago, but it seemed silly now; I was using Joe Brainard and Frank O'Hara to fuel my own career rather than learning from their example and living a life of generosity, care and community, throwing myself into the world as an enthusiastic amateur. I shook my head, trying to dislodge the thought, and stared again at the black kitten with a thought-bubble containing a small ice-cream in a cone.

I worked for most of the afternoon. There were, by the evening, many more pictures from Pride on the internet, some gathered into slideshows with explanatory captions. I saw the usual children with their faces painted, dressed in rainbow tutus and smiling, the usual adults in leather or thin singlets, arms smeared with glitter. I saw a group of people in red t-shirts that read *One Pulse*.

Gays Against Guns were more theatrical, shrouded in white, each member of their contingent veiled and wearing a white dress or white trousers, with the name of a victim on their chest. They held hands with one another in the sun.

On Instagram, I found photos of a die-in, like an echo of the 1980s, and then, scrolling further, saw two dogs in rainbow bibs, their tongues hanging out, with the caption *love is love*. It seemed especially trite this year, only weeks after the shooting. Often queerness wasn't about the luxury of love, at all, but simply about trying to exist, and there wasn't much comfort in those platitudes. I scrolled further and it got worse, with a Hillary Clinton contingent of white women smiling in t-shirts reading *Love Trumps Hate*, with the awkward caption *#werewithher*. In the background, a man wearing rainbow wings queued for a Chase Manhattan ATM.

The Stonewall Inn had just been declared a national monument. It was celebrated in all the newspapers, but I felt the loss of the resistance that the site had represented, though I knew it was already in tourist guidebooks, had been co-opted into the main-stream long before that was made official. I'd seen pictures of policemen marching in the parade, and I imagined, with a shudder, policemen inside the Stonewall Inn, drinking at the bar.

I missed Emily and wanted her here, sharing my contempt for all of this. Our judgement, when we were younger, used to build together, and I'd felt recognised by her expletives and her jokes.

I'd softened, now, though. I wasn't sure that I necessarily opposed the inclusion of Stonewall as a historic site. It flattened history, but it also meant that those living in conservative states might have to acknowledge this history, that kids might read about it in guidebooks or see it in the paper. I wanted to check my opinions against Emily's opinions, though it had been years since I remembered needing this.

I kept scrolling. There were so many topless white men, all looking as if they belonged to expensive gyms. It showed a lack of imagination, I thought, to embrace this aesthetic, but perhaps there was comfort in being a cliché.

Robert had sent another letter, but I couldn't bring myself to open it. I felt as if to do so would be to find myself transported to the forest and I felt, for some reason, as if I didn't deserve this respite, as if I had to learn to exist independently or create my own community. I supposed that I'd need, after opening it, to send Robert another email or slip a letter into one of the boxes he'd pick up along the way, to articulate my own experience of my environment. I didn't know how to do that, so I left the letter on the table, with the bills.

———

I went back to the Nan Goldin exhibition, idly, whenever things were quiet at work. I lingered on one of the photographs laid flat in a glass vitrine, entitled *Cookie and Vittorio's Wedding.* Cookie Mueller appeared throughout *The Ballad of Sexual Dependency.* Goldin had written that she'd felt if she photographed somebody enough she'd never lose them, but later realised that the images instead showed her how much she'd lost. I'd read this, recently, and it heightened the pathos of the images of Cookie and Vittorio's funerals, which came later in the slideshow. This image of their wedding felt haunted by their deaths from AIDS, in 1989, as if the white of Cookie's dress hinted at her spectre, particularly once I'd remembered that white was a mourning colour in most cultures.

I loved Cookie's outfit in the photograph, though it wasn't stylish to twenty-first century eyes. I loved it because it read like a costume, camp and carnivalesque in a way that made me question the association between white wedding dresses and heteronormative respectability politics. I registered the streaks of bleach in Cookie's hair, framed by an enormous veil that fountained out from an embellishment atop her head, and the stiff, shining white fabric of her dress and jacket. It wasn't worn with irony, but an authentic desire for this type of wedding that seemed to speak to the complexity of queer love.

Cookie sponged her eye with a tissue, in the photograph, and her fingers peeked out from fingerless white fishnet gloves. Cookie's fingernails were very short, with pearlescent polish, and there was a tattoo of a flower on her left forefinger, like a child's drawing, and it was this detail that I loved the most. Beside her, Vittorio looked down tenderly, as if her audience or her assistant, content to bask in her brilliance, wearing a black silk shirt with ruffles. They looked very happy. I admired Cookie for her ability to remain so obviously herself in any situation, even a wedding to a man, and admired Nan for her ability to capture this, to create a portrait of a loving marriage in which it seemed so obvious that nobody was straight.

I didn't know if I was projecting, though. I didn't trust my mind anymore.

On Monday, Trevor told me he'd had no luck with the cute boy he'd met at Pride, who'd disappeared into the crowd too quickly.

'I was going to go,' I said. 'I don't know why I didn't.'

'I kind of hate it when straight people go to Pride,' said Trevor.

I checked my email, quickly, but there wasn't much there. I'd written some biographies of mid-century artists for the Publications Department, and they'd sent a follow-up about edits, but nothing else in my inbox required attention.

'No offense,' Trevor added, a few minutes later. 'It's just, like . . . we're not a spectacle. It's not entertainment. It's a protest.'

I didn't know what to say. I was still mad at myself for masquerading as a straight girl and being taken as one seemed a fair punishment. Kelly, the other intern, stared furiously at her computer screen, lost in her own world or in her work, as always.

16

It was July. The sound of fireworks reminded me of Boston, rumbling like a tourist's suitcase dragged across the cobblestones of Beacon Hill. I heard the popping of a balloon, the beating of a drum, the high pitch of sirens, but saw only fragments, the sky needled with glittering, sugared shards that melted as they descended. It was warm in an easy way, even in the evening, and I felt the heat building each day, knew that soon it would cease to be pleasant, become oppressive.

I'd turned down Lucy's suggestion of a party in Gowanus. I was at home, sifting through job advertisements on the New York Foundation for the Arts website, though almost all of the positions were unpaid internships. I'd missed the deadlines for this year's academic positions, and it didn't seem like museums were advertising many jobs. I felt the end of my fellowship looming.

I thought of the previous summer, when Robert and I had gone to a barbeque in East Williamsburg. We'd painted pictures with water on asphalt and watched them evaporate. I remembered returning home that evening and falling onto our bed, kissing, at the point at which the afternoon ended, so that, beyond our bodies, I saw lights turning on in the apartments opposite, the sky above softening as I breathed the scent of sweat and body lotion. I had heard the chimes of Mister Softee, carried on the wind, far away and then closer, right outside the window, and then further away again, replaced by the rustle of traffic, a sigh of satisfaction, our breathing becoming slower.

I wanted to stay still, I thought, because everything else seemed to be in motion. I could not determine what was real and what was, as Emily had called it many years ago, when I told her I was leaving Australia, a form of running away from myself. I had, in Australia, been called *troubled*, though Robert never believed this; he told me that I was well-adjusted, that Australians just hadn't appreciated me enough.

I went outside to see if I could spot more fireworks. It was raining lightly, not enough to disrupt anything. When I looked up toward the sky, a drop hit the inner edge of my eye, as if New York was dispensing some sort of medicine. I hoped that the eyedrop had fallen from the sky, not an air-conditioning unit. I couldn't see any fireworks at all, just the usual fire escapes. I went back inside.

My phone buzzed and I picked it up to see that Cara had sent a message, a photograph of yellow and red towels laid out on sunny rocks beside a river, of two people, half-submerged, splashing one another with water. She was in Asheville for the long weekend. It was hard for me to imagine Cara outside New York. It was as if she'd emerged from a dark corner of the bridal shop. Cara seemed like the gleams and shadows of the city itself; she had the hardness of steel and the playful mystery of light bouncing off glass. I closed my laptop. Work, after seeing this photograph, after meeting Cara, seemed less central to my life, to my experience of New York City, and finding another job for September seemed like something I could delay.

In Pennsylvania, Robert was struggling with rocks. He'd mentioned it only briefly: *it's flatter, here, but rocky.* I'd googled it and learnt that hikers called it *Rocksylvania*. Pennsylvania ruined everybody's hiking boots and, looking at the pictures, I could see how this happened; every second image was of a pile of rocks, almost a cliff, steeply ascending after a bridge over a river. Robert had written, also, though, of the quality of fruit in the Cumberland Valley, of the mist rising over farmland in the morning, and, while I'd never visited that part of Pennsylvania, I felt a vague, nostalgic longing. I remembered early mornings in fields elsewhere and the ways in which all my senses came alive as I was drenched by those mists, transformed into a shaking leaf, covered with dew.

I was, that summer, discovering a new joy in the city, a way of looking that embraced the play of light on steel frames and glass. I noticed that the leaves scattered in the street glowed as the sun set. On the eleventh of July, Cara and I dashed to the centre of a crosswalk, with a crowd of others, to watch the sunset between the buildings before the traffic lights changed and the cars started moving.

'What's going on?' asked a bus driver, leaning out of his window.

'It's Manhattanhenge,' said a tall person in blue dungarees and a white t-shirt, standing in the crosswalk. 'It's the day when the sun lines up with the street grid!'

'I guess the sun's setting,' said the driver, shrugging toward his enquiring passengers.

There was a certain demographic, it seemed, for celestial events. We raised iPhones into the air, straining our arms to capture the street and sky unobscured by the audience of onlookers. I scrolled through all the other images on Instagram, later, occasionally pausing to consider the orange sky and the way it sometimes made buildings seem bluer and sometimes scorched the lens such that the entire scene was obliterated by yellow light.

I let my eye linger on details. I thrilled at a line of shadow thrown across my leg as I waited to buy coffee; I felt the electric dullness, the smudged yellow buzzing, of the bulbs on the subway platform. It felt as intentional, as perfectly considered, as paint on canvas. It felt, when I looked up and caught the glint at the top of a building flash as I stepped into the street, as if the city was winking at me.

It was warm into the evenings and everything was sultry.

I saw other people, sometimes, who seemed to be looking for something, too. They gathered on corners in unspeaking clumps, phones in their hands. I was searching for answers about my future, feeling out of sync with postmodernity, but they were playing Pokémon Go.

It had seemed, initially, as if this game could be something good: Pokémon in the world, luring people out of themselves, asking people to engage, informing them about murals and corporate lobbies that were, by law, open to everyone, giving people a sense of ownership of public space.

'It's so awesome,' said Emma, at lunch. 'My little brother went outside yesterday for the first time in forever.'

'That's so sad,' said Jessie, to the rest of us, after Emma left.

Nearby, people waved their phones at the Pokémon living in the sculpture garden.

It was a low bar for the world, I thought, if we saw Pokémon Go as a good thing because it lured people outside, still swiping at their phones. I wondered if there were Pokémon along the Appalachian Trail, if groups of teenagers gathered in the woods, looking for something unreal superimposed on the real. I wondered if that was all anybody ever did, search for illusions that offered a sense of meaning, and if the only differences were in the technologies we used and the forms that our illusions took.

I walked up toward the Met, one evening, to meet Lucy for dinner, and suddenly a crowd of people rushed past, clutching their phones and elbowing one another, eager to capture some creature on their screens. I wished the key to my future could appear like this, as a notification on my phone that gave me something to run toward.

Lucy and I had a drink on the roof before we walked east for dinner, and I told her about the crowd. I asked her if people had been playing Pokémon Go at the Met.

'It's embarrassing, Soph, but I'm actually addicted,' she said. 'My sister got me onto it.'

'When do you play it?' I asked.

'All the time,' she said. 'It's the worst. I can't stop. It's draining my phone's battery, too.'

'Are there Pokémon in the Met?' I asked.

'Yes,' she said. 'I try to catch them when no one's around, so my colleagues don't laugh at me. It's awful.'

I'd seen screenshots of Pokémon in galleries, which worried me. What was to stop people from crashing into the artworks? I wondered if it was modern to be ascetic about Pokémon, to want physical spaces to remain unembellished by the virtual. It was entirely dependent on the definition of modern, whether we were using the word in a more classical or contemporary sense, and the choice of definition, too, depended on whether we were puritanical about it. It was the kind of question that could have derailed any staff meeting at MoMA.

'Oh, by the way,' I said. 'I asked Anthea to add your name to the list for an opening at PS1 on Thursday, if you're free.'

'Thanks,' she said. 'I should be, if I'm not falling asleep at six o'clock. I'm so exhausted from work these days.'

'I invited Cara, too,' I said. 'That artist I mentioned.'

'Are there Pokémon at PS1?' asked Lucy.

'I wouldn't really be surprised.'

I thought only, when I posted on Instagram, about what Cara might think. I posted a picture of Cornelia Parker's house on the Met's roof, the colour of cherry flesh against blue sky. I'd already posted pictures of it in Spring, and I toyed with the idea of deleting my newer picture until I saw that Cara had liked it. I wondered, after she'd liked it, if she had liked it *enough.* I was never sure if she genuinely liked the things that I posted or if she was simply easy with her compliments. When she commented with an emoji, I felt as if I'd achieved something significant. She didn't, this time, though.

I liked most of Cara's pictures and she liked most of mine and I was anxious whenever she missed one, but then I was anxious, too, when she didn't miss them. I felt relief only when Cara messaged me. I posted things that I felt would get responses from her, without quite realising that I was doing this until I felt my muscles relax as I saw that '1' in the upper right corner of the app and knew, or hoped, that it was Cara.

I imagined, that night, Cara lying on my bed, her blonde hair against my pale pink bedspread. I was, in my mind, lying there, too, and so it was not like a painting in which the figure was framed, limited by the edges of a canvas, but rather something that surrounded me, a daydream too restless to fix in art. I thought of Cara's self-portraits, which were not what I wanted. I thought of Walter Benjamin's ideas on aura. It was substance that I wanted, though, not aura; it was relational, built on senses beside vision.

It couldn't be analysed, anyway. There was nothing nicer, I thought, than having one's legs tangled up with another woman's legs. It wasn't the same with men; power and convention, our social roles, made things complicated. I missed the simplicity of limbs. I didn't know what it meant to be missing this, but I let myself dissolve into it.

I cried, lightly, after masturbating. I stared at the ceiling and swore at the intensity, at my own confusion. I couldn't disentangle sexuality from sadness. I worried about the slippage between the private and the public, about the way in which my life and my desires felt fragmented by geography, each sense of myself smashed as I switched continents. I felt suddenly pooled in emotions. I noticed my hand was covered in blood. I'd been told, once, like almost every woman I knew, that my irregular periods were a sign of stress. I couldn't stop my body from acknowledging whatever it was that stayed unconscious, feeling whatever it was that I pushed down lest I become submerged.

I couldn't really deny, after this, that I was attracted to Cara.

17

I almost never went to PS1, MoMA's sibling institution in Long Island City, though each time that I did I remembered it wasn't hard to get there, that it was only two stops on the E from Midtown. I felt nervous about seeing Cara, afraid that my feelings for her would be suddenly visible and make everything awkward. I was worried, too, about my friends meeting Cara. She'd visited me at the museum, but hadn't met any of my colleagues, and now she'd probably meet Anthea. She'd meet Lucy, too, and I worried that Lucy would find me transparent, would pinpoint my attraction to Cara and force me to talk about it.

I was trying to figure out what my interest in Cara meant. I felt desire as a tumbling through space; I didn't know the gravity of it, how I'd balance or where I'd float, if I'd find something that I could grip. I didn't like to feel untethered. I couldn't figure out how Cara felt about me, or about anyone. She seemed to want to spend time with me, but she was languid, sometimes, in a way that might have been southern or might just have been boredom, and her moods were hard to predict.

Everything was fine, I told myself. I didn't need to know how Cara felt, because it didn't matter. It wouldn't change anything. I didn't need to act on all my feelings. I'd had a crush on Sally, once, and that was gone. My desire for Cara would disappear with the season, I thought, or as I came to know her better. It wouldn't matter at all once Robert returned.

I loved the theory of exhibition openings, but less so the practice. I felt awkward, perpetually outside the circles in which other people stood. I felt alert to the shape of gatherings, to the subtle shifts of shoulders which rendered one inside or outside a group. I'd had too much practice, when I was younger, standing outside circles. I had a headache, having drunk three glasses of wine in quick succession so that I could queue at the bar and look as if I had a purpose.

'Why don't my colleagues ever seem to want to talk to me?' I asked Anthea.

'You look like you're about to cry,' she said. 'They're probably giving you space because you look upset.'

'I'm anxious because they're not talking to me.'

'Well, yeah,' she said. 'It's not that different for me. I guess it's also that they know we're Fellows. We're leaving soon and most of them are leaving, too, sooner or later, so what's the point?'

It was the opening of the Young Architects Program's Summer Commission, an installation by two architects from Mexico who were always in the elevator, smiling much more than anybody who actually worked at the museum. I'd looked up at the coloured rope canopy as I arrived, walking across the main courtyard. I'd liked it. It felt festive: the rope was in neon colours, and the sun threw a messy set of shadowed lines across the ground. It was much more open than the usual commissions, with no structures blocking sight lines, and gave the outdoor area an expansive quality that it had previously lacked.

'It's clever,' said Anthea. 'They've used the holes in the concrete from when it was poured, the formwork ties, so it really is a sort of weaving, embellishing the courtyard and working with it rather than just building something to sit inside it.'

We were standing at the top of the stairs, looking down at the loose canopy of rope.

'Have you seen the mist room?' Anthea asked.

'No,' I said. 'Is that inside?'

'It's in one of those smaller courtyards,' she said. 'Just off to the side, that really tiny one. They've put nozzles that spray water in tie holes, too, so it feels pretty magical. Like, this mist just coming out of the concrete. There's also a wading pool in the medium-sized courtyard, and the sandpit, of course, which I guess you've noticed.'

She gestured with her hand to the hemisphere of sand on one side of the main courtyard, separated from gravel by a row of wooden benches.

I spotted Cara coming toward us, beneath the neon rope, wearing a white short-sleeved shirt and black jeans. When I'd invited her, she'd thanked me, excited about coming to an opening at PS1, but I'd felt that I should be the grateful one. She was evidence that I had a life outside the museum, that people who were poised and stylish wanted to spend time with me. I'd realised, also, that I was grateful for her company; I just wanted her around. She made her way up the steps.

'This is Cara,' I said to Anthea. 'This is Anthea.'

'Hi,' said Cara. 'God, it's cool to see this place without that weird igloo they had in winter.'

She turned and looked out at the crowd spilling down the steps, in a mix of office clothes, expensive t-shirts, handmade dresses and feathered jackets reflecting the combination of museum employees, architects, artists and donors.

'How many people do you know?'

'Not many, I said. 'Anthea's in Architecture, so she knows more than me.'

'Do you know anybody else here?' asked Anthea.

'Yeah, a few,' said Cara.

I glanced at Sally, further down, leaning against the brick building, smiling and laughing, talking to a guy I recognised from Registrar. I wondered if Sally was glad that Cara and Anthea were here so that she didn't have to talk to me. I wondered if Anthea had been right when she said that I looked upset. I rarely felt at ease at openings and my face – which never really smiled easily or automatically – probably showed it. It was a self-fulfilling prophecy, I supposed. I had formed my own sort of circle, with my involuntary expression of sadness keeping people out. I envied Cara, who was smiling as she surveyed the crowd.

I'd invited Lucy, too, and I introduced her to Cara when she arrived. I scanned the crowd, nervously, while they talked. I had friends here, now, but I was still so aware of the distance between myself and my colleagues, afraid that I'd never close it, afraid that it meant I didn't belong in the art world, that I'd never get another job.

'I worked in a shop when I was younger,' said Lucy. 'It was strange. I had to use all these short phrases, this clipped language, to keep people moving when the queue was long. It messed up my ability to have normal conversations for a while. I was so used to brief interactions, ending things quickly.'

'That sucks,' said Cara. 'It's not like that in a wedding boutique. We don't have queues, for one thing.'

There were speeches, the usual expressions of gratitude to the wealthy, and then people began to wander out, junior staff trickling away before senior staff while those with more tenuous connections to the museum, for whom it wasn't a work function at all but a party, showed no signs of intent to leave. I watched each person take photographs of the pavilion as they drifted beneath it toward the exit, catching the orange streamers against the blue clouds of twilight.

Lucy hadn't stayed long and Cara and I said goodbye to Anthea after about an hour, when we started feeling hungry. We left slowly, taking our own photographs of the installation as the sun set and gave the concrete vibrancy. I uploaded an image of the bright canopy, lit by the setting sun and framing the bricks of the school above, in shadow, to Instagram, and Cara uploaded an image of me caught in a cloud of mist in the smaller room. I was thrilled to think of people seeing the image, clicking the tag to learn my name, of people knowing that I was a part of her life.

We went to a bar nearby, hoping they'd serve food but getting only bowls of peanuts and olives. I'd been careful, since my messy first year of graduate school, to combine alcohol with carbohydrates, but somehow, with Cara, I forgot this rule. I didn't care about the future, didn't think beyond each drink.

'Want to go to a party?' she asked. 'I mean, another party. Since you don't have to work tomorrow.'

I was taking Friday off to go to the Hudson Valley and meet Robert for the weekend. I didn't have work, but I had to wake up at six am to catch the train.

The next morning, though, was hours away.

On the subway, I thought of Cara and Lucy's conversation about working in a shop, and of the other boutiques I'd visited, of the way that the shop assistants spoke. The interactions weren't brief or clipped, but it still felt as if the conversations taking place might act as guards against intimacy. There were so many assumptions about the shapes that relationships took that I imagined all the women working there would struggle to untangle their own desires from the norms perpetuated by the wedding industry. I wondered why Cara's boutique was different and could only conclude that it was because of her, because her curiosity about weddings was genuine and informed by her own position as an artist, drawn toward beauty rather than convention. I'd never seen her interact with another customer, though.

I rested my head on Cara's shoulder, silently, sleepily, and she smoothed my hair with her hand.

I had imagined students in New York lived in expensive dormitories, like the ones I saw clustered around Union Square, or in tiny spaces in obscure neighbourhoods, like Cara, but the party was at a Clinton Hill duplex, shared between six students, with a backyard. It was crowded. Cara seemed to know everybody. I was drunk enough, after the free drinks at PS1 and a cocktail at the bar with nuts and olives, that my anxiety had disappeared. I knew nobody at the party but Cara, and it was liberating; there were no professional consequences lurking.

There was an energy, here, that I remembered from parties I'd attended when I was in college. Everybody was drunk on adrenalin alongside alcohol, eating chips and skittles from plastic bowls and waiting for something to happen, full of anticipation, only faintly aware that these conversations, this blur of drinks and snacks and standing near the door, were life itself rather than its preamble. I found myself smiling for photographs with strangers, borrowing somebody's hat so that I'd have a costume, Cara having neglected to mention that the night was themed.

The party, as is often the case with parties, became a set of fragments.

I remembered, later: hassling the DJ to play a Bruce Springsteen song for one of Cara's friends; dancing in a circle as if I were a Springsteen obsessive, too, as if these were my friends, too; sitting on the couch with a boy whining about his ex-girlfriend, asking me why she wouldn't speak to him, how he could win her back, while I watched, through a doorframe, Cara talking to the girl who I had recognised, earlier, as Stacey. I remembered going into the kitchen in search of water and guzzling it from a beer glass emblazoned with *Samuel Adams*; I remembered lying on the floor with Cara, both of us staring at the ceiling, tired from dancing, strangers stepping around us as they left, and the odd sense of intimacy that the proximity of our bodies, relaxed, collapsed on the floor, seemed to suggest. It reminded me of when we'd looked at paintings together, our separate gazes fixed on the same point. It felt lazily romantic. I didn't remember my trip home, my tumble into bed, but my alarm blared at six and I felt sick, the sugars of wine and beer, potato chips and skittles, churning in my stomach.

18

Across the river, a tiny freight train crept beneath a steep rock face. The mountain's shadow stretched toward us. This part of the state was familiar to Robert, close to his parents' house, but to me it felt shrouded in magic despite my hangover. I'd been to Cold Spring before, many times, but I was always astonished by how separate it felt to the city; Midtown was just over an hour away on Metro-North. I'd caught the train up that morning and Robert had met me at the station.

We were sitting in the small park by the Hudson River. I was happy to be with Robert again, but the sun was too bright and my stomach felt fragile; I wasn't good company. If my head hadn't been hurting to the point of distraction, I would have asked Robert what it had been like to hike into the landscape where he'd grown up, his own first forests. It was weird to think that he'd walked here from Georgia, but I couldn't quite arrange my thoughts into sentences.

I felt Robert's eyes on me, disappointed and chastising. I didn't go out regularly, didn't drink often, and yet I'd drunk too much the night before meeting him in Cold Spring. I'd sent him a text message from the train, warning him that I'd stayed out too late and had little energy, trying but failing to make a joke about city girls recovering in the mountains.

Robert took hangovers too seriously, I thought, and I wasn't really sure why. I'd gone to parties more frequently when we'd started dating, in those first months of graduate school when most of us had focused on making friends rather than on our coursework, but Robert always seemed faintly concerned when I drank too much, despite the culture. He'd tell me that I was lucky that I hadn't been hurt, and that I needed to take responsibility for myself rather than expecting him to save me, to take me home. I was a graduate student, I'd thought; graduate students were always drunk. I'd liked, then, that he'd worried about me, but it annoyed me today.

'You can't keep doing this,' he said, now, as if it were a pattern.

'I'm sorry,' I said.

I couldn't see, though, why it mattered to him. I was the one with the headache.

'It's okay,' Robert said. 'I just worry about you.'

He picked a daisy from the grass beside us and tucked it into my sunglasses, beside my ear.

'Let's talk about something else,' he said. 'How's your mid-century girlfriend?'

'What?'

'Grace Hartigan. How's work going?'

'It's good,' I said. 'Or, well, you know, summer. Uneventful. I'm still hoping Sally's job will be advertised, since she's leaving in October.'

Barbara had picked Robert up, yesterday, from somewhere near Manitou. We had his mother's car today, and could drive anywhere that we wanted, but neither of us really wanted to go anywhere. I was too tired to make my usual suggestion of Dia Beacon, and I sensed Robert was tired, too, so once I'd had a sandwich and enough coffee to be cogent, I asked about the Appalachian Trail.

'Fucking Bear Mountain, Soph. I'm glad that's over.'

Robert loved and hated Bear Mountain more than any other place he'd known. We had a picture of it on our wall, in Manhattan, but he'd always refused to take me there, depressed by the zoo that caged the same native animals that lived in the forests around it. He'd told me of the miserable bears who'd become tourist attractions, separated from their peers.

'The trail goes through the zoo,' he said. 'It was the first part of the trail to be blazed, back in 1923. It has such a history. It's the most-visited section of the entire Appalachian Trail. But it's real crowded and I feel so bad for those bears. I'm glad that's not the part of the trail that you're doing.'

'What do the other hikers think of it?'

'They love the views of Manhattan. And I get that. I'd probably feel differently if I hadn't grown up around here. I think the animals are rescues, now, ones that couldn't survive in the wild, but I don't think they were when I was a child. They were just native animals in cages . . .'

I was going to hike some of the Appalachian Trail, with Robert, over the weekend. We'd be slack-packing, as the hikers called it, taking only a small daypack with lunch and water, and spending the nights with Robert's parents, who would drop us off and pick us up at the trailhead.

'Do you think I'd like Bear Mountain?'

'I don't think so, but it's always possible. We can go, sometime, if you want. I hope it's not like I'm holding you back from your dream of seeing Bear Mountain.'

I shook my head. I was curious about Bear Mountain, mostly, because it roused such passion in Robert. I loved Manhattan despite the changes that had taken place since the 1950s, was fascinated by the city as a site that was always in flux. I wasn't turned off by the gentrification of the Lower East Side, even as I feared the impending demolition of the Essex Street Market and hated the shiny new buildings that were being erected. I didn't believe in authenticity. Robert, though, seemed to view Bear Mountain as a hallowed site and his heart was broken by the pantomime of wilderness that he felt had replaced the real thing.

'Don't you think, maybe, that Bear Mountain is what Benton MacKaye envisaged for the Appalachian Trail?' I asked.

I'd been thinking, since Robert's presentation in May, about the history of the Appalachian Trail, about the fact that it had been intended as a site where city-dwellers might reset, a chain linking camps and bucolic resorts, but had become a more gruelling pilgrimage for worshippers of wilderness.

'You might be right,' he said. 'But I disagree with him on a lot of stuff.'

Cold Spring was a small town and soon, after we'd walked down Main Street and along the waterfront, holding hands, like tourists, it felt as if we'd have to get into the car and go somewhere. Robert drew me to him, though, and hugged me, again, as he'd been doing frequently since I'd arrived that morning, despite my hangover and our brief spat.

'I don't want to go home and deal with Mom just yet,' he said.

I wanted to be alone with him, horizontal, or near-horizontal, or simply in a place where we didn't have to worry about onlookers.

Inhaling the scent of his t-shirt, I wished that we could just have sex immediately. I felt an urgent need to be touched, a certain tautness of muscle spreading across my entire body. I imagined Robert's hands and hipbones pressing into me, pushing me to the ground, and closed my eyes. I wondered if he'd missed sex while hiking, if he'd thought of me in his tent at night.

'I've missed you,' he said, lifting my head from his shoulder and kissing my temple in a way that seemed to answer my question.

'Do people ever have sex on the Appalachian Trail?' I asked.

Robert laughed.

'Yes, of course,' he said. 'I don't, obviously. But people do.'

He brushed a strand of hair away from my ear and kept his hand on me, lightly running it past my ear onto my neck, tracing my collarbone with his fingers.

'We could camp instead of staying with my parents,' he said, half-joking.

'They'd be furious. Walk all the way from Georgia just to sleep in the woods.'

'Oh, they're used to that. I've slept in every clearing out here. But they'd miss seeing you.'

He kissed my neck, again, and held my waist beneath my t-shirt, his thumbs against the base of my ribs, and I wished we were in the forest or a bed.

I couldn't tell if this stirring of desire was really about Robert. I felt, when he was beside me, that I'd really missed him, that I really wanted him, that nothing else particularly mattered, but when he left, briefly, to find a bathroom before we drove away, I thought of the evening before.

I had never felt so lucky to be lying on a dirty floor, I thought, remembering the party. I recalled, through my fading headache, that there had been a distance that I hadn't felt in my own anxious youth, when everything had been so fresh, so proximate, that I couldn't endure it. I could be young, with Cara, without the inhibition and pain that I'd felt when I was actually that young. I observed more, now, and the stakes were lower. I wondered if Cara was as clueless, secretly, as I had been at twenty-two. She didn't appear clueless at all. I should have been more mature than Cara, given I was almost thirty, but I wasn't. I didn't mind. She was finishing her undergraduate degree and I'd just finished my graduate degree. We were the same; I liked that.

In New York, I hadn't been thinking about my wedding. I'd been thinking, instead, about the wedding as an abstract idea, a framing device, rather than something that required organisation and would actually occur. Barbara had given me a list of things to consider, which I'd left in a pile with my unopened mail on the kitchen bench. I remembered Robert shaking his head at all the envelopes when he'd visited in May.

'What if there's something urgent?' he'd asked.

I worried, now, that Barbara would ask me about something on the list. I'd bought a dress, but it wasn't the sort of dress that Barbara would approve. I wasn't sure, anyway, that a dress was enough. I hadn't thought about flowers, cakes, venues, dates. I hadn't thought about music, invitations, guest lists, bridesmaids, table settings. I hadn't thought about shoes, food, vows, photographers. I wondered if Robert had thought about these things, was expected to think about them. I sat in the car, wondering how to broach the question, as we drove toward his childhood home.

I thought of Cara as I carried my suitcase up to Robert's old bedroom, left unchanged for his visits. Cara was a tantalising possibility, like a lemon tree seen over a high fence. I felt torn between following my desire and doing what seemed sensible, permissible. I wondered if desires always threatened a downward spiral.

I reminded myself that a crush didn't change anything. My feelings for Cara were totally irrelevant to my feelings for Robert, my feelings about marriage. I could compartmentalise. I had made a decision, and adult relationships were about carefully considered decisions, not impulses or passing attractions. I had a good relationship; I didn't need another. I had wanted Robert for years and I'd known Cara only a few months. It was silly, I thought, juvenile, to feel torn.

Robert's parents' house felt, to me, like something from a film. It was in the south of Putnam County, in what was technically a wealthy suburb of New York City, but the area didn't feel at all suburban to me. It felt like the countryside, but like a particularly luxurious version of the countryside, with roads that wound out into views over the river, with elegant libraries and fancy pizzerias in villages that could have been on film lots. The houses were large and each had a forest, instead of a fence, to shield the residents from neighbours and the occasional passing car.

There was space in the garage for two cars, and a basketball hoop hung above the driveway. There were two separate staircases, at either end of the house, and a basement in which to shelter from storms. It was large enough that Robert's parents hadn't noticed when Robert and his sister climbed out a second-floor window to sit on the roof as teenagers. There was a fridge with a built-in icemaker, a kitchen island and a casual table beside a bay window that looked out onto a large deck and the woods beyond. There was a formal dining room, too, and beside it a space called a 'Butler's Pantry' which the family used to store wine. I'd looked up Putnam County real estate, once, and found that most of the nearby houses had all these things, too. I'd never get used to it.

'This is the first time we've all been together to celebrate,' said Robert's father, Jack, at dinner, raising his glass for a toast.

'Michelle's not here,' Robert pointed out.

His sister lived in San Francisco.

'We'll celebrate again when she's here,' said Barbara. 'It's a major event.'

'Birth, marriage, death,' said Jack. 'This is the only one that you get any control over. Celebrate as often as you'd like, I say.'

I felt uncomfortable, but I always felt uncomfortable at dinner with Robert's family. I remembered my own family dinners, each of my siblings piling a plate eagerly, wanting to secure food before it was gone, gobbled hastily at the kitchen bench or in front of the television. In Robert's house, the dining room table was laid with placemats, knives and forks, multiple glasses at each setting, and the food was carefully measured and arranged on plates, carried from the kitchen, and nobody began to eat until wine had been poured and glasses knocked against one another. It felt too structured to be a celebration, but then, I wondered, what would celebrating an engagement look like? I had no idea. I couldn't imagine a context in which I'd feel comfortable.

'What about the wedding march?' asked Jack.

'Um,' I said. 'I presumed that famous one . . . I don't know the name.'

I hummed it.

'Do you know what happened in that opera, after that wedding?' asked Robert.

'I didn't even know it was from an opera.'

'It's the Bridal Chorus from Lohengrin. Elsa dies, basically.'

'Oh,' I said. 'You can choose the music.'

It was so easy to see the stars in Putnam County that it took away any sense of accomplishment, but Robert and I still clambered out onto the roof, after dinner, as we always did when visiting. I tried to talk to Robert about his parents' comments, asking if he felt nervous at all about marriage, if he'd reflected on the decision.

'Do you think we need to talk about it?' I asked. 'Because we didn't, really.'

'I don't think I need to reflect on anything,' he said. 'I know I want to be with you. Why wouldn't we get married?'

It felt cruel to respond to this with a list of reasons.

'What about yesterday?' I said. 'I drink too much. Isn't that something to think about?'

'We've already discussed that,' he said. 'We're past it.'

I had never wanted men in the same ways that I wanted women. I had never glanced at men and felt instantaneous attraction. It had grown as I'd come to know them, or so I told myself. I couldn't quite remember wanting Robert, now, as I wanted Cara, but it felt deceitful to say that I hadn't, as if my past were lying to my present. It was a different form of desire, one that had developed rationally, in pace with the relationship, rather than overwhelming me before anything began.

I didn't know how to approach marriage. I didn't feel excited about it, but I didn't feel afraid of it, exactly, either. I felt only that I had been asked a question for which I hadn't studied, and that I might have given the wrong answer. I hated that marriage was a binary position, that the answer had to be either *yes* or *no*. It reminded me of the nightmares I'd had before my qualifying exams during graduate school, of my fears of showing up to discover the questions were all on paintings I'd never seen or that the whole test was composed of trick questions.

Robert hadn't been as stressed as me that year. I wondered if he'd ever been asked a question for which he wasn't prepared, a question that hadn't already been thought through at the family dinner table.

Barbara dropped us off at the trailhead early the next morning. We walked uphill and then the trees thinned out into fields and fog structured everything, hanging like stripes of white paint slathered boldly across the landscape. I loved the way that the fog shifted with the wind, with the dawn, lifting like a veil. We weren't far from roads and houses and I saw a figure, clad in black, running through the midground, a damp silhouette untethered from the earth, running through a cloud.

It didn't feel like summer this early in the morning; it felt like autumn. The sheep matched the fields, still frosted with dew, and everything seemed softened into pastel, into the sweet colours of saltwater taffy. It seemed staged, like a theatre set in which different layers dropped down from above, and I felt euphoric, understood why Robert had been so eager to spend months on the Appalachian Trail.

We stayed mostly silent, that morning, and my giddy feeling gave way to rational thought; my urban preoccupations returned. I was wondering why desire, if it were ordinary and human, always felt as if it had to stay hidden. I didn't think that I could tell Robert of my feelings for Cara, but it seemed odd to leave it unspoken. It was as if the secrecy rendered the feelings taboo and made me wonder if they were dangerous when I knew that they couldn't be, that it was only that Robert would worry unnecessarily if he knew. It felt as if desire were only permissible in art, where it could be dramatised, made beautiful. I wondered if this was why I had been drawn to curatorial work. I was represented, in a gallery, by the work of others, rather than through my own body; I was as interesting or attractive as whatever I chose to display, invisible yet elevated by the links that I made.

I thought of my writing about Grace's work. I'd always justified my fascination with her as professional interest. I was also infatuated, though, and my infatuation with her seemed to become greedier as I leafed through printouts of her paintings, taking notes. I was distorting Grace's substance, transforming her into an object of study that I might possess through interpretation, creating some sort of bond through the writing of a text. It felt so cruel, sometimes, to be an art historian.

'I paint things that I'm against to try to make them wonderful,' Grace had said, once, about *Grand Street Brides*. I wondered if I, too, could find a way through my discomfort via art. I thought of Grace's brides, haunting but beautiful, and of Sheila Legge's *Surrealist Phantom of Sex Appeal*, a performance in which Legge, masked with flowers and wearing a white dress, carried a pork chop around Trafalgar Square. I'd tried to determine why it was that Grace kept painting weddings while living in a community where relationships were casual and everybody ignored, or scoffed at, bourgeois values. If I looked beyond her social circle, though, she was far from the only artist who borrowed from and subverted their visual language. I wondered if there was a way to link my own wedding to this tradition, if serving pork chops at the reception would be too subtle.

It was rational, after all, to marry Robert, and I was a sensible person.

I hadn't been hiking in a long time. I followed Robert easily; it wasn't difficult terrain. I liked hearing the cracking sounds when he stepped on twigs. Robert glanced back, often, and smiled at me, and when we paused to drink water he stroked my hair and hugged me.

'I wish you were out here with me every day,' he said. 'It's nice just sensing your breath alongside mine.'

I'd walked through the forests of New York with Robert often, in past years, but I hadn't had an excuse to leave the city since he'd flown to Georgia. I thought, looking around at all the different shades of green, that I really liked hiking; I just didn't think that I'd ever be brave enough to wander through the forest alone.

I thought of all the same things, mostly, that I thought about in the city, but everything felt measured. My mind didn't outpace my body as it did on the concrete sidewalk. I wasn't sure if this was because of Robert or because the uneven surfaces, bursting with roots and sudden uphill shifts, forced me to pay attention to my relationship to the world. It forced an embodiment that I lacked in Manhattan, where everything was at or above my eye line.

We stopped, for lunch, beside a small lake.

'Is it always this lovely?' I asked Robert.

'It's lovelier because you're here,' he said. 'Plus it's not raining.'

We didn't need to talk much, and I realised that I'd missed the way that Robert's presence brought me back into my body. It wasn't only hiking that did this. It was also that he didn't speak simply for the sake of speaking. He pulled out sunscreen and passed it to me, quietly. He stretched his legs toward the water. I remembered that I, too, had legs that I could stretch, and that there was pleasure to be taken in doing so. He tucked the sunscreen into the backpack that we were sharing and moved it so that it was no longer between us, then shifted so that he could wrap his arms around me. I remembered, with Robert, what it felt like to be loved – it wasn't simply verbal affirmation.

We stepped back into the shadows after lunch. It was exhausting to think about the length of the trail, even if I wasn't walking much of it. I kept thinking, too, of Cara's work, and of Cara herself, and fixating on small details. I wondered if these strange, sudden obsessions were called crushes because, as with berries underfoot, a skin might break, rupturing the boundaries between one life and another. It felt risky to desire, as if compartments inside me were vanishing, oozing, overheating with the charge of adrenalin. My desire for Cara was new, or newly identified, untested, and I was not sure I could contain it.

In times of crisis, we must all decide again and again whom we love, Frank had written. I held the line close, as guidance, though he'd written it in a light-hearted poem on the film industry. It seemed, out of context, so profound, but it was his ability to blend depth and levity which made him, to me, so representative of Midtown Manhattan. I thought of my lunchbreaks at MoMA, of the clash of cultures on the nearby streets, flooded by tourists and corporate workers, sales assistants, pretzel vendors, other women, like me, who worked at the museum or, slightly northwest, in publishing.

The path tacked and twisted through the forest, and my thoughts did, too. I thought of Australia. In July, in Sydney, camellia blossoms lay soft and magenta, squished at the edges of sidewalks in Newtown, their petals turning brown. I liked things better here.

Robert stopped, suddenly, and I looked up.

'Are you okay?' he asked.

'Yes,' I said. 'A bit tired, maybe.'

'We're almost there,' he said. 'But look.'

He crouched beside a log and pointed toward a small mushroom, bright red amongst decomposing leaves. I crouched, too, to look at it more closely. It looked more like an emoji than a living thing.

'Oh, wow,' I said. 'Do you see these often?'

'I have to remember to look,' he said. 'There's a group of guys I hike with, sometimes, who know all sorts of stuff about mushrooms. It's great. I need to read up on it.'

Robert stood up and stretched his hand down to help me to stand, too. I rested against his shoulder and he kissed my temple.

'I kind of do wish I were hiking the whole thing,' I said, though this had only been true for a minute and I was sure, my ankles blistering, that it wouldn't stay true for much longer.

I got a seat on the right-hand side of the train and looked out at the river and the leaves, at Bear Mountain, at the Tappan Zee Bridge, at the small boats moored at the water's edges and the barges carrying crude oil from North Dakota or tar sands from Canada down via the Great Lakes. The landscape was beautiful, but blurry, and the window was too dirty for clear photographs. I felt that my life, too, was moving so quickly that I struggled to make sense of it. It was exhausting to resist, to switch paths, and yet I kept thinking about it and this, too, was exhausting. I wondered if my relationship with Robert had been premised less on desire and more on fear, on how alone I'd felt when I first moved to Massachusetts. I kept thinking of Cara. I kept thinking of the shooting in Orlando, wishing I were part of New York's queer community, wishing for some kind of collective mourning. I felt a different kind of loneliness, now, from that which I'd felt arriving in Boston, when I was eager to talk to anybody; I was eager, now, to be recognised, in all my messiness, rather than reduced to the easiest, or most palatable, version of myself. I felt, with Robert, as if I might be playing a role, but I'd never wanted to be an actress.

I felt, for a minute, when the train slowed at Yonkers, as if my thoughts were resolving into a neat picture, as if I was gaining clarity. I didn't want something that was predictable and tidy. I would break up with Robert, I thought. I wanted to move with my desire rather than resisting it in favour of the sensible. I kept thinking of how happy I'd felt, on Thursday night, lying on the floor with Cara, being young and drunk. The train started moving again, though, and by the time we entered the railway tunnel at 97th Street, close to a bar that Robert and I had always treasured, I'd completely changed my mind. Thursday night seemed so long ago.

19

I needed to talk to someone and so I decided to talk to Lucy. We met at a Mexican restaurant in Midtown East with an exhaustingly long menu and an expert's list of tequilas. I didn't know how to start the conversation. I was used to presenting myself as neat, assured and tightly together when it came to my relationship. I was used to talking about work instead of love. I was used to being rational and suddenly I wasn't being rational at all.

'Robert sent me a letter,' I said. 'I didn't open it for a week. Is that weird?'

'It sounds like you're going off him,' she said, casually enough to frighten me.

'No,' I said, panicking. 'I think it's a coping mechanism. I think it's because he's away. I think I have to switch off my feelings or I'll miss him too much.'

'Sure,' she said. 'I'm going to have quesadillas.'

I wasn't sure if I was trying to persuade Lucy or myself. I hadn't thought, until this moment, that the distance between Robert and I – not much in miles, but further in mystery – could change the way that I felt. I'd never been good at opening mail. Robert, in fact, was usually the one who insisted that I do it, reminding me that the envelopes piled up on the table might include phone bills that would increase if payments were late.

'I don't know how I feel,' I said. 'I can't figure it out. There's no real reason for me to feel ambivalent.'

'I think you and I are the same,' said Lucy. 'We try to solve these things with logic, rather than by going with intuition. It makes things difficult. I mean, that's what happened with me and Charlie.'

'What did you do, in the end?'

'I guess eventually we broke up,' she said, shifting her eyes away from mine.

'Was that what you wanted?' I asked, but Lucy didn't answer.

'How's the sex?' she asked instead.

'He's in the forest,' I said. 'So, you know, non-existent.'

'You just visited him.'

'We didn't have sex.'

'You must not really be into him.'

'I don't think that's it. I mean, we were staying with his parents. I think I just have too much to worry about,' I said. 'I think my mind's just put him to one side for that reason. I can't think about job applications and miss Robert simultaneously. It's too much.'

I knew this was an easy way to change the subject. Lucy was applying for almost six jobs a week while fighting with the curator who wrote her letters of recommendation for all these jobs. She would tell me about the threats that he'd made, about her inability to report his actions to HR, who always protected the curators and never kept anything confidential, and I would feel lucky, again, that Antoine was at the Venice Biennale or

Art Basel or the Tate Modern, or somewhere else in Europe, and rarely replied to my emails. He asked me to write my own references and allowed his assistant to ink his signature on letters with a custom-made stamp.

'I looked up that artist you're friends with,' said Lucy. 'Cara Weathers. Do you like her work?'

'Yeah,' I said. 'What did you think of it?'

'It's a bit naff,' said Lucy. 'Juvenile. I guess she's young. But I don't know why you like her so much, really. She seems kind of self-obsessed. Like at PS1, she didn't ask me any questions, she just talked about herself. Anyway, I shouldn't say that, since she's your friend. Sorry. But I found her work like that, too . . . navel-gazey. I'm surprised you're into it.'

On the bus that went down Second Avenue, my mind wandered to the thought of Robert breaking up with me. I would be freed, then, from the possibility of making the wrong decision.

I knew, though, that Robert wouldn't break up with me. If our relationship was a path, he would stick to it, even if it took a counterintuitive route, because that was what Robert did. He excelled at doing what was expected of him. I thrashed around, trampling plants as I searched for something original, something that felt right, while he was content with achievements that were conventional rather than ground-breaking. I called myself 'creative' when really I was just making a mess. Robert was content to be happy, successful, while I needed to be modern, to find some new variation on truth, even if that meant I lost my sense of security, all semblance of stability, in the process.

I was tired of all this thinking. I wondered if there was a way of testing what my life might be like without Robert, of ascertaining whether my desire for Cara was real or simply a projection, a longing provoked by the looming threat of marriage. I had known, in Australia, people who had open relationships or were polyamorous, but this seemed to require something that I didn't have, a conviction about myself that I did not possess, an embrace of clear boundaries. That wasn't what I wanted. I did not want to solidify, to become fixed. I loved feeling as if I didn't know who I might become in the future, and yet I couldn't quite bring myself to embrace this interpersonal uncertainty. I still wanted some security and hated my sense that I didn't know who I was in the present moment. I was too busy, and too insecure, to be the person that I wanted to be.

I wondered about Lucy's suggestion that I wasn't really into Robert. I'd wanted to talk to Lucy about my uncertainty, but I'd been so defensive when an opening emerged. I had jumped to defend my attachment to him. She'd never been in a long relationship and compared everything to what had happened with a guy named Charlie who she'd dated casually for eight months.

I wasn't overwhelmed with feeling all the time, but I had been, when I was younger, when I'd first met Robert, and I might be again. I couldn't make an important decision based on how I felt at a given moment, because I might not feel the same way at another moment; relationships had periods of romance and periods when things were bland. It was possible, even probable, to love somebody and yet develop crushes beyond the relationship. The danger, perhaps, was in inscribing importance to those crushes. I didn't feel overwhelmed by love for Robert, right now, but I knew that most people thought I should feel that way.

I couldn't figure out how to be overwhelmed by a feeling that was expected, by a feeling that I knew I was supposed to have.

I looked at Cara's Instagram account once I was back at home. I hadn't especially minded when Lucy criticised her, which I supposed was because I wasn't sure about her work, either. I wondered if I only liked it because I liked her. It hadn't occurred to me that Cara might be self-involved, and I liked this suggestion, too, because it made my appreciation of her feel more significant, as if it was less that everybody liked her and more that we had a particular connection, something that couldn't easily be replicated.

I didn't want to linger on the pictures, though, because I felt as if I was seeing them through Lucy's eyes. I was testing, perhaps, whether I was able to agree with her, trying to see if I could talk myself into it. It might have made things easier.

20

On Thursday evening, Cara and I went to some openings in Chelsea. It didn't feel stressful because it was summer, because everybody knew that the really important people were in the Hamptons or Europe, so the really important shows weren't opening right now. It was relaxing to go to openings and actually look at art, free from worries about whether I was being introduced to people who might later interview me for jobs.

Cara and I drank wine in the bar at Hauser and Wirth and then wandered through the Philip Guston show, which had evening hours. It was about to close and I'd seen it before, twice, because Guston had been friends with Grace Hartigan, had shown alongside her in *12 Americans*. They kept in touch after she moved to Baltimore, long after she'd had her falling out with Frank. Grace liked Guston, and their work in the 1970s hit similar notes, so I wanted to like him, too, but his paintings intimidated me. I'd thought his figures were cartoonish ghosts, for years, and dismissed them as whimsical, before realising, embarrassed, that they were members of the Ku Klux Klan.

We wandered through Chelsea, dipping into galleries when something called to us. I wondered what other gallery goers assumed about our relationship, and wondered if Cara, too, thought of that. It felt intimate to look at art alongside Cara, even as my job involved constant scrutiny of gallery walls; I should have been inured to it. I felt happy, as if my throat were coated in honey, sweetening the everyday act of breathing.

'Let's walk downtown,' she said, as things began to close.

We walked down Ninth Avenue and along Hudson, and then Cara suggested more drinks. I was fuzzy enough, from the gallery wine, to overlook the memory of my headache a week earlier. I couldn't have said no to Cara, anyway.

I'd never been into Henrietta Hudson before, though it was clear that Cara had. I'd seen the interior on Instagram, occasionally, when I tried to imagine myself into New York's queer scene. I felt proud of myself, ordering a beer, as if I'd achieved something. I felt oddly relaxed. It was enough, here, simply to be queer, and queerness was the norm, was instantly assumed. It wasn't necessary to have a relationship that demonstrated one's sexuality; I could just be myself, independent of other people, of the constraints of mutual desire.

It got later and we drank more beer and everyone was dancing and it didn't feel like a Thursday in New York. It didn't feel like 2016. It felt like 2007 in Sydney, except I wasn't pressing myself against a wall, too shy to mingle, watching Emily laugh with somebody she'd met five minutes earlier. I was dancing, now, alongside everybody, alongside Cara, and there was a woman doing the splits in the middle of the dancefloor, and a stranger in a blue jumpsuit turned to me, smiling, and yelled above the music.

'Doing the splits in a lesbian bar – good move!'

I laughed and smiled and it was easy. It didn't feel like a performance. I realised how much I'd missed this, though I couldn't pinpoint what it was about the bar that registered as *this*. It was a sense of community, in part, but more than that. I missed uncertainty and potential, the sense of existing outside categories and institutions that had felt easy and exciting with Emily. I felt, as another person whirled and everybody clapped, that uncertainty was far more creative and communal than certainty, that marriage was an institution that sought to tame, to strip away the electricity of desire.

I wanted the electricity.

I turned to Cara, but she'd moved back slightly, toward the wall, and was looking sullen. I followed her gaze and saw Stacey, across the room, in conversation with somebody. I looked back at Cara and she shifted, caught my eye.

'It isn't fair that she gets the whole queer community,' said Cara. 'Just because she's the outgoing one.'

'This isn't the whole queer community,' I said. 'It's one bar.'

Cara rolled her eyes.

I empathised with Cara's sense of estrangement but envied her the ex-girlfriend across the room, a proof of belonging that she could carry with her into the future, beyond the bar. I felt another envy, too; I wanted the attention that Cara gave Stacey, though I'd had her company all night.

I felt shaky, then, and it was late, and Cara didn't feel like dancing anymore.

It didn't seem safe to catch the subway back to Ridgewood, so Cara came to the Lower East Side with me. She rested her head against my shoulder in the taxi and linked her arm in mine as we got out. I unlocked and opened the door, then she leaned against the doorframe, and looked into my eyes.

It felt as if Cara were willing me to move toward her, to press her against the wall with my hips, to brush her hair from her face and keep my hand at the back of her neck. I almost kissed her, but then I thought of how she'd looked at Stacey at the bar and shifted my gaze. Instead, I let Cara fall asleep beside me, in my bed, wearing one of my t-shirts.

I'd expected that Cara would still be asleep when I left for work, but she was awake and in the kitchen when I emerged from the shower. She'd started making coffee, using Robert's drip coffee machine rather than my French press, and was looking through a book on the history of the colour black.

'Your apartment's so nice,' Cara said. 'Given the price, I'd figured it had to be awful. I always thought rent control only existed on TV.'

I shrugged and let her believe in it. I wasn't a morning person and couldn't remember if I'd told Cara the full figure or just the half I paid. It was, either way, much less than anyone would expect for the location.

'I should look at art books more often,' Cara said, turning a page. 'Learn from history. But I get turned off by all the reproductions. You lose the texture of the works. I'd rather go to a museum.'

She kept flipping through as I put bread in the toaster, pulled margarine from the fridge.

'The fabric shows up well, here, though. Maybe it's just oil paintings that photograph badly.'

I peered over her shoulder at a satin dress, photographed on a runway. It was black, predictably, and the straps crossed at the front, evoking a knot at the bodice. It hung loosely on the torso, meeting the body again at the hips, where two lines of stitching created the illusion of a belt. The fabric hung closely, draping downward, the play of light on creases indicating the shape of the thighs.

I remembered the comment Cara had made about black wedding dresses and imagined marrying her, both of us in black dresses, surrounded by a sea of guests in white and pale pink. I found that the idea didn't terrify me; it made my pulse points prickle, like I wanted to rush toward it. I'd been so critical of marriage. Why had this changed, suddenly, when I was thinking about Cara? I wondered if it was simply because she was a woman. I nodded at the dress and tried to smile, but I was too overwhelmed by my own feelings to speak, and then the coffee gurgled.

Cara was right, I thought, that evening, when I found the blue ribbon she'd worn in her hair lying on my bedroom floor, imagined pairing it with the dress I'd moved into my cupboard. What sort of modernist was so hooked on tradition that she didn't even consider black instead of white? It was so simple and yet it had never occurred to me. I felt stupid. I wondered if I could dye my dress or if I'd have to find a new one. I put the ribbon on my bedside table, tucking it under a bracelet so that it didn't fall away.

I noticed, as I lay down in my bed, the lingering scent of Cara's perfume. I thought of her cheek, the previous night, pressed against the pillow, and her body imprinted on the sheets. I reached out for the ribbon, ran my finger down it. I felt close to knowing what I wanted.

21

I needed to start applying for jobs. I didn't have much to do at work, so I took my laptop to the MoMA library and scrolled through listings on NYFA. I checked my email and saw that Sally, downstairs in our office, had forwarded me a link to the museum's own website.

Looks like you might be able to stay! She'd written.

It was an advertisement for Sally's job, which was similar to my own but with a longer contract and more responsibilities, a curatorial assistant position with an emphasis on working with the museum's collection. It was perfect for me; I was perfect for it. I loved all the tasks listed in the job description – performing gallery checks, writing dossiers for acquisitions, researching future exhibitions, liaising with Graphics and Conservation – and I fit their preferences, with my attention to detail and speciality in modern American painting, extremely well. I often compiled checklists for collection shows and saved them in the shared departmental folder for fun. I knew the institution and I knew how to do the job and the transition from Sally to me would be seamless. I could finish this job and start that job, simply shifting from one desk to another, and I'd have four more years in this museum that I loved, enough time to figure out what I might do with the rest of my life.

I replied to Sally's email, thanking her for sending the link, and began to write a cover letter.

We had, that night, our annual dinner with the benefactor of the fellowship program, or rather a senior member of the family whose foundation funded it. His apartment was one of those improbable places on Fifth Avenue that can't be imagined from outside; the building looked like all the others, with a canopy extended over the sidewalk, plants around the entrance and a doorman, and yet the apartment itself was completely singular, such that it seemed impossible that it could be contained within an unexceptional exterior form, a routine example of the type. The benefactor's private lobby, with black and white tiles and two mannequins dressed in elaborate kimono on an elevated platform, looked somewhere between an exhibition at the Met and the entrance to a ride at Disneyland. He waited for us there, looking almost like an actor, tall and bored in a tuxedo, flanked by three servants. The first servant took our coats and handed them to the second servant, who whisked the coats from the room, and the third servant offered each of us a glass of champagne or sparkling elderflower soda.

I, like the others, thanked the benefactor for the invitation, took a glass of champagne and filed into the living room, which was larger than my apartment. The view of Central Park, framed by chintz curtains and softened by the light-resistant gauze that coated the windows, looked as if it were painted.

He lives here alone, I thought, though there were staff everywhere and I assumed they did not all disappear when the guests left. Or, perhaps, the guests almost never left and the quiet hours were simply spent on preparation for the next group's arrival.

The benefactor didn't collect much modern art and so the fellows at the Met and the Frick gathered around the paintings, asking about their attribution, while those of us at MoMA just stared wide-eyed at the apartment and quietly gossiped.

'I've heard he has a dinner every night for different organisations he gives money to,' said Emma.

'I've heard his table accommodates twenty-eight people and he doesn't even have a smaller table,' said Anthea.

'Is that a Renoir?' said Jessie, who was better with the nineteenth century than the rest of us.

We were ushered into the next room for dinner. I counted the places; there were twenty-six, with various professors from universities with which the fellowship was linked invited alongside us. Our names were written on small cards and the benefactor sat at the centre of the large table. I was seated next to a man I hadn't met.

'I'm Sophia,' I said. 'I'm in Painting and Sculpture at MoMA.'

'Nice to meet you,' he said.

'Where are you from?' I asked.

He laughed.

'I am the Head of Art History at Yale,' he said, as if the sentence itself was a reprimand.

I knew, then, what his name was; it didn't seem crazy to me, though, that I might not know his face. *I study modern painting*,

I wanted to say, *and you work on medieval architecture.* Instead, I smiled politely. I wasn't even sure that he did work on medieval architecture; I simply associated him with the word *byzantine.*

Joe, a fellow at the Met that almost nobody liked, who never socialised with the other fellows but instead emailed senior curators as if offering them a rare delicacy, inviting them to lunch with him in the American Wing's café, smirked at me from the other side of the professor and asked his thoughts on a recent article in *The Burlington Magazine.*

I turned to Abby, on my other side, one of the two fellows at the Frick. I'd known Abby since my first year in graduate school; I'd hoped, when we both moved to New York for the fellowship program, that we would develop the friendship that we'd always teetered on the edge of, but Abby was, as she'd been in Massachusetts, an extremely busy person. I never knew if Abby and I had a rapport or if Abby was just charismatic. She always seemed delighted to see me.

'Sophia!' she said. 'I'm so happy we're sitting together.'

I'd kissed Abby, once, at a pub after a departmental party early in my first term at graduate school, which was the first term of Abby's second year. I had wanted to keep kissing her, but she was drunk and kissing everybody: classmates and strangers, even a poster on the wall that advertised a musician playing a show that had taken place two years earlier. I remembered noticing, after Abby had moved to France for her dissertation research, her lipstick still smeared on the musician's poster, still hanging on the wall over a year later.

'You have to come to the Frick soon,' said Abby. 'I have to show you the bowling alley in the basement before I leave.'

'Do you know what you're doing next? I know that's a dreaded question.'

'No, it's fine,' she said. 'I have a postdoc at the University of Toronto.'

I'd noticed, when Abby had introduced speakers at departmental seminars, years earlier, the way that her long hair weighed itself straight until it reached her shoulders and then bounced into waves that lay across her breasts, shining against the rough wool of her sweaters. I had talked to Abby at parties in that first term, wide-eyed with desire and trying not to embarrass myself. After I'd met Robert, we'd become confidants who only really saw one another when tipsy, promising lunches that never eventuated.

Abby had slipped, now, immediately, back into gossipy intimacy. She was complaining that all the men she met on dating apps were bankers, and that her flatmate, Elodie, didn't understand why she preferred hipsters.

'Elly doesn't get it because she grew up with all those people. She went to art school. She's tired of it. She doesn't understand our desire for arty boys at all,' Abby said, assuming I shared it.

'It's more arty girls that I'm interested in,' I said.

'I didn't know you were interested in women.'

'Oh,' I said, trying to understand her tone of voice.

'We can find you an arty girl,' she said, consolingly.

'I do have Robert,' I reminded her.

'Oh, that's good,' said Abby. 'I didn't want to ask about him in case you'd broken up or something. I'm glad you're still together. You have your hipster boy.'

'I wouldn't call Robert a hipster.'

'Well, he's not a banker.'

The benefactor tapped a spoon against his wine glass, calling us all to attention, and announced that he wanted each of us, going around the table, to share what we were working on and our plans for once the fellowship was done. Anthea, across the table, made eye contact with me and scrunched up her face.

Over the next few days, I kept thinking it was frustrating that even a girl I'd once kissed had assumed that I was straight. I didn't know if she even remembered kissing me, though; she'd been quite drunk and we'd only just met. I tried to assume that everybody was bisexual, but it felt safer, sometimes, to believe that women I'd kissed were straight, and I had to privately admit that I'd assumed that of Abby. I'd always felt mad with envy when Abby mentioned girls she'd hooked up with, though I'd never tried to pursue her, afraid that my crush might destroy the possibility of friendship. I struggled to believe that anybody who showed interest in me really felt it. It seemed, often, too good to be true; I kept expecting these beautiful girls who tilted their chins toward mine, and touched their lips to mine, to pull back. I replayed the scenes, later, in my mind, always fearing that it had been a performance for some man elsewhere in the room.

The other fellows, following the dinner, kept talking about their plans for September. Those of us at MoMA discussed other departments in museums, romanticising the world outside Curatorial, and everybody seemed surprised when their applications for Education or Events were overlooked. We had thought, snobbishly, that it would be easier in departments which didn't insist on PhDs. Emma had lined up some exhibitions at various downtown spaces. She was hoping for something a little less institutional but was applying for institutional fellowships nonetheless – freelancing barely paid and offered no health insurance. Anthea was applying for jobs as an architect, back in the UK and in Germany, but hoping she wouldn't have to take one. Nobody knew whether to renew the lease on their apartment.

'Everyone seems happier in LA,' said Emma. 'I want to move there.'

'I can't be picky,' said Anthea. 'I'm applying for everything, everywhere.'

'Well, yeah,' said Emma. 'I applied to a fellowship in Indiana yesterday and I can't drive. Don't even know how I'd get there.'

I stayed silent and ate my sandwich. I still hadn't applied for anything and was channelling all my energy into my application for Sally's job. I'd done the same thing two years ago; I'd applied to only three fellowships, against everybody's advice, and secured the one that I wanted most.

'The curatorial assistant I'm working with is leaving,' I said. 'I've been hoping, for ages, that her position would be advertised. I'd worried that it wouldn't be, because of the expansion and everything, and because they just hired an extra curatorial assistant six months ago, but they just put it up. It's so perfect.'

'You really can't count on that,' Anthea said. 'MoMA don't like to promote from within. I've heard so many stories. They'll suck out your expertise before you leave and then hire somebody working in a different area so that they can cover that, too, and get some new connections.'

'It's true, Soph,' said Emma. 'MoMA are notorious for it. The curators in my department are all bitter about being passed over for one another's jobs. Everyone's disposable and nobody ever gets rewarded.'

I'd heard similar things, before, from Lucy, whenever I'd told her that I wanted to stay. She'd told me that I had to move on, that I couldn't get attached to places, that museums were cruel and ate their young. I'd heard this from other people, too, but the phrasing was always so impersonal, always pinned on the institution rather than the individuals who shortlisted and interviewed candidates. I'd done my job well and I had institutional knowledge; I knew I could do Sally's job very well and I didn't believe that Antoine, or any of the curators, would throw that away due to a reluctance to hire somebody they knew. My contract was finishing, too, so it wasn't as if they could keep my expertise while acquiring somebody else.

'It's a sad truth of the world, Sophia,' Anthea said. 'Qualified, clever people are not a hot commodity. It's people who will connect you with power that are in demand. That's always what they want.'

'They fired a curatorial assistant last year,' Jessie said. 'And I'm pretty sure it was just so they could hire a gallerist's daughter who'd just finished her Masters.'

I'd heard all of this before, too, but I'd also heard counter examples. There were people in Archives and Conservation who had leapt from one fellowship to another; in Education, a foreigner on a one-year contract had secured a permanent position. The gallerist's daughter, while finishing her Masters, had been an intern in the same department. Emma's boss, despite her personality, had been hired at PS1 from MoMA, which was basically an internal promotion. I just needed to write a perfect cover letter, I thought; the life that I wanted was in such close proximity.

22

Can we go for a walk tonight? Cara messaged, a few days later, around lunchtime.

Sure, I replied. *I'll meet you at the shop.*

It was starting to rain as I left the museum, so I borrowed an umbrella that had been sitting behind my desk for months. I didn't know if it belonged to anyone. Cara was locking up as I arrived and looked doubtfully at the sky.

'Maybe a walk wasn't the best idea,' she said.

'We can get a drink,' I offered.

She scrunched up her face in displeasure, though I didn't know if this was in response to my suggestion or the drops gathering in her hair. It wasn't pouring, yet, but it was almost the end of July. We both knew that flash floods were likely.

'Here,' I said. 'Come under the umbrella.'

She shuffled underneath. I thought of the umbrella's architecture, of the way the edge operated like a threshold. It felt intimate to share an umbrella, as if we were living together in a small, domed house. Cara's face was close to mine and softened in the diffused light. We were held by the same frame, with no distancing mechanism. I wasn't sure where we were walking, but it didn't matter to me. I was content.

'Frank O'Hara called this *fragrant after-a-French-movie-rain*,' I said.

'I just wanted to say,' said Cara. 'This is awkward, maybe, and I don't know if I'm totally off-base, but I hope I'm not leading you on.'

'Oh,' I said.

'I mean, because, we're friends, but maybe I've given you the wrong impression. Like, I've been so upset about Stacey these last few months that I don't really know how I've come across. We've spent a lot of time together, and sometimes things seem blurry. I've kind of relied on you and maybe it seemed as if I wanted something more than friendship.'

It sounded rehearsed. It also sounded as if Cara were certain of how I felt, less as if she'd been questioning her own behaviour and more as if somebody else had warned her of my feelings. I knew this couldn't be the case, though, because I'd confided in nobody, and my friends weren't her friends anyway. I was shocked to realise I'd been so obvious.

'No,' I said. 'I think we're friends.'

'I am getting a bit wet,' she said. 'I hate umbrellas. It's, like, you're half inside the umbrella and half outside and all the rain gathers and rolls and pours all over your shoulder. Worst invention.'

'I am attracted to you,' I said, feeling an obligation to be honest. 'But it's fine. I know we're just friends.'

She came into my flat. I boiled the kettle, poured out cups of tea, and we were both silent, as if the conversation were paused until the tea had brewed. I felt, now, that I could confide in

Cara; she was, officially, a friend, which meant I had less to lose through honesty. I didn't need to be what she wanted.

'Why is it always like this for me?' I asked. 'I mean, in undergrad, my friend, Emily . . .'

I noticed the steam rising from my tea, hanging in the air like a ghost, dissolving, and stared at the circles on the Bakelite cup, composing photographs in my mind, as I waited for it to cool, instead of looking at Cara. I'd trailed off, expecting her to prompt me to continue, to ask questions or comfort me, but she didn't. When I looked up, Cara had almost finished her tea, which confused me, because I hadn't, and soon she was standing, telling me she had better go, that I didn't need to walk her down the stairs or to the subway, that she didn't even need to borrow an umbrella. She gave me a hug, quickly, and then she was gone.

It should have been something bigger, I thought.

It felt as if the conversation had lasted only five minutes. I had been blinking away tears, playing the part of a reasonable person, pretending that it didn't particularly matter if Cara didn't want to date me, even as I knew I'd almost ended my engagement over her. I felt rejected and sad, and I kept forgetting Robert, but I was still engaged to him and felt guilty for having these feelings of rejection, for pinning my desires on somebody who didn't desire me, looking outside my relationship like an adolescent looking to avoid adulthood, acting out. I'd been looking for an answer to my questions about Robert, about whether life might be better if we broke up, and I supposed that this was that answer.

I hadn't lost anything, I reminded myself. It was nicer to be friends, anyway. There was security, depth and longevity to friendship, which wasn't always the case with romance. Cara hadn't let me tell her my secrets, though, before she finished her tea and slipped away. I'd wanted to confide in her, to find evidence of the friendship that she professed, but she'd brushed that off. She hadn't left any space for intimacy, even the platonic kind.

I thought of Grace Hartigan's friendship with Frank O'Hara, platonic but closer than any romantic relationship that Grace had in her youth, more significant than her marriages. It's common to read hypotheses that Grace was in love with Frank, thwarted by his sexuality, though he had been the one who suggested to her, once, that they sleep together. *And ruin this?* she'd said, reportedly, turning him down. Frank O'Hara poured all the devotion he couldn't show the men he chose, who were always at least a little bit unavailable, into his friendships with women. There was, I thought, as much love in friendship as any other sort of relationship. It was so reductive to believe that all love was sexual or that the highest forms of love were those that asked for commitment and consummation. Grace Hartigan, after all, discarded most husbands very quickly. It was impossible to read Frank's poems without seeing friendships as sites of very deep love; a line he'd written to Grace was etched on his gravestone.

It was the season for rain, the point in summer when the sky became tender, easily provoked. It might look fine, in the morning, and then a storm would arrive in the late afternoon and suddenly drench everything. The flash floods brought the car exhaust that usually hovered above the streets, filling the spaces between skyscrapers, down to the asphalt. I was new enough, still, that New York's downpours left me awed, standing at the window staring as the water poured like syrup from the overhang onto the sculpture garden or pausing at the museum entrance to photograph the headlights of cars, kaleidoscoped by water, my phone's camera stilling a sort of doubled motion as drops pooled into rivulets, running down the windows as the traffic streamed past, tyres leaving a wake.

Umbrellas were useless when it rained like this. They showed their flimsiness, sending water cascading down off the edges and around the body, which was never still enough that the umbrellas could protect even the torso; water bounced off somebody's shoulder onto somebody else's face, grabbed at the collars of jackets and dribbled down the backs of shirts. Every drop felt dirty. It was worse around the legs, ankles, feet, where water came from every direction, crashing in horizontal waves as cars whisked it from the gutter or leaping up underneath skirts when it was flicked from nearby shoes. If this powerful rain came toward the end of the day, everybody stood together at the window, watching, rather than leaving work, bound together by water so dense that the air before us became opaque.

It felt as if the conversation had been quick, as if Cara had been in my flat for only five minutes, and yet I spent hours, that week, running over everything she'd said.

'Like Escher staircases,' Cara had said. 'Our desires don't match up . . . It's so rare for desires to match up. I mean, Stacey was the first person I'd ever liked who liked me back.'

I'd felt so envious, then, of Stacey. I pictured her in my mind as I'd seen her at the bar: tall and self-contained, half-smiling, with good posture and smooth skin, her eyes glancing easily around the room.

I wondered if I'd opened up to Cara too quickly, if she'd realised that I was always sad, and possibly mad, incapable of making any kind of decision. I wondered if I should have hidden my insecurities, if I'd shown her my weaknesses too quickly, scaring her away with the intimacy that I'd imagined.

'I'm sorry,' she'd said. 'You've really done nothing wrong. I really think you're a great person. And friendship's really important. It's not just a consolation prize.'

She had said nice things, but when I'd tried to tell her that this wasn't the first time that something like this had happened to me, when I'd tried to tell her about Emily, she'd looked down at her watch.

'I think I should probably go,' she'd said, which didn't feel like friendship.

I hadn't cried. I'd felt, instead of sadness, a strange relief that I knew, now, what was going on, that I no longer needed to worry about misinterpreting Cara's actions, no longer needed to make decisions about my life and what I wanted.

It was only after she'd left that I realised I'd gone along with her suggestion that I wanted more than friendship and that I'd never thought to mention Robert. I wondered if there was a certain narcissistic confidence in her presumption that I'd wanted more. I had a fiancé, after all.

23

I started trying to catalogue all the rejection I'd experienced in the past, hoping for an explanatory theory. I thought mostly about Emily, who hadn't ever told me she didn't want to date me, but who had made it obvious that what was between us was only friendship through countless small gestures. I had known that my love for Emily was unrequited from the speed with which she turned away from me, in bed, and from the way that she fixed her eyes on the dishes she was washing, rather than on me, while we talked. I'd had an intuitive awareness that I had to be careful lest she pull away further.

I'd expected to keep in touch, after I moved to Massachusetts, and I'd emailed regularly for a while, but Emily was slow to respond. I realised, eventually, that she didn't need to hear from me, that I was setting myself up for disappointment each time I contacted her. I met Robert and Emily gradually faded into the past, into Australia.

While *Grand Street Brides* was Grace's best-known painting, *Bride and Owl* had been painted first. Her work on this had been interrupted when Frank O'Hara was shot in his hallway by a burglar, the bullet in his hip sending him to hospital. Grace aimed, in *Bride and Owl*, for a certain austerity, a reliance on line over colour. I thought often of a photograph that Walt Silver had taken of Grace painting while Marion Jim posed with a white owl which was only just visible, and easy to miss, at the edge of Grace's canvas. In the end, it was the combination of the natural – the softness of the owl, of the woman's face – and the abstract – the hard lines intersecting the owl's eyes, the vast expanses of black atop the pale canvas – that gave the portrait its pull. After *Bride and Owl*, Grace wanted a larger canvas as a battleground, and began to work on *Grand Street Brides*.

I was trying to channel my sadness into my work, but I wasn't entirely succeeding. I tried to draw parallels between my own work and Grace's paintings. I supposed that my fellowship at MoMA might be my *Bride and Owl*, but I was still wondering what came next, which museum might provide me with a battleground for curatorial masterpieces. Grace had been such an excellent observer of her own work, filling her diaries with descriptions that I wished I'd written. I wanted to live up to Grace's work, rather than simply to report on it, repeat it.

I was waiting to hear from Cara, but I feared that she might fall out of my life as quietly as Emily had done. I didn't miss Emily so much as the youth that we'd shared; I'd felt alive with the pain and pleasure that she'd provoked, but she'd provoked so much of it that I'd fled the country. It had been eight years since I'd lived with her, but I remembered sharply the ways in which we'd communicate in group settings, secretly, through quick glances or turns of phrase that were loaded only to the two of us.

Emily had known everything that was inside me, which made it easier for her to dissect me, to dismiss me. I was always too much for sensitive people to handle; they knew that to be in a relationship with me would be more trouble than it was worth. It was the people who saw through the myth of coping that I really wanted – the people who caused me to dissolve into tears and confessions of childhood secrets soon after I met them. I'd seen a therapist, once, who suggested that I was addicted to loss, that I chose people who would hurt me in order to process trauma, and then he asked about my childhood and I didn't make another appointment. I didn't want to be analysed by a stranger. I just wanted to be in love.

Robert had never seen me as sad. It had made me feel powerful when we'd first met, but I wondered now if it was because he'd fallen for something he'd projected onto me, some image of the ideal girlfriend, rather than for me. He thought that I was happy, confident, well-adjusted. I'd been intoxicated by the light in which he saw me. He still thought that I was fine, told me I was being melodramatic whenever I suggested that I might be depressed. I remembered, now, that he had never asked about my family; months into the relationship, he had avoided my hints, changing the subject, talking about himself instead.

'It didn't seem polite to pry,' he'd said, almost a year later, when I'd finally asked.

This seemed, then, like soft, sweet reasoning, though love needed communication more than good manners. Robert's reticence had allowed me to be to be the stronger party, which I had enjoyed, but I wondered now if it meant that the dynamic would always be one in which I was a little abandoned. I knew, though, that it was easier to long for somebody I couldn't have than to long for Robert, with whom my relationship was real rather than imagined. I knew Cara only as a friend, couldn't see the instincts that romantic intimacy might unlock in her, while Robert's flaws were familiar. Robert was somebody that I knew that I would, or could, or did, have, somebody that I knew had chosen me. It seemed ridiculous to want someone who didn't want me when I had Robert. I wasn't sure that he could handle, or even see, my emotions, but those who recognised them couldn't – or, rather, wouldn't – handle them either.

I thought, now, of what Cara had said about Escher staircases and wondered if what Robert and I had was rare, if I'd never find another person whose desires matched mine, even if the match wasn't exact. I kept reminding myself that I was lucky. I kept pushing my sadness away, but it kept coming back, overpowering me, and pinning me to the floor. I had to learn how to inhabit it, how to stop wanting more, wanting too much. I'd been doing so well before I met Cara.

24

I was trying to focus on work, on art, on anything but love. Robert was in Connecticut, now. I wished that I was with him, that he might give me a hug and tell me the histories of trees, whisper an Alice Notley poem into my ear. I stopped listening to my favourite songs, afraid to associate them with this sadness, and listened to Metallica instead.

I read exhibition reviews in *Artforum* and sent them to my friends from graduate school, scattered at various museums and universities across the world, asking if they'd seen the shows. I considered catching a train to Boston for a weekend and staying with friends who were still in Somerville, but nothing on the ICA's exhibition schedule interested me and the trip didn't seem justifiable without art as an excuse. I emailed Emily, and some other friends from Australia, writing that it had been a long time and that I'd like to catch up on all their news; none of them replied.

—

I was still struggling to focus, as I had since April, but the intrusive feelings, now, were of disheartenment rather than possibility. Cara had said that we were friends, that nothing would change, and yet I felt already that it had. I missed her. I waited for her to message and she didn't. I felt that I couldn't message her, that to do so might be misinterpreted as unrequited desire. I didn't know, anyway, what to say. I wondered if she was just trying to let me down easily. If she wanted to be friends, why hadn't she messaged me?

I kept hovering over Cara's name on Facebook. I watched her Instagram stories and she watched mine, but she never clicked *like* on the pictures that I posted, even when they were images that I'd felt sure would appeal to her, images that I'd chosen in the hopes of some recognition. I had always thought of friendship as offering increased intimacy, as an ongoing discourse, but it seemed that she'd told me that we were friends only to immediately withdraw the practice of friendship.

There was a certain light in August that made everything seem distant. The air was thick with illuminated dust particles and drinking glasses on tables cast long shadows. In the evenings, everything was filtered blue, stretching dusk for hours. If I left the lights off, the street lamps seemed to float upward, projecting the shapes of window frames onto the walls. The street outside felt like a ravine, rough with rocks and a river of traffic.

I knew that soon the leaves would crisp and fly across the pavements. I knew that somebody would draw a curtain and then everybody else would begin to notice night falling and draw their own curtains. My neighbours would, as they turned their lights off to sleep, see the city through veils, with streetlights caught in the fabric, the shadows of fire escapes flattened and abstracted.

I slept with the blinds open, watching dusk fade into night. I wanted the city to come inside, to enter into my dreams. Robert hated this; he always complained that he couldn't sleep with the lights outside. I wondered what it was like to sleep in a tent under the moon, if it became impossible when the moon was full. I looked over at my white dress, hanging like a ghost in the half-light of the open closet, and then out the window. The moon, glimpsed through a gap between buildings, glowed like a shaking soap bubble.

On Thursday, Cara finally messaged. I had been starting to accept a life in which I might not hear from her, in which we'd drift apart quietly, sadly but without drama. When her name reappeared on the screen of my phone, I felt nauseous.

Hey Sophia, how's your week going?

She had sent the message, I supposed, to show that she was still thinking about me, that she did care, but it felt empty. I had no choice, really, but to reply with something equally inane. I tried to wait half an hour before replying, to signal indifference, but lasted only eighteen minutes. I hated myself for my inability to resist something that seemed so simple. I felt as if my limbs might fall away from my body; the air bubble in my stomach had gravitated to my throat.

Hey, it's going well, thanks – how is your week going?

I couldn't ask too much, be too much. I didn't know if Cara was writing because she missed me or because she felt a sense of responsibility, a need to prove that she'd meant it when she said that she cared.

Cara took much longer than eighteen minutes to respond to my reply, leaving me feeling more powerless still, hooked on her for the entire afternoon. She messaged back three hours later and her response felt hostile in its brevity.

I'm good, thanks.

I knew, after this meaningless exchange, that there would be another week without her, that Cara was doing the bare minimum, a surface charade of caring. I knew, too, that I wasn't entitled to more than that charade, that nobody was ever entitled to anything. I could be mad at Cara for her absence, but that that wouldn't mean she was at fault.

25

I uploaded a picture of my breakfast table to Instagram, composed so that the sun slanted in through the window and illuminated the decorative tea towel that hung above it, a pink replica of *The Advantages of Being a Woman Artist* by the Guerrilla Girls. I caught the subway to work and uploaded a picture of the museum's sculpture garden, the neat chairs and messy foliage mottled with shadows, captioned *early morning*. I checked the app, anxiously, each time I went to the bathroom, but Cara didn't click 'like' on either photo. I spent the morning proofing acquisition dossiers.

Emma, Jessie and Anthea were almost finished with their lunches when I went down to the sculpture garden. I joined them at their table, in the corner, where Emma looked like she'd been crying.

'She's literally not your boss anymore, though,' said Anthea.

'Yeah,' said Emma. 'But I don't understand everybody else being like that.'

'What happened?' I asked.

'I went to Hope's goodbye breakfast and nobody spoke to me.'

'Nobody spoke to you?'

'Nope,' she said. 'They all ignored me for the entire hour.'

'They probably all felt they had to do what Hope was doing,' said Jessie. 'I wouldn't take it personally.' She paused. 'Also, I heard a rumour that Hope tried to get the museum to pay her replacement less than she'd been paid.'

'Wow,' I said. 'That's absolutely evil.'

'Yeah, I definitely wouldn't take any of this personally, Emma,' said Anthea.

'How am I going to get another job if Hope hates me?' said Emma.

'Well, I think a lot of people hate Hope,' Jessie replied.

I went back to the cafeteria to buy coffee on my way up to the office. There was a long queue, so I pulled out my phone and checked Instagram again. Cara still hadn't liked either of the morning's photos. I hadn't liked her more recent photograph, either, which was an image of somebody seated on a chair, cropped just below the knees and above the waist, with a large bouquet of roses in her lap. I saw that somebody else, a stranger to me, had commented with five flying heart emojis and that Cara had responded with the emoji that showed hearts floating around a smiley face, the crab emoji and the sparkle emoji. I was saddened, then, by the thought that we were no longer one another's primary audience, though perhaps I'd never been that audience to Cara.

I scrolled down, looking at Cara's older posts, and suddenly realised that the photographs she'd taken of me at PS1 and in Chelsea were gone. I blinked, wondering if I'd simply scrolled past them, and checked the section for photographs in which I'd been tagged. They weren't there. I felt a bolt of adrenalin, of anger or disorientation, and went back to Cara's profile. She'd deleted all the photographs that she'd taken of me.

I returned to the strange side project that I'd given myself: researching marriage in modern art.

I read about Yayoi Kusama's 1968 performance of New York's first 'homosexual wedding', held on Walker Street. She created a wedding gown designed for two people, explaining that *clothes ought to bring people together, not separate them*.

I just didn't seem to care. I couldn't concentrate.

I looked at Cara's Instagram again. She'd deleted quite a number of images, I realised. She'd deleted all her earlier photos of Stacey, too. It was a compliment, I told myself, to be included in the same category as Stacey.

On Saturday, I went to the Guggenheim to see the Moholy-Nagy show. I wore a pleated skirt pulled from the back of my wardrobe, hoping I might be able to hide my insecurities in the folds of fabric, and a white t-shirt that felt dirty, sweaty, by the time I'd caught the subway uptown.

It was the worst museum to visit when one wasn't in the mood for art at all. The major exhibitions were in the central rotunda, requiring visitors to walk up a sloped incline, slowly, for hours, with little relief. The piece that I was most interested in seeing, a silver kinetic sculpture beneath lights that changed colours, called *Light Prop for an Electric Stage*, was right at the beginning, too, so I didn't have anything to look forward to as I edged up the spiral ramp.

Lucy and I had dinner, that night, at Dimes. We met at six, before the crowds came, and there was a group of people loitering outside, hoping for the pink table that always looked good in photographs. There was no wait at all for the other tables. Our table was small and orange.

'The wheatgrass margarita is meant to be really nice,' said Lucy. 'But I can't ever bring myself to order it. It just sounds so . . . Los Angeles.'

I felt lucky, sometimes, to be a foreigner. In Sydney, I would have been self-conscious ordering a wheatgrass margarita, and would have wondered, sitting in a restaurant known for them, if I was a class traitor. In New York, I just felt like a tourist or, better, like a denizen of the Lower East Side. I'd had the wheatgrass margarita before and I'd liked it.

Lucy ordered a cocktail named Desert Flower, instead, and the roasted cod, while I ordered the black rice bowl with pickled salmon and a cocktail named Gift of Summer that tasted of watermelon and rum.

'Do you think we like this place because we're art historians?' asked Lucy. 'The food's always so beautifully presented.'

I considered the subtlety of my dish's colour scheme, the range of greens and pinks set against the deep black backdrop of the rice. I looked across at Lucy's cod, garnished with a piece of lime twisted into a serpentine line at the centre of the bowl.

'I think the chef started out as a painter,' I said.

I'd decided to tell Lucy about Cara. It was easier to speak about, now, perhaps, because I wasn't risking my engagement. There was nothing at stake, really, and I wanted comforting.

'I've been a bit of a mess, lately,' I said. 'I don't know if you've noticed. I sort of developed some feelings for that girl I met, Cara. I didn't know what to do about it and then she realised and rejected me, anyway, which hurt more than it should have.'

'Oh, I'm sorry,' said Lucy. 'That's rough.'

She paused. 'But, wait, what does this mean? Are you bicurious now?'

'I've always been bisexual,' I said.

'Sorry,' she said. 'You've just been with Robert for such a long time. A little crush, then?'

It felt as if Lucy minimised it when she called it a crush, rendered it something safe, sweetly adolescent. There was nothing safe, though, about feeling teenage. I'd felt, during those years, in mortal peril, and attractions to girls in my small town had been one of the worst parts of this. I knew that crushes could crush people, that they were passionate, urgent, out-of-control, something to contain or conceal. I knew that desire, if it flared in the wrong place, could cost a girl her life. I didn't want to think about it.

'I wish I had a crush,' said Lucy. 'It would be nice to have somebody to daydream about at work.'

'Crushes against capitalism,' I said, and she laughed.

'Do you think it's cold feet?' asked Lucy. 'My cousin had a total crisis before her wedding. She took a ton of drugs at her bachelorette party and ended up in hospital. They got married, though, and they're still together.'

'I suppose it must be,' I said. 'But what does cold feet even mean?'

'I think it's just that people freak out, knowing it's permanent and, like, we're getting older,' said Lucy.

'It is such an adult rite-of-passage, marriage,' I said.

'Cara is, like, nineteen,' said Lucy. 'Are you trying to be nineteen again, relive your youth?'

'She's twenty-two,' I said.

I didn't want to be twenty-two again, in love with Emily and living with her, hoping sex alongside friendship would turn into romance. I didn't want a crush. I didn't want anything that would carry me into the past.

'I know it's silly,' I said. 'It feels like a breakup, even though we were never going out. She said we'd stay friends, but then she deleted the pictures of me on Instagram.'

Lucy paused, her fork above her plate.

'Maybe she did like you,' she said. 'It's weird to delete pictures. Like, symbolically, it's a kind of repression.'

'Thanks, Freud,' I said. 'It's probably just what people do, though.'

'I'm more of a Jungian, actually,' said Lucy. 'Do you want to be friends with her?'

'Yes.'

'I'd be angry if I were you. It's kind of deceitful, the Instagram thing.'

'You don't even really use Instagram,' I said.

'I do,' said Lucy. 'I'm up to four thousand followers.'

'You only use it for work,' I reminded her. 'It's not the same.'

'Still,' said Lucy. 'You don't have to be friends.'

'She didn't do anything wrong,' I said. 'Why wouldn't I want to be friends with her?'

'Well . . .' Lucy shrugged. 'Just make sure it doesn't get masochistic.'

'Robert and I saw Adrien Brody here, once,' I said, changing the subject. 'Robert thought he looked familiar, so he nodded to say hello, thinking it was probably a lit scholar he'd met at a conference somewhere, and then realised it was Adrien Brody and was mortified.'

It had been at brunch, just before Robert had left. I'd eaten the 'love toast' with raspberries arranged delicately atop two triangles of bread coated with tahini and honey, sprinkled with lavender. We'd been given, with the bill, a postcard on which Bernie Sanders and Hillary Clinton had been photoshopped into Dimes. Bernie sat at a table by the window, his hands together and a cup of coffee at his elbow, looking over at Hillary, smiling on her phone at the next table over, a salad before her. I wondered if we'd get a different postcard now that Hillary was the definite nominee.

I supposed that Lucy was just being a good friend, criticising Cara to make me feel better about myself. I knew, rationally, that people deleted photographs to help themselves heal after breakups, but we hadn't broken up. I didn't know why Cara would need healing. It did seem, as Lucy had said, like a repression, but perhaps I just wanted to assign myself greater significance in Cara's life than I deserved. It felt as if she was determined to erase memories of our pleasant moments, ashamed to admit that we'd spent time together, as if she was trying to create a narrative of her life in which I meant nothing.

It was possible, probable, almost certain, that I'd meant nothing. It hurt, though, and there was nothing at all that I could do about it.

I was still trying to think through this question of marriage and modernism. I felt like it would, if formulated and answered, make everything clear to me. I wondered if part of the problem was modernity's emphasis on the individual; marriage forced a dependence, perhaps.

I missed being able to talk about these things with Robert. I thought of him, walking a literal track, but I thought, also, of the ways in which he seemed to provide a path for me, something steadying and level. Robert would, if asked about marriage and modernism, have some perfect quotation; one of the writers he'd studied would have articulated my idea in language that I'd never have myself.

I tried to think about it in relation to Frank O'Hara, and remembered 'Poem Read at Joan Mitchell's', written for the painter's wedding. I leafed through O'Hara's *Collected Poems*, which I kept in an untidy pile of books at one end of the sofa, until I found it.

It is most modern to affirm someone, I read.

I typed the phrase out on my phone and sent it to Robert. He hadn't replied to my earlier message, which probably meant that he didn't have reception wherever he was camping, so I plugged the phone into the wall and went to bed.

It's so original, hydrogenic, anthropomorphic, fiscal, post-anti-esthetic, bland, unpicturesque and WilliamsCarlosWilliamsian!

I read, in a text message from Robert, when I awoke on Sunday morning. *It's definitely not 19th Century, it's not even Partisan Review, it's new, it must be vanguard!*

Reading this, I didn't know why I'd ever felt uncertain about marrying Robert. He had memorised my favourite poems and could send me the perfect quotation, the one that fixed the link between marriage and modernism, even while walking through the forest.

26

I woke up, next Saturday, to the telephone ringing.

'Sophia,' said Barbara. 'I haven't heard from you in a while. How is wedding preparation going? Do you want me to come down to help?'

I had forgotten, again, about planning this wedding. Robert had said that there was no urgency, that he would talk to his mother, that we would talk about all of it, together, when he was back. I had bought a dress, but that was it, really. I hadn't decided on a season, considered venues, drafted a list of guests. I felt that this was fine and Robert agreed. I was terrified of Barbara, though.

'Well, what have you been doing?' she asked.

'I've been thinking about it a lot,' I said. 'I've done a lot of research.'

I swung my legs out of the bed and sat on its edge. My eyes fell on Cara's blue ribbon, still lying on my bedside table, atop a postcard showing a young girl with doves that she'd given me. I hadn't had any coffee. I wondered why I'd answered the phone.

'I've been thinking there should be birds . . .'

'I don't think that's very practical,' said Barbara.

'In cages, so they don't fly away,' I added, and then immediately regretted it. I hoped Barbara's interest in the Metropolitan Museum was superficial enough that she didn't know what birds in cages signified in art. I tried to shift the conversation away. 'I'm going to look at cakes tomorrow.'

'Where?' said Barbara.

'On Grand Street. Near Grand Street. I can't remember the name of the place.'

'That's a strange neighbourhood for cake,' said Barbara. 'I suppose things have changed since I lived in the city. I think you should ask about a croquembouche. They always have those at weddings in France and they're lovely. Do you know how to spell it?'

I hated when I was woken by the phone. I said things that didn't make sense and that I regretted. I couldn't break my promise to try cakes, because Barbara would almost certainly call to ask about them. She would probably write to Robert about it, too, and he – probably salivating, on the trail – would be excited about cakes. It was, at least, an excuse to eat nice things.

It could be, also, an excuse to call Cara.

She'd said, after all, that we were friends, even if she had deleted those photos.

I called Cara.

'Are you working tomorrow?' I asked. 'Do you want to come to try cakes with me?'

'Why cakes?'

'Wedding cakes.'

'Like, for your wedding?'

'Yes.'

'Sure,' she said. 'I'm not working.'

I needed to make more of an effort with Robert, I thought.

In graduate school, my advisor had suggested that having a secure relationship, the kind of relationship that could just fade into the background, was useful for getting work done. I'd wondered, at the time, if I'd ever take Robert for granted in this way, allow my relationship to fade into the background. I worried, now, that I had. I wondered if all of this was, as Lucy had suggested, 'cold feet'. I did love him.

I saw an advert for an underwear line called 'Wish You Were Here', I texted. *Near Canal Street. xx*

I set an alarm on my phone to remind myself, later, to look up advice on text messaging in long-distance relationships.

Cara seemed a little subdued when we met. She was wearing a sleeveless blue dress, white sneakers and silver earrings that caught the light. She was typing something into her phone, leaning against the painted brick fence that separated the street from the small soccer pitch between Forsyth and Chrystie Streets, and didn't see me until I was beside her.

'Oh,' she said, and tapped her phone screen before tucking it into a pocket. 'Hi.'

'How are you?' I asked.

'Pretty good,' she said, squinting into the dappled light. 'I should have brought sunglasses.'

'We'll mostly be inside,' I replied.

It was only a few blocks to the first bakery on my list. I had wanted to start with a place near Grand Street, so as to retroactively excuse my lie. I had trouble finding places on the internet; I didn't want a cake from Momofuku Milk Bar or anywhere too obviously trendy. I wanted a cake from AW or Fine Bakery City or one of those other places that tourists failed to notice when walking past. Nonetheless, it turned out the Italian bakery I'd found on Google was an icon. It had wooden panelling and a long counter, selling gelato alongside pastries, with paper napkins that read *Since 1892*. I ordered a small raspberry and white chocolate chimney cake and split it into two with a knife.

'I'm not really sure how to do this,' I said. 'I know there's some formal way of organising cake tastings, but I haven't done that, so I thought we'd just go to cafes nearby and eat cake.'

'Sure,' she said.

It was like this for almost half an hour. Cara would say almost nothing, save the word *sure* when I suggested something. She seemed to like the cake, taking dainty spoonfuls and lingering over them, but she wasn't really talking much. I was reluctant to press her; I knew she was acting strangely because our friendship had been complicated by the last time we'd met. I'd acquiesced to everything, though; I didn't know why Cara seemed to pull away.

'You didn't tell me you were getting married,' she said, eventually.

'I'm not sure if I am,' I said.

'Why are we tasting cakes, then?'

'I'm not sure.'

'Are you engaged?'

'I suppose.'

'You *suppose*?'

'I mean, officially, yes,' I said. 'I guess I'm engaged. I thought you knew that. I came into your bridal shop.'

'Sure,' said Cara.

'I mean, didn't you?'

'Sure.'

'I'm sorry.'

'It's just kind of fucked up, don't you think?'

'Marriage?'

Cara laughed without smiling, tugging at the sleeve of her pink jacket, looking over my shoulder and then down around my elbow and out toward the back of the cafe, never meeting my eyes.

'I'm your friend, right? We see each other all the time. I kind of sensed there was something weird going on with your boyfriend, because you never talk about him, like, whenever you say *boyfriend* you flinch, like you didn't mean to say it but your tongue slipped or as if you're being forced to testify under oath, but . . . and, like, I'm not sure I've ever heard you say *fiancé* . . .'

She trailed off and then kicked up her chin to look directly at me.

'Isn't it a bit . . . Isn't it something that you'd tell me, that you're engaged? Especially given my work. Especially when, well . . . I thought I was the one leading you on.'

'I thought you knew,' I said.

I was looking at the ground, now.

'That doesn't make sense. We've had all these conversations, like we've talked about wedding dresses and performance art, all sorts of wedding rituals, that painting of brides at the Whitney . . . It's weird you never linked any of that to your own relationship.'

She was right. It would have been natural, even easy, to talk to Cara about all of it, and I'd held back for fear of the consequences.

'I'm very sorry,' I said, suddenly on the verge of tears. 'I haven't really been talking about it with anyone. I don't want to think about it. I don't know if I want—'

'It's okay,' she said. 'We don't need to talk about it.'

I didn't know what else to say, so I looked across at a family at another table. There were two teenagers wearing baseball caps, slumped back and staring at their phones as their parents leaned over the table, pointing at a map in the guidebook between them and talking quietly. The softening cream in their half-eaten cannoli oozed toward the edges of the plate. I noticed, in my peripheral vision, Cara's gaze follow my own and then turn back, fixing on my cheek with what seemed like sympathy.

'This really isn't the best way to go about tastings. I don't think you want cannoli at your wedding,' said Cara. 'I know a girl who makes cakes.'

27

I hadn't expected to agree with Barbara, but when I looked up *croquembouche* on the internet it seemed perfect. *Profiteroles piled into a cone and bound with spun sugar*, I read. It wasn't a cake, technically, but a crowd of pastry, which I quickly theorised as an argument for the collective over the individual. It looked, I thought, a little bit like a mountain, but it was also sculptural and modern, first appearing in a cookbook in 1915. It married Robert's interests and my own, binding them with spun sugar.

Cara had given me Alice's email and she'd replied, quickly, with a set of detailed questions about taste, budget, colour scheme, venue and guests, over half of which I couldn't answer. I googled her name and couldn't find any information on her wedding cakes; I guessed that she was just starting out. I replied, asking about the croquembouche and apologising for my uncertainties on the other counts, and she replied, quickly, again, to say that it was fine, suggesting Wednesday evening for a tasting and giving me her address. I messaged

Cara, asking if she wanted to come along, and she replied, saying *yes*.

Robert and I had settled into a rhythm, now, with emails and phone calls. He didn't feel as far away now that he was in the North-East. I'd seen him in the Hudson Valley and would see him again, soon, in North Adams. The Appalachian Trail felt less distant, less different, in the states that I knew. It wasn't really wilderness, but a weekend trip.

Robert rang from Kent.

'I'm going to test cakes tomorrow,' I told him.

'Thanks for appeasing Mom, Soph,' he said. 'It's obviously not your job to do all of this stuff. She was the same with Michelle when she got married. Mom thinks men can't plan events. I swear she's forcing you to do all this planning now so everything's all set and I can't invite my hiking buddies or something.'

'It's fine,' I said. 'I like eating cake.'

I looked up Kent after I hung up the phone.

Kent had a beautiful waterfall and rivers full of trout. It appeared idyllic in a bourgeois way that left me slightly uncomfortable. *In Connecticut, the Unwashed Meet the Upper Crust*, read a headline about the town. I supposed that towns like this made almost everyone feel like an outsider, offering an impossible image of the world as neat and tidy that couldn't be matched by many psyches. It had a museum dedicated to antique machinery and the town's most popular tourist attraction was a covered bridge over the Housatonic River.

Kent sounded insufferable on paper, but Robert had told me that the locals were friendly, that a woman outside the chocolate shop had offered him a Cointreau truffle and a lift to the trail-head. I'd always seen Connecticut as a state for wealthy white people who just wanted large swathes of land on which to keep the expensive things that they inherited or bought. Robert had laughed when I'd told him this, once, on the train down from Boston, and said that I was forgetting about all the roads, that Connecticut was fifty-percent traffic jam.

Robert was going at a slower pace, now, taking more 'zero days', as hikers called the days when they didn't walk, stopping in town libraries to research sections of the trail and their environments. I suspected he was doing this because it was almost my birthday, because we had a plan to meet in North Adams and he didn't want to get there too soon and see the town before me, but it was possible that he was just tired of rushing or had reasons to read and research in New England. I was looking forward to seeing him in Massachusetts, anyhow.

Cara and I met outside the DeKalb Avenue subway, near Alice's flat. She was friendly but impatient, skipping as much as walking, and kissed Alice on the cheek after she opened the door, almost dancing past her and whirling around, smiling, to introduce us.

'I've had so much coffee this morning,' she said to Alice. 'This is Sophia, my friend.'

'Hi,' I said.

'This is Alice,' said Cara, and paused, as if considering something. 'My muse.'

'I'm not your muse,' said Alice, tilting her head.

'Not *yet*,' said Cara, and Alice laughed and turned back to me, shrugging her shoulders.

'Congratulations,' she said.

I had assumed that pastry chefs had large, dedicated spaces, but Alice's kitchen was in her flat, or, perhaps more accurately, *was* her flat. It was a studio and her single bed was pushed into a small corner behind a rack of clothes, her shoes lined up underneath. There were a lot of cardboard boxes around, in varying states of assemblage.

'Sorry about the mess,' she said. 'I'm moving next week. I've just been staying here while I looked for a place, but I unpacked everything anyway. It's a sublet; I obviously couldn't afford to live alone in New York.'

Alice, like a storybook character, matched her name. She had a blonde fringe and velvet headband. She was dressed in a plain pink t-shirt and blue jeans. She wore no makeup and no nail polish, though her cheeks and eyes had a natural brightness. Alice didn't look tired, like most people in New York, despite her impending move.

I hoped that Alice wouldn't coo or ask questions like the women who worked in bridal shops, and she didn't. She asked, mostly, about life at the museum, proffering strange questions about rumours that I hadn't heard.

'Is it true that Mies van der Rohe's frozen head is in the Architecture and Design archives?' she said.

'That doesn't sound true,' I offered.

'Is it true that somebody took a Picasso drawing on the subway, once, and left it there?'

'I think that one actually is true,' I said. 'Where did you hear all this stuff?'

'I went to art school before culinary school,' she said, lightly. 'I'm a career advisor's worst nightmare.'

Cara stood by a shelf, examining Alice's jewellery.

'I'll give you some competition,' she said, looking up. 'I'm thinking of training as a florist.'

Alice had made an entire croquembouche for the consultation. She carried it over from the counter, balanced on a flat ceramic plate in royal blue, and placed it on the small table. Cara wandered back over and pulled out one of the wooden chairs, sat down and gazed at the croquembouche, as entranced as I was. Alice stood awkwardly, for a moment, and then pulled out her own chair.

'I wouldn't usually make a whole thing for a tasting,' she said. 'I'm new to this, though.'

The croquembouche looked like a mountain in miniature. It tumbled upward, with spheres of hardened sugar crowded beneath a blanket of icing powder, white and soft. If I had to get married, I thought, this cake was the one that I wanted. Cara and Alice kept talking, but I lost track of the conversation and fell into a chain of thoughts about the cake. *Croquembouche*, I'd read, translated to *crunches in mouth*. That made sense for a mountain, too; mountains appeared soft, pillowed with snow, but were hard, made of rocks, as deceptive as the cake. There was something different on the surface than at the centre, and maybe the surface was the best part, but the centre was usually inaccessible. Mountains, really, were shapes in pictures, inaccessible to almost everybody. Cara and I were sitting in a small kitchen, though, testing a mountain, consuming it, feeling the snow dissolving, the rocks of sugar cracking, discovering that the core was soft, tender, delicious.

'I'd like to get married just for this mountain,' I said.

Cara and Alice stopped talking to one another and looked at me, confused.

'I mean, this cake. Sorry. It looks like a mountain.'

'It's good, isn't it?' said Cara. 'Everything Alice makes is perfect.'

'You've only tried one other thing,' said Alice, smiling at her.

'I'd like to try everything,' said Cara, smiling back.

'I want to make some drawings of Alice's cakes,' Cara said, as we walked back to the subway. 'They're so beautiful. I'd pair them with photos of fruit that look sort of abstractly pornographic, like halves of oranges on a plate on a bedspread or a raspberry in a glass of champagne.'

'Very Marilyn Minter,' I said.

'Hmm. Yeah. Maybe. I'll have another idea, something new. Maybe somebody will write an article about Alice's cakes and I can illustrate it.'

'How did you meet her?' I asked.

'At an afterparty for that show I was in, the one you saw. This girl was making red velvet cookies in the middle of the party while everyone else just drank beer. I thought that was so cute. It wasn't even her house, but she was making cookies at, like, midnight and offering them to everyone.'

When I was back at home, I googled *cakes in art*. I expected Wayne Thiebaud's paintings to appear, and they did. I'd always wondered what Thiebaud thought of Grace. He was a Californian painter, but had come to New York for two years in the 1950s, had been friends with Grace's friends, had likely met her. She'd painted *East Side Sunday* – which was bright and layered like pickles, mustard and ketchup – in 1956, the year that Thiebaud had arrived and MoMA had shown her work in *12 Americans*, which he must have seen. Thiebaud had wanted, before he came to New York, to be an Abstract Expressionist, but he started painting these cakes, afterward, and it was easy for me to connect his shift toward this painterly realism with Grace's influence. She was, after all, the member of that group who had taken the first and most concrete step away from abstraction.

Thiebaud's cakes were creamy and decadent, with paint heaped like frosting, in pastel colours, whites and blues and pinks underpinned by geometry, by triangles and circles, careful lines. These paintings were often described as evoking a nostalgia for diners and lunch counters, perhaps the automat. I hadn't grown up with these places, but I longed for them, anyway. I savoured the windows of the Italian cake shops that remained in lower Manhattan, taking photographs of their gloomy wedding cakes with white icing, though I'd never stepped inside or considered buying one.

It was strange to want that nostalgia for diners, for the delights of cakes piled high with cream in unknown hamlets. This version of small-town life only differed aesthetically, perhaps, from the girlhood that I'd had, where the *Women's Weekly Cookbook* was pawed over, each year, in advance of a birthday. It was brightly coloured fondant wrapped around a Barbie doll that I remembered, rather than cross-hatching atop an apple pie, but I wasn't nostalgic.

I loved Thiebaud's cakes because they were dreams of cakes, made for looking rather than for eating, allowing the promise of fantasy without the disappointments of reality. These paintings reminded me of Cara, perhaps, of the promise that came with our first meeting and the way in which my desire curdled into disaster when it was exposed to reality. It was nicer to allow some things, or people, to remain fantasies. I supposed, in committing to Robert, I could keep my dreams.

I think I wanted Alice to make the cake because she was adorable, like a character from a film. She had studied art and literature before going to culinary school, and had written her senior thesis on dancing vegetables. Alice and Cara had seemed to have a playful rapport, and I had felt a second-hand thrill mixed with envy, a desire to attain the same intimacy, to count Alice among my friends. I wondered if this might make my friendship with Cara easier, allowing for a sort of buffer. It hadn't really been a girlfriend that I'd wanted, after all; I'd just wanted more connection to my own queerness, which came through friendship as much as love.

Alice seemed interested in being my friend, too; she sent me an email, a few days later, inviting me to a housewarming next Friday.

28

I knew the cliché of losing weight before a wedding, but I'd expected to avoid it. Barbara and I went for lunch on Sunday, and when I said that I might order a sandwich, she looked at me over her menu.

'Sophia, you're certainly not fat, but I would think you want to look your best for the wedding,' she said.

I had never encountered this sort of message from another person before. It came at me through the media, in films and magazines, but in those places the messages were directed at all women; I'd always assumed an attitude of outrage, which was easy because I had always been relatively thin and so the idea that women should aspire to a certain aesthetic was largely theoretical for me. I'd never felt the pressure of it before and I didn't know what to say to Barbara. She had the authority of an older woman, of Robert's mother, of the person who would be paying for lunch, and it seemed obsolete to argue by telling her my dress size, given she'd said that I wasn't fat. I ordered a salad.

'If you're careful now,' she said. 'You won't have to starve yourself at the last minute.'

We hadn't even set a date for the wedding, but I felt chastised, as if I was failing to be a woman, allowing my body what it wanted rather than setting limits, enforcing rules. I had been making an instinctual choice rather than a rational one. When somebody at the next table received a large beige macaron filled with sliced strawberries, I couldn't help thinking of Cara, and the ways in which everything might have unravelled if I'd been allowed whatever my body wanted.

I'd returned to my usual routine, in which life centred upon the museum. There was so little to do, though, with only a month until my contract ended. I wanted to prove my worth, particularly given my application for Sally's job, but everything was winding down. I was excited by the possibility of staying, but I knew that I had to presume I was leaving, and so I felt anticipatory loss, a recognition of the flimsy foundations of my belonging. I was still invisible to the motion sensor that turned the lights on in the office bathroom. I'd waved my arms about, once, hopefully, but now I just endured the semi-darkness, resigned. I felt embarrassed when Sally, with her hair that stayed perfectly in place, immune to August humidity, walked in after me and lit the room up without trying. Did I really think that I was good enough for Sally's job?

—

I felt uneasy about Barbara's comment, which I hadn't challenged. *You won't have to starve yourself at the last minute.* In lieu of work, I searched the internet for wedding diet plans and found myself in a world of calorie calculators and torsos encircled by tape measures. I lived in a world removed from women's magazines, a world in which we all countered our histories of disordered eating with body positivity, in theory if not in practice, and I'd expected the phrase *wedding diet* to bring up warnings, reminders to eat healthily, to feel happy with one's body rather than fighting to change it, but there was none of this. There were, on the internet, only strange rules that promised physical perfection.

I thought of Sophie Calle's *Chromatic Diet*, in which Calle ate food of a different colour each day, following a scene that Paul Auster had written in a book; they were playing a metafictional game. I remembered when, heartbroken at twenty-one, I had agreed to eat only when Emily was with me, and only ever pink food. She would sit beside me, trying to coax me to eat strawberries whilst telling me that I was her best friend, that we lived together, that the people she met at parties were no threat, that she loved me more than anyone, that my insecurity was mad. I did go a little mad when I hadn't eaten; I was constantly alert, watching for danger like a malnourished animal, and reaching out, a little desperately, to anybody who might offer protection. I remembered that everything felt heightened; starvation made my senses vivid.

I wanted, reading about wedding diets, to provoke that madness in myself, to use the tools of the marriage industry to probe the boundaries of the institution, to determine what I felt when I was empty. I wanted, I suppose, to embrace being female, with all its exaggerations and vulnerabilities. I felt as if there were a part of me that always wished for chaos, and I struggled with the temptation to give into those self-destructive urges, felt I might be a little more charismatic if I was a little less sensible. I felt haunted by all the wedding imagery, kept thinking of gardens as cemeteries, bouquets as funerary flowers, all those white dresses as ghosts. I needed Robert as a stabilising force.

I wrote an application for a teaching fellowship at the Whitney, though I didn't know if they accepted applications from foreigners. I emailed my dissertation supervisor to ask her for another letter of reference, wondering if I was wasting her time and my own. It was exhausting to be an American Art specialist without blanket permission to live in the United States. I'd never even considered anything else, though. I'd thought that everything would be easy after graduate school, that I'd be able to stay in New York, forever, but it all felt contingent on Robert, now.

I'd been alive for long enough to know that I needed to eat properly. I knew that my mood plummeted each time I tried to diet. It induced a strange depressive euphoria, like alcohol. I ran on adrenalin and burst into tears suddenly. I had learnt, years earlier, that I needed to resist calls to starvation; the idea of eating less, for me, would fast become the idea of eating less than less, and then I would find myself unable to work, unable to think, unable to do anything but cry. I don't know why, then, I toyed with Barbara's ideas that week. I'd spent all summer trying to be healthy, perhaps, and it hadn't made me less confused. I didn't buy lunch and my mood dropped each day.

I felt, often, as if there was an expectation that I would be invisible, refusing to take up space. My desk was in an out-of-the-way corner, which made it easier to feel that I was succeeding, though the corner felt vaguely humiliating, sometimes, positioned near the photocopiers. If I got Sally's job, I thought, I would have a real purpose, beyond research, and then I would feel more comfortable taking up space in the office.

It was necessary to have an income, but the quest for it felt more like anguish than aspiration. I was lucky, too, in that the museum didn't demand much of me. My work was largely self-imposed, intended to prove my employability and enhance my CV. Still, it felt as if life beyond work was a luxury – I tried to make space for it, but I was exhausted. It was work that lay next to me when I woke up in the morning, often having left my laptop on my bedside table; I ate breakfast, or rather drank coffee, with my emails and caught the subway with exhibition proposals and academic articles. I was accompanied by my work even when I caught the train upstate to visit Robert, always aware of all the projects, present and future, that might be informed by whatever landscape I saw out the window.

I kept thinking that I'd read, once, that one could have a satisfying career and a relationship but no friends, a relationship and friends but no career, or friends and a career but no relationship. In theory, I had all three, but in practice? I couldn't figure out what I had; I couldn't figure out what I'd choose.

———

I caught the elevator down to the cafeteria, ordering coffee in lieu of lunch, and then caught it back up, returning to my desk. I couldn't afford to take a lunch break when I was applying for Sally's job. I had to show them that I was serious, that lunch meant nothing at all to me.

I didn't know if I was equipped to handle the rejection that came of being in the art world. It was a place where one was always yearning. I kept hoping that I was tough enough for it. I had asked Robert, once, if he thought I had a heart of felt, easily moved yet flexible, or a heart of stone, hard to break, cracking rather than bending, and he had told me that I was hard-hearted. I kept wondering what would happen if I were rejected by the museum, if there were a glue that might repair the shattering I anticipated.

But why was I worrying about this before the rejection had actually arrived? Sally seemed to think it was possible I'd get her job, after all, and she was the one with whom I worked most closely.

It was hard not to cave to Barbara's suggestions because I wanted more control that week. I wanted to control my body, because my desires had been so unruly, so misaligned with the events of my life. I was trying not to think of Cara, now, but the sting of her rejection, and all the questions I had about our subsequent interactions, about her deletion of those photographs on Instagram, resurfaced when I wasn't busy, wasn't working. I felt thirsty, as if I were catching a cold. I kept pushing back lunch in order to do more work, and then it was five-thirty.

29

It felt as if the week had dragged on for ages. On my way home from work, on Friday, I dropped into the bridal shop to ask Cara if she wanted to catch the subway to Alice's party together.

'Oh, you're invited to that?' she said. 'Yeah. I guess. We can.'

Cara was quiet on the train and separated herself from me almost as soon as we arrived at the party. I had expected that she, like me, would know almost nobody. I had thought that we could navigate the crowd together, imagined that it might be like the party we'd gone to in Clinton Hill in July, where we'd danced to Bruce Springsteen and collapsed on the floor alongside one another.

Alice's new apartment was quite different to her old one. It was uptown, near Columbia, where both her housemates were working on PhDs. It was cheap, she told me, because it was technically university property, designated for families, but none of the families had taken it because it was a walk-up, difficult with a stroller. It was sparsely furnished, but piled with books, and had a large kitchen, which I presumed had attracted Alice.

Cara didn't seem to know people, but she was confident in introducing herself. She never looked at me and seemed to leave conversations as soon as I entered them. I had made Cara promise, earlier, that we would leave together, catching the subway back to midtown where our paths diverged.

'Sure,' she'd said.

I felt, after one drink, drunk and anxious. I wanted to blame myself for something, so that I had something to correct, but the only thing that struck me was Cara's unfriendliness and I wasn't sure what I'd done to cause it. I felt so uncertain at parties, though alcohol made things more comfortable; it made control seem less essential. I didn't drink that much, in general, despite what Robert had suggested in Cold Spring, and alcohol went to my head quickly, especially when I was hungry.

There was a lot of food here, though; Alice was, after all, a pastry chef. I picked up a biscuit, labelled *lime-ricotta*, unsure if it was sweet or savoury. I took a bite, tentatively, and found I still wasn't sure. It reminded me of sourdough pancakes. I didn't feel like eating, but I didn't want to put the rest of the biscuit down, awkwardly, so I swallowed the rest of it.

I wandered from room to room, smiling uncertainly at strangers.

Thankfully, Alice appeared sometimes, taking me by the hand and introducing me to people nearby before drifting away again. She was a good hostess, though her new housemates stood together in a corner, arguing about Kant. I wondered if they knew Robert.

'How do you know Alice?' said Sydney, a very tall person with blonde hair, after Alice introduced us and floated away.

'She might be making my wedding cake,' I said.

'Might?'

'I'm still deciding.'

'You should definitely pick Alice.'

'No. I will. I mean, I'm still deciding if I should get married. I don't know if I believe in it.'

'It doesn't matter,' Sydney said. 'You can always get divorced, right? That's what you need to believe in if you're going to get married. Not marriage.'

Alice had made a whole array of cakes for the party, including small meringues with a sort of raspberry flavour which she'd labelled Sweet Nothings; when I tried one, it seemed to dissolve as soon as it touched my tongue.

I wandered into the kitchen, at some point, and found myself looking at a shelf of cookbooks. I took down *Modern Art Desserts* and leafed through it. I'd been struck by the cake on the front cover, resembling a Mondrian, with food dye used to colour different squares of cake, chocolate icing replacing Mondrian's black lines. Inside, I was impressed by an attempt to create cakes that imitated Wayne Thiebaud's paintings. The recipe ran for thirty pages. It was strange to think about going to such lengths to create a cake that would resemble a painting of a cake. I loved the idea of a Thiebaud painted with a palette knife rather than a brush, of cutting into an image and finding strawberry sponge and layers of jam and cream.

'Be careful with that cookbook. I don't think we need any more baked goods,' laughed Sydney, leaning against the kitchen counter.

'True,' I said. 'But it's a beautiful book. Have you seen this?'

I held up the book, open to a photograph of the Thiebaud cakes on their stands.

'Here's a question,' said Sydney. 'Do you choose cakes for how they look or for their flavour?'

'For how they look, mostly.'

'Damn. I thought I'd catch you. Most people say they make decisions based on taste, not appearance. I was going to tell you this whole anecdote about a study that showed that they were kidding themselves.'

'I'm an art historian,' I said. 'I'm biased. But you can tell me the anecdote anyway.'

I found Sydney easy to talk to. It reminded me of when I'd first met Robert; it was a relief rather than an anxious connection. I didn't want to end the conversation and yet I didn't fear, as I had with Cara, that any small error would mess it up, would lead Sydney to vanish abruptly, leaving a hole in my life.

'I used to live in Sydney, actually,' I said.

'I thought I noticed an accent.'

'I can't get rid of it.'

'You wouldn't want to. It's cute. I can't stick around and appreciate it, though. I have another party to get to.'

'Popular,' I said.

'I've got the good anecdotes,' Sydney said, and winked.

I was always impressed by people who could make a wink look playful rather than forced.

'It was nice to meet you,' Sydney said, slipping toward the door.

In the main room, Cara was reading something to Alice from her phone. I drifted over to them, trying to appear casually interested rather than desperate for friends.

'Hey there,' said Alice. 'Are you having fun?'

Cara glanced at me but didn't say anything.

'Okay,' she said to Alice. 'Next question. On what occasion do you lie?'

'We're doing the Proust Questionnaire,' Alice told me.

'And don't say that you don't lie, Alice,' said Cara, smiling at her. 'That's just boring.'

'I think people who say that they don't lie are usually the ones who lie the most,' said Alice.

'Geminis,' said Cara, and they both laughed.

I went to the hallway, where Alice's flatmates were standing, looking as if they'd finished arguing about Kant but were about to turn to Hegel. They were both wearing collared shirts, marking them out as sociologists; one shirt was a pink that looked as if it had once been red while the other was white with a green pattern that reminded me of a spreadsheet.

'Sophie, right?' one of them asked.

'Sophia,' I said.

'Max. This is Robert.'

'Oh,' I said. 'That's my boyfriend's name.'

I was trying to make a practice of bringing Robert up in conversation. It wasn't terrible, after all, to be in a relationship; I didn't need to avoid mentioning it.

'A good name,' said Robert. 'Where's he?'

'Hiking the Appalachian Trail.'

Robert laughed.

'Ignore him,' said Max. 'He's a politics nerd.'

'What?'

'It was a thing, a few years ago,' said Max.

'I'm sorry,' said Robert. 'It was just the way you said it.'

'Remember, that guy—'

'Mark Sanford,' interrupted Robert.

'He told the newspaper that he was hiking the Appalachian Trail, but he was actually having an affair,' said Max.

I did remember this. I'd made jokes about it to Robert at the time, but they'd faded away as the trip approached. I'd almost completely forgotten. It was the anecdote that everybody mentioned, but it didn't have much to do with the trail at all.

Cara kept her promise to catch the train downtown, but barely looked at me. She chattered eagerly to a new friend, Amanda; I felt invisible. They were both catching the L Train, but only Amanda said goodbye when I peeled off toward the D. It felt as if Cara was trying to prove that we were not friends and yet she had said, so many times, that we were.

I called her when I got home.

'Hey,' she said, sounding tired. 'What's up?'

'You ignored me for the whole evening,' I said. 'It's hard to believe you actually want to be my friend. You don't have to, you know.'

'I am your friend,' said Cara. 'I didn't ignore you. It's a party. I spent as much time with you as with anybody else and nobody else is yelling at me.'

'I'm not yelling at you,' I said. 'I just wish you'd tell me if you didn't want to be friends.'

'This is really unreasonable,' said Cara. 'I shouldn't have to babysit you at a party. I didn't do anything wrong. You've got to realise that. I was just trying to talk to Alice. You're the one who isn't acting like a friend.'

I tried to explain myself, but felt like I was failing, making everything worse.

I lost track of the conversation. It ended.

I thought I'd cry myself to sleep, but I couldn't fall asleep agitated. I flipped my body from side to side, gradually pulling the sheets from beneath the mattress, tangling myself in them, and finally passed out, exhausted.

I did realise, the next morning, that I didn't have these sorts of fights with my other friends. I'd been the one who started it with Cara. I knew that it wasn't reasonable and yet I felt compelled to clarify things, afraid that she would leave me, afraid that she was already leaving me. I wanted a friendship that was all-consuming, almost proprietary, without boundaries, like I'd had with Emily, but without the yearning and sense of lack. I supposed that was why I'd been mad at Cara, because she treated me as one of many possible friends rather than as a special friend, particular and irreplaceable, with the power to make almost any situation better. It seemed strange that she'd ignored me, but perhaps I'd been too clingy, had brought it upon myself.

Maybe Robert was right, I thought. Maybe drinking was dangerous.

30

In Dyker Heights, I drove past a teenage girl loading flowers into the trunk of a car outside a funeral parlour, and then I was stuck above Gowanus, on a shaky stretch of elevated highway. It did not feel as if I were escaping from the city so much as wrestling with it or waiting for it to give. I'd picked up the car in Brooklyn, because it was cheaper, but it seemed to be adding hours to the trip. I was stuck, a while later, underneath the Promenade at Brooklyn Heights, trying to manoeuvre into the right lane as we turned upward and around, onto the Brooklyn Bridge, and then I was stuck on the bridge, below the tourists, and then suddenly the city did give. The other cars went elsewhere and Manhattan felt small as I traced the island's western contour before finding myself waiting, again, as the traffic merged off Willis Avenue Bridge and splintered onto the Bronx's many roads.

I saw a huge graveyard to one side, then a sign reading *FedEx Freight*. As I drove up into Westchester County, I saw buildings covered with Tyvek, as if wallpapered on their exteriors, turned inside out. It was all preferable to the Taconic State Parkway, which I joined near Tarrytown. On the Taconic, everybody drove too quickly, the cars shooting like curling stones on ice. Robert had told me that it was statistically more likely that a person would die driving to the trailhead than die hiking. I didn't feel at all surprised given those drives often included the Taconic. Everybody but Google had suggested I take a different route, to go up through Connecticut, and I wondered why I had listened to the computer rather than to my colleagues.

It was so green on the Taconic, though. It was still August, but it felt like the end of summer, with my fellowship finishing in less than two months, now, and I imagined that when I returned to New York it would be autumn or fall, either cosy or ghastly, cider and fires or the skeletal branches of trees.

I drove into North Adams from the East. I'd been thinking of the Appalachian Trail all day, though I hadn't crossed it since Westchester. I felt a sense of the trail, though, on every wooded hill and in every quiet valley. I knew that it was close, and I thought of Robert walking as I drove.

Robert would be on Mount Greylock, walking down the slope that led to the street on which we planned to meet. It intersected the main road that led into town and it was strange to turn right and see, suddenly, a man with a beard, pack on back, skin and clothes a scuffed beige, walking at an even pace, looking at nothing but the space ahead of him while I looked, spellbound, at his brief incursion onto a suburban street. This thru-hiker seemed weary, disinterested in Phelps Avenue, while even the white blazes painted on telephone poles felt wild to me. It was strange to think that this man, a stranger to me, was probably somebody that Robert knew, that they might have slept at the same shelter or exchanged greetings earlier in the day.

I looked ahead of me, again, and there was a deer, springing across the road in two beats, gone before I could fully register the animal's appearance. I parked the car at the point where houses gave way to forest and watched a child jumping and tripping on a trampoline while I waited.

I was supposed to be turning thirty. I *was* turning thirty, though I couldn't quite believe it. I was turning thirty and I'd cried on the Taconic and I was, now, pretending to be fine. I'd listed things about Robert that I'd loved while driving up here – his readiness to provide literary examples to match whatever I was wondering about, how grounded and steady he always was, never rushing or tumbling – but I still knew I'd rather be in New York with Cara. I didn't know why I felt this way, and I'd tried to tell myself that I didn't, and I willed it to change. I didn't know why I wanted somebody who made me feel like a teenager when I had a good life as an adult. I reminded myself to look into therapists, perhaps, once things were a little more stable with work. For now, I had to think of Robert, of my luck in having him. It was Saturday, and soon he'd walk down the street, toward me, and we'd find our hotel and have dinner, sleep, and then it would be Sunday, my birthday, and we'd go to MASS MoCA, and then it would be Monday, no longer my birthday, and I'd hike with Robert for a day, and then it would be Tuesday and I'd drop him off in the forest and return to New York, officially older than when I'd left.

Robert liked that we could see Mount Greylock from our room. I did, too. We turned the lights off, at dusk, so that we might stand and look at it. Robert had woken up on the mountain. I wanted to ask him about the way he saw it, which I felt sure was different to the way I saw it; Mount Greylock, to me, represented something unexplored and potentially threatening, a sort of unconscious. I wondered what it meant to Robert, but I couldn't formulate the right question.

I was trying to determine whether the Appalachian Trail was changing Robert, but it was hard to evaluate this because I couldn't really remember what our relationship had been like before he left, though it had been only a few months ago. I didn't trust my memory and I wasn't sure how I'd changed, either. I lived in the present, which wasn't really a good thing.

I wondered if, for Robert, the Appalachian Trail was a means of bookending his youth, a walk into the future. I wondered if I, too, were part of this, if marriage was a ritual, for Robert, like finishing his PhD or hiking the Appalachian Trail. Everything that Robert had done seemed to coalesce into the foundations of an organised adult life, while everything I'd done was provisional and easily undone. I wasn't sure about anything and Robert always seemed certain of everything.

I thought of Robert's thesis, of the idea of hiking as following a narrative structure, of the Appalachian Trail as something with a beginning, middle and end.

'Do you think marriage is an ending?' I asked. 'Like, in narrative terms. In novels.'

'*Novels, shirking the disagreeable reminder of Death, end with Marriage, as the only admissible and effective crack in continuity,*' he said, sort of flatly, as if it wasn't something he really believed.

I must have looked confused because he added, 'It's from *The Edwardians*. Vita Sackville-West.'

'But what do you think?' I asked.

Robert often seemed to avoid expressing his own opinions by having quotations at the ready. He'd told me, once, that he'd spent his teenage years reading dictionaries of quotations, which I'd found endearingly precocious. His sister had told me that when he was younger he used to quote, regularly, from books he'd never opened, but she supposed studying literature had forced him to actually read the books.

'I'm not sure,' he said. 'People have written about it. The marriage plot.'

'Jeffrey Eugenides,' I said.

'No,' he said. 'I mean, well, yes. But the title of that book is a reference to a genre. You know. Jane Austen's the most obvious example.'

I realised, later, that Robert hadn't expressed any real thoughts about marriage at all. I wondered if he had thought about it, while walking, or if the purpose of marriage seemed so obvious to him that he didn't need to contemplate it. I wondered what it was that he did think about while walking, but I'd asked about this before and learnt that hiking was too embodied to lend itself to easy explanation. I didn't know how Robert could be so invested in the concept of narrative, in interrogating texts and applying theory to them, and yet seem nonchalant about the framework within which he lived his life.

I hadn't thought about marriage much, either, until he had proposed to me. It had forced me to see our relationship differently – not as a succession of small moments, like individual paintings, but as a part of something bigger, an exhibition or collection, that I needed to construct and manage so that it wouldn't simply pass by, becoming cluttered like a disorganised storeroom. Or maybe my painting metaphors failed there. Maybe life was in danger of playing out like a film left on in the apartment while I went to eat lunch around the corner. I did not want to say *yes* once and find myself performing a script that I hadn't written. I wanted to keep saying yes and maybe to say no, sometimes, to make the decision daily, so that my love for Robert remained always in the present. Robert, though, had always seemed to see his choices as linear and untroubled, like the steps he took on the trail, accumulating toward a goal.

We left the curtains open, that night, so that we might wake to the sun on Mount Greylock.

Robert was used to early nights, after months of hiking, and fell asleep easily. I lay awake considering the fact that I was turning thirty. *Time to begin to fulfil the 'promise'*, Grace had written.

I considered whether Grace had actually begun to fulfil her promise by thirty. It had been a good year for her. She had a solo show, *Paintings by George Hartigan*, open at Tibor de Nagy just before her birthday, and it was written up positively in the *Times*, with her work described as offering *artistic salvation in generous swabs of handsomely harmonised color which loop and frolic in and out of each other*.

Grace hadn't seen it as a good year, though. *Any kind of 'success' as far especially as sales are concerned seems farther away than ever*, she wrote, complaining about public apathy, bitterness and jealousy amongst the artists and *on top of all this one's own torments and weaknesses*. She became more depressed, later in the year, when Eisenhower won the election. I thought about this, wondering what it would be like if Donald Trump won the election, but reminded myself that I was catastrophising; all the analysts said that this was impossible. I could be glad, at least, about that.

Grace had spent her thirtieth year learning to follow her own instincts, chastising herself for being too self-consciously analytical. She'd moved away from abstract expressionism and turned toward art history, doing studies of Titian and Tiepolo, Rubens, obsessing over Cezanne. She left the club that defined the downtown art scene, after criticising Clement Greenberg and accusing a panel of *being boring and pedantic*, and filled her diaries with scepticism about Jackson Pollock and Robert Motherwell. *Revolt against deadness*, she wrote.

It seemed as if thirty was an important year for Grace, though perhaps she couldn't have known that until later. She sold her first work to MoMA, *Persian Jacket*, when she was thirty-one. Her strongest works, including *Grand Street Brides*, came just after this, at thirty-one or thirty-two, but wouldn't have been possible without her critique of abstract expressionism or her studies of the Old Masters. It was when she was thirty, I thought, that Grace moved from being a talented minor painter to a painter with real potential.

She'd been so depressed, though, and partially due to her unknown future. She wrote of *complete self-doubt & despair, inner turmoil, the pain of it all*. She whined about Frank's devotion to Larry Rivers, describing it as *nothing short of treason*, complaining that everybody but her had powerful champions, even as Frank remained her champion, despite Larry. It was her partner, Walt Silver, who kept her steady. *I hope I can always keep sight of what I need & what Walt gives me – peace, emotional security, and enough calm & inner aloneness so I can learn & discover myself.*

I looked at Robert, lying next to me, and felt the same way.

I didn't know how to start my birthday, so I got out of bed and went into the bathroom to look at myself in the mirror. I found my first grey hair, nestled amongst the more familiar brown hairs at my temple. I didn't know if the hair was new or if this hotel mirror was simply sharper, cruel in its clarity, than the mirror at home.

I hadn't expected to look different, to notice change on my birthday. I must have wondered about it, though, given I went straight to the mirror upon waking. I had hoped, perhaps, for a sudden maturity. I wanted to know where my life was going and I wanted to be happy with it, but I still felt uncertain about everything beyond September, when my job would finish and my visa expire. I felt almost as uncertain as when I was twenty-three, but I was now thirty, and the only thing I really knew was that time would continue to pass even if I ignored it. The grey hair, after all, was evidence that something inside me had changed.

I wasn't sure that I hated it.

I thought, perhaps, that the strand was a little bit beautiful, glacial.

'I'm a crone,' I said to Robert, returning to bed.

'You're a millennial,' he said.

'I'm a millennial crone,' I said.

I liked the way that that sounded. I was young and old at once, like a witch. I had outsmarted time. I had strands of hair that glittered, free of pigment. I kept repeating *millennial crone*, joyfully, until Robert asked me to stop.

'I don't want to think of you as an old woman,' he said. 'I don't think crones are sexy.'

I had never cared, though, about being sexy. I did not think the concept of sexiness had done women any favours. I wanted to be cool, modern, with the zeitgeist, and I knew that witches were very much of the moment. If modernity was the disenchantment of the world, witches were heroines of the re-enchantment. I wondered what Cara would say about this. Robert, though, was lying beside me on the bed, pawing at my hip, wanting to start the day with something other than critical discourse.

On the way to breakfast, I saw a sign in a shop window, in kitsch, curled lettering, that read *I have lost my husband and my cat. I want the cat back*. I thought of the sweatshirt that had appeared in my Facebook feed, recently, placed there by some algorithm that had intuited my engagement, reading *STUCK WITH -- FOREVER*, advising me that I could provide my fiancé's picture to be printed on the sweater between *WITH* and *FOREVER*. I thought of the other jokes I had seen, comparing wives to balls and chains, to gaolers. I couldn't see why anybody would ever want this, considered what this widespread embrace of marriage as a trap might mean. I wanted to be sure that it would always be easy for me to leave and to be left, to know that Robert and I were with one another because we wanted to be rather than because we felt locked into place.

'Do you think you'll compare me to a ball and chain one day?' I asked.

'No,' said Robert. 'That's not going to happen.'

'Do you ever worry that you'll feel stuck with me?'

'I don't think anybody could feel stuck with you, Soph.'

'What do you mean?'

'I don't know,' he said. 'I don't feel like I'll ever be sure of you, even when we're married. You're here, but you're also always somewhere else, thinking about something else, like Grace Hartigan or whether radical new spaces dedicated to feminist practice are more important than including women in mainstream institutions or, like, even now, you're probably wondering whether your breakfast is modern or not.'

I looked at my pancakes, their round shape echoed by the plate and by the glass of orange juice, its colour a complement to the turquoise linoleum table. It reminded me of an early Stephen Shore photograph.

'This breakfast is pretty modern, I think.'

Robert smiled.

'It's, like, you're living this life, with me, but you're also living another life, without me. I know I'll always come second to art history.'

'Isn't that a good thing? It's not healthy to build your life around another person.'

'Yeah,' he said. 'But I'm not likely to take you for granted. I'm never going to compare you to a ball and chain. You don't need to worry about that.'

I felt, at MASS MoCA, as if my world and Robert's world were suddenly in close proximity to one another. Sound vibrated through a corridor, with single hums at different pitches creating an eerie cloud of tones. I imagined dashes of lightning, falling trees, rain getting heavier, skies greyer, and then a sudden hollowness, with wind shaking the branches and clearing the atmosphere, rays of light swilling through, and then a quivering, as the tunnel seemed to hover between cloister and forest, changing with each step.

'You're a work of art,' Robert whispered into my ear, half serious, trying to be romantic, slipping his arm around me as we stared at a rectangular void edged with a strip of violet. I cringed. I hated the cliché of his phrasing, and I hated my own awareness that he hadn't thought the metaphor through: to be an artwork was to be an exercise in control and release, something calculated, not quite human. I did feel, though, an affinity with the acidic neon, which must have felt like an argument against the eyes after the forest. Robert was being sweet, natural, and I was jaded, postmodern, an installation that threatened to shock, buzzing with electricity.

I read everything, here, through a screen of reviews and references I'd encountered elsewhere, familiar with everything except the sound pieces, which I felt more impressed by for this reason. I tried to feel something, but I was exhausted by my life in museums, by the accumulation of right angles, a repetition of exhibitions. There was a man standing in front of a Sol LeWitt wall painting, a rainbow swirling across a flat surface; his black shirt and navy-blue shorts were staid before the backdrop. There was another man crouching before him, at crotch level, taking his photograph.

I'd seen so much Sol LeWitt in so many places. There was a Sol LeWitt outside the entrance to the museum's restaurant, back in New York, and often visitors didn't even register it as an artwork. It was always like this, with people posing for photos, creating records of their appearance, transforming conceptual art into backdrop. Sol LeWitt was an intellectual artist, but he'd been transformed, lately, into an Instagram photo wall.

All day, I kept trying to see MASS MoCA as Robert must have seen it. The spaces were clean and the walls white, a celebration of sharp corners. I felt the inadequacy of the artificial in the place of the natural, felt that the art worlds, and everybody in them, were desperate for feeling, but retreated inward, away from life, replacing the dirtiness of reality with fake mists and flat colours, with a lack of depth.

Robert didn't see it this way.

'I really liked that,' he said, as we came out of a dark room. 'It was such a heavy darkness, so much darker than anything you find in nature. It's so dark that anything seems possible. It tests the limits of reality and plays tricks on your eyes. I guess that's the point, isn't it? I started thinking I saw a grey orb drawing streaks of purple light toward it, in rings, like a will'o'the wisp.'

I didn't tell him that the video piece that was supposed to be playing in the room had been turned off. The darkness he had experienced as transcendental was a technical fault.

I wondered, when Robert left the table for the bathroom at dinner, why he had said that I would always put art history first as if this were something particular to me. He, too, put other things first. He was hiking the Appalachian Trail. He'd applied for jobs all over the country. I couldn't imagine he'd ever turn one down because of me. I thought that this was healthy, that our relationship allowed each of us to operate independently, rather than losing ourselves, each overwhelmed by the other. I thought that our separate spheres meant that we each brought something to the other's life. He'd always said that he'd agreed.

We were back, the next morning, on the street where we'd met in North Adams. It was early. Somebody Robert knew had arranged a lift for us to and from the trail. There was a sign beside the little footbridge on the north end of the street, reading *NO PARKING FOR APPALACHIAN TRAIL*. On the bridge, we could see a backyard filled with children's toys and an American flag on a pole, the edge of the town pushed up against the stream. We would cross the bridge and disappear into the forest.

In actuality, we crossed the bridge, disappeared into the forest, crossed a railway track and found ourselves at the edge of another major road only minutes later.

But then, after we crossed that road, we were in the forest.

I thought, as we walked, of all the pictures that I wanted to take, of all the details I wanted to stop to consider, of how much I wanted to dwell in experience rather than moving through it, past it. I wanted to separate it into individual images. It seemed, here, that the light was always broken, that the wind was splintered into whispers by the solidity of the trees. There were, as we walked, no vistas, no distance, just imperfect shelter and second-hand rain, from overnight, tumbling from the canopy of leaves in sloppy drips.

'You can't take pictures of everything, Soph,' said Robert. 'We'll never get anywhere.'

I took a picture of a deer, though, two minutes later, and Robert didn't challenge that. It looked like all the photographs of deer that I'd seen on the internet, with those soulful eyes staring into the lens, challenging the camera's gaze. I thought of this deer, standing still, all day, and the deer I'd seen springing across the road days earlier, less like a fairytale but harder to believe.

I wanted to be the sort of woman who loved hiking, but I wasn't. I felt inadequate in my hiking top, clinging close to my body so as to wick sweat away. I was the sort of woman who loved people who loved hiking, who loved the idea of a wilderness beyond the city, of the forest's mystery, but I hated everything that had to be given up in order to hike. I hated, most of all, that I couldn't hold onto places, couldn't stop constantly and take pictures. I hated that when I was hiking I was always moving forward, leaving beauty behind me. I would, at the end, just wish for the beginning. I wondered if Robert, spending the whole summer on this trail, was unwittingly walking toward a world in which he had accomplished too many of his goals, had less to which he could aspire.

31

I returned to New York alone and confused, trying to reconcile my head and my heart. I knew that whatever I was feeling was less about Cara or Robert than it was about me. Robert hadn't done anything wrong; I'd known Cara for less than six months and she, too, had done nothing major. I knew that events triggered feelings, but also suspected that the feelings were already there, waiting to latch onto whatever happened and anoint it the cause. I couldn't identify, though, what I was feeling. I might have been anxious, sad, overwhelmed, frightened, infatuated or nonplussed. I might have been looking for a distraction from job applications. I didn't know how I felt or what those feelings might indicate regarding what I wanted.

I met Cara for dinner near Washington Square after work. She was wearing a pencil skirt and her makeup was neat, her hair slicked back, her lipstick purple. She was statuesque, seemingly cold and aloof, though I'd apologised for our fight after Alice's party over Facebook and she'd accepted the apology, suggested this dinner. The restaurant was Italian and cosy, with a fireplace, brick walls and green curtains.

'You're dressed up,' I said.

'I had a job interview earlier,' she said. 'Happy birthday, Sophia.'

I loved it when Cara said my name. I supposed that I always loved it when people said my name; it sent a rare thrill of recognition through me.

'How is it being another year older?' she said.

'I'm a millennial crone now,' I told her.

'Millennial crone,' she said. 'You should find a familiar, like a raven or something, and send it to do your bidding. You can meet it on your fire escape. I could take photos, with one of those nineteenth-century view cameras. It'll be beautiful. I'd like to be a millennial crone. I can't wait to be in my thirties. Such a glamorous decade.'

'It's really not,' I told her. 'I thought it would be, too.'

'It seems like women in their thirties always know exactly who they are,' said Cara.

Cara had ordered wine before I arrived; the waiter brought it over. I would never have been confident enough at her age to order drinks before somebody else arrived. I didn't tell Cara this, internally wincing at our age difference, which I hoped that she forgot, mostly, as I did. In truth, I wouldn't have been brave enough even now, had I arrived before her, to order a bottle of wine. I wasn't sure I knew who I was, or perhaps I knew but wasn't quite living up to the person that I wanted to be. I didn't like to admit that I was cowardly.

'I just wish things got easier as I got older,' I said. 'I had expected that they would, but it just seems to get harder and harder and lonelier and lonelier and people fall away. I wonder if that's why people get married, at the end of their twenties. As a way to stop the erosion.'

'God, that's melodramatic,' said Cara. 'That's not why people get married.'

'Well, okay,' I said. 'But it still feels quite difficult. I don't feel like I've accomplished anything. I've lost touch with so many people, too.'

I was never sure how honest I was supposed to be with friends. I didn't think honesty was romantically or sexually loaded, but I felt sometimes that my understanding of friendship was distorted. I was always trying to determine, with everyone, whether I was on the right side of an invisible line. If asked, I'd always argue that the problem was with normative approaches to intimacy, though I'd never actually been asked. It had worked for Grace Hartigan and Frank O'Hara, I thought, and then I remembered that it hadn't. I felt, talking to Cara, that perhaps I was veering into something too unstudied, but I wasn't sure that that could stop me today. I wanted comfort; I wanted to feel close to somebody.

'I suppose I'm lonely,' I said.

Cara shifted her chin and angled her eyes toward the corner of the restaurant, as if concentrating on what to say, and then looked back at me.

'That's a bit unfair,' she said. 'There's always two ways to see things. Like, we're having dinner together and you're telling me that you're lonely.'

'I'm sorry,' I said.

It hadn't occurred to me that she could interpret things in that way; I had been thinking, rather, that perhaps I was too attached to Cara, that I needed other friendships. She continued speaking, though, as if I'd neither hurt her feelings nor apologised for it.

'And, I mean, the idea that you haven't accomplished anything is bullshit and I'm not sure what to say, because if things are harder now, it's because you're doing harder things, like, you work at MoMA. That's kind of how life is, and you'd be just as disappointed if things were the same now as they were when you were sixteen or twenty-two or whatever.'

'But emotionally,' I said. 'I have more than I wanted as a teenager. I work at the best museum in the world. I went to graduate school at an Ivy League college on a scholarship. I have a fiancé, so I must be lovable. It doesn't fix anything. It's useless to have a PhD and my job ends soon. I'm still as miserable as I was at sixteen.'

'I'm not a therapist,' Cara said, with a hard tone to her voice.

'I know,' I said. 'I'm sorry.'

'No,' she said, softening her shoulders. 'I didn't mean it like that. I just meant – I don't know what to say. I mean, if I have a life like yours when I'm thirty, I'll be thrilled, but I . . . like, I already know I'm not going to get a scholarship to an Ivy League school. I don't think I'd even be accepted to an Ivy League school. I wouldn't—'

'You probably would,' I said.

'I mean, it's beside the point,' said Cara. 'I just mean you're doing well.'

'I'm just pretending to be normal,' I said.

'God, I hate normal people,' Cara said.

'I suppose,' I said, because she was only twenty-two and she looked irritated and the waiter was coming over, about to ask if we were ready to order.

I didn't want Cara to be a therapist; I just wanted her to be my friend. I thought platonic intimacy sprang from, or at least allowed, sharing weaknesses. I wondered if I should go to therapy. I remembered, though, that I had once asked a therapist, in Australia, what it was that made people happy, and the answer had been *love*.

Cara walked me home through the East Village, past planks of wood and clear plastic chairs left out for collection the next morning, past the queue for a ramen shop just off St Marks, past the building that bankrupted the Cooper Union, past the New Museum and slim couples in jeans eating black-coconut ice-cream outside Morgenstern's.

'Should I be worried about you?' Cara asked.

'Everybody who knows me well is worried about me,' I said.

I could see why she'd accused me of melodrama.

'Do you think you maybe *like* people worrying about you?' she asked.

'No,' I said, but I wasn't sure that it was true.

We cut across to the Tenement Museum and down Orchard Street. *We are a balloon in a world full of pins*, I read painted on a door. The phrase was bright and cheerful when I noticed it during the day, but ominous in the evening's semi-gloom.

'I should walk you to the subway,' I said.

'No,' she said. 'It's your birthday.'

'It's not,' I said. 'It's late. Do you want to stay here?'

She shook her head and kissed me on the cheek.

'Happy birthday, Sophia,' she said, waving as she walked away.

She had boundaries, now, and I hated it.

I squeezed my fingers into fists, feeling my nails against my palms, and then unlocked the door. I thought of the moment earlier in the evening when she mentioned her desire to find a girlfriend and live in a cottage upstate, whittling and reading beside a fire, and I felt a sharp pain inside my chest, as if a delicate, feathered needle had been shot through me.

I wanted things to return to the way that they had been before Cara had realised that I was attracted to her. I remembered the party where we'd danced to Bruce Springsteen in a stranger's living room and then lay on the floor of the corridor together. I'd worn her jacket home and accidentally stolen it.

'No urgency,' she'd said, when I told her it was in my closet. 'I like that you have it.'

It felt as if this period, this perfect beginning, had lasted for a long time, but it had been less than two months. It had been such a quick connection. I thought of the jacket, still hanging in my closet, which seemed, now, an embarrassing sign that I clung to things and people, while Cara didn't mind if a jacket or a friend drifted away; she trusted that they would return or that they weren't needed.

It wasn't love, I'd been told when I first cried over Emily, at nineteen, and went to the college counsellor. One desires what one lacks and some are drawn to unrequited love; it is a safe kind of suffering, an avoidance of surrender. It is a desire to stay in the past, rather than to face an unknown future. I'd been sceptical, then, and I was sceptical, now, when I tried to apply the same logic to my infatuation with Cara. After all, I'd fallen for her before I'd known that she didn't want me.

We'd just celebrated my birthday and I was supposed to be happy, but instead I felt suddenly exhausted, made of concrete. I wanted to sink down upon the couch, into abjection, and I did, and then I wanted to stay there, forever. Only Frank O'Hara seemed to understand. *If he will just come back once and kiss me on the face*, I thought, reciting his poem in my head, *then I can put on my clothes, I guess, and walk the streets.*

I remembered thinking of this poem, feeling it for the first time, when I was with Emily. It was the poem through which I'd fallen in love with Frank O'Hara and the New York School. I was back to thinking about the ways in which I never seemed to change, to grow up. I lacked narrative; I was like a painting rather than a novel. My movement forward lacked a motor and even a wedding seemed like a costume party rather than a climax, a conclusion, evidence of adulthood. My mind recorded itself in messy brushstrokes, the same style repeated across different canvases. I felt closer to Cara when I analysed my longing for her, just as I felt a connection to Grace Hartigan when I opened the folder that contained my thesis documents.

It wasn't love, in theory, but I had loved Emily, in the end, so it was hard to say whether I might love Cara, sooner or later, platonically or romantically. I didn't flee from Grace Hartigan because I loved her; instead, I studied her.

Grace was dead, though, and nothing good had come of loving Emily, just years of mess, and Cara wanted a girlfriend who wasn't me. I was used to the unidirectional gaze, but that didn't mean that I could handle it.

32

I opened up Instagram and noticed that Alice had started following me. I clicked to follow her back and scrolled through her pictures, a messy mixture of cakes, selfies and other people's pets. I noticed Cara's username beneath each of them and it seemed suddenly obvious that something might be happening between them. I didn't know how I'd missed it. Alice was prettier than me, funnier, light-hearted; she had a fringe that flopped over her eyes. I tried to figure out when Cara had met Alice, to see if this correlated with any shifts in her behaviour toward me. I remembered Cara teasing Alice in her kitchen as I considered the croquembouche, remembered Cara's irritation when I'd asked her to catch the subway home from Alice's party with me. I wondered if she'd been hoping to stay with Alice that night, if I'd been in the way inadvertently. I wondered if Cara thought I'd been trying to sabotage their courtship. I wondered how Alice felt about it all. I couldn't imagine she wouldn't be interested in Cara.

I felt sad that Cara wanted something beyond our friendship, which felt so consuming to me that I didn't really have space for a relationship. I couldn't imagine having both Cara and Robert in the city. It should have been obvious, I supposed, that Cara would desire a relationship, but I'd projected my own ambivalence about romantic love onto her. When she said she wasn't interested in me, I'd figured that she wasn't looking to fall in love at all, but of course that made no sense. I thought of Cara's drawings, which dwelt on beauty even as they were disquieting, and I replayed her comments on love as transcendent. She'd told me that she wanted to have a wedding one day. I hadn't considered the idea that she'd meet somebody else so soon. I suppose I'd imagined that if Cara's life was going anywhere in particular I'd be going there, too.

I decided, that evening, to drop into Cara's shop on the way home. She was on the phone when I stepped inside and she smiled, held up a finger, and turned away, speaking quietly. I picked up a beaded comb from the table near the window, ran the spikes across my fingers.

'Hey,' I said, when she was off the phone. 'Are you up to anything after work? Want to get dinner?'

'I can't,' she said.

'What are you up to?' I asked.

'I'm tired,' she said. 'I just want to go home.'

I felt sure that she was acting differently. She'd been eager, before, to do things after work. She never really wanted to go home.

'Have I done something wrong?' I asked.

'What? No. I'm just tired.'

'I didn't mean to get so upset, yesterday,' I said. 'I just thought . . . aren't we supposed to be friends?'

'We are friends,' said Cara.

'But now you're saying you don't want to get dinner.'

'That doesn't mean we aren't friends, Soph. We had dinner yesterday. I'm just tired.'

'It just really doesn't seem like you want to be friends, and if you don't want to be friends, you shouldn't have said that we were friends. And, like, last night. You just left so abruptly.'

'I didn't leave abruptly.'

'It really doesn't feel like you want to be my friend.'

'You're the one yelling at me because I'm tired,' said Cara. 'I don't think this is about friendship at all . . . I don't want to tell you that you want more than friendship because, like, I can't tell you what you want. But in your apartment, that night, when we were drinking tea . . . I could have stayed that night and told you how much friendship meant, and I really do mean that, but it just seems like what you want is something else. I do value you and you don't seem to believe it, and it's frustrating. None of this is fair. This whole thing makes me crazy. Like, didn't we have this exact fight last week?'

She said this as if the departure were something that hung over her, as if it had been a momentous decision, that decision to keep the conversation brief, to leave abruptly, before I confessed anything to her.

'I don't want to hurt you,' she said.

I bristled at this. It implied that she had power over me while I lacked the power to do any damage to her. Why was she saying she didn't want to hurt me? I didn't want to be protected, shielded from life. I didn't want her to see me as vulnerable, pitiful, as somebody that she might hurt.

'I think I've been a good friend,' she said. 'I don't know where all your aggression is coming from.'

I just looked at her, shrugged. I realised I'd started crying as we were speaking and I was exhausted, now, too. I didn't know what to say, so I shrugged again and left, slamming the door, hearing the bell jingle behind me.

I knew, once I'd calmed down, that none of it made sense. I'd become hypersensitive to Cara's rejections; I never would have accused Lucy of being a poor friend if she'd felt too tired for dinner. I'd thought that Cara was attracted to me and I'd been proven wrong and the result, now, was that I didn't trust that she liked me at all. I presumed that there had to be a clear reason why she didn't want me and that this reason would disqualify me from friendship, too, even though I knew, rationally, that this wasn't how desire worked.

I wondered, also, if I'd bristled particularly when Cara said she worried about hurting me because the comment suggested that she had a tenderness, a care for others, that I lacked. I had never thought about whether my desire for Cara was hurting Robert or, for that matter, anybody else. Emily had hurt me, when we were younger, but I was fairly sure I'd never hurt her. I didn't think about hurting people because I didn't have the power to do so. I envied Cara that power.

Cara was right, though, I thought. I hadn't been fair. I didn't know how to apologise.

I rifled through Frank O'Hara's *Collected Poems* until I found something that fit.

I want you to be very very happy like Central Park, I sent, in a text message, and hoped she understood.

Cara didn't reply.

I wondered, again, if I should break up with Robert – not for Cara so much as for the possibility of being electrocuted into being by another person, for the possibility of renewal, for the kind of romantic transcendence that Cara kept telling me might exist. I thought of the trees in New England, dropping their leaves in autumn to make way for new leaves, not yet sprouting, that would come later. I thought of a poem, by Rainer Maria Rilke, that Robert had once read to me: *immemorial sap mounts in our arms when we love.* I wasn't a tree, though, even if my arms felt heavy with sap, and it seemed short-sighted to give up a relationship that was secure, to hurt somebody I loved who had done nothing to me, for the possibility of fresh sensations. I didn't know the answer, yet, but I had formulated the question.

Perhaps, I thought, that was something.

I knew Cara would say that it was nothing at all, that action was everything.

33

A few days later, Robert called to tell me that he'd just been offered, and had accepted, a tenure-track position at Dartmouth.

'Where exactly is Dartmouth?' I asked, though I'd searched for it on the internet while he was speaking and had the location in front of me, was using one hand to zoom into the map on my laptop while I held my phone with the other.

'It's in New Hampshire,' he said. 'Hanover. It's a small town. The trail goes through Hanover, and I'll be there, actually, really soon. I might stop for a week or so, look around, get a sense of where we might live. But I don't think I'll meet with anyone from Dartmouth, not while hiking.'

Hanover was closer to Canada than to Boston, which looked like the closest city. I knew already that I did not want to live there. I wanted to ask Robert about the university museums, but I suspected it might sound cutting.

'Congratulations,' I said, instead. 'We'll have to celebrate somehow. Are you going to celebrate tonight, on the trail? Oh, do you want me to book a restaurant? Is there somewhere you've always wanted to go?'

'I always just want a burger when I'm out here,' Robert said. 'It's hard to imagine being at a real restaurant.'

'Little Prince?' I asked, remembering a French restaurant in Soho that always seemed a little too expensive for us.

'Sounds good.'

'I'll book for October. We'll have so many things to celebrate. You'll have hiked the Appalachian Trail and gotten a job. And we still haven't properly celebrated the engagement.'

'It's a big year,' he said.

There was a tradition of artists coming to New York, but there was also a tradition of artists leaving the city. I thought about writing a research proposal exploring this, looking at Grace Hartigan and Joan Mitchell and the ways in which exile had shaped them, and applying for postdoctoral fellowships. I looked up deadlines for the Terra Foundation and the Smithsonian Archives of American Art fellowships. I checked staff profiles on the website of Dartmouth's Department of Art History, imagined driving for hours to visit the archives in New York and DC. I could see the appeal of the forest, but I didn't know how I could permanently live or do my work there. I'd felt such relief, at seventeen, moving to the city and knowing that I'd never have to live in a small town again. Was a North American small town different, though? Could a town with a university really be considered a small town, or would it be something else, a sort of hybrid?

It was possible to romanticise departure, and everyone I knew who was decamping to LA seemed to do this, but Grace had romanticised departure, wondering if she could create her own creative community in Baltimore, where the rents were lower, and regretted it, later. She described leaving New York as 'the disaster of my life'.

It had started, for her, too, with marriage, with marriages. She'd only been married to Bob Keene for a few months when she told him she'd never loved him and left him for Winston Price, an epidemiologist at Johns Hopkins who had bought *August Harvest*. She'd only known Winston Price for three days, if I remembered correctly, when she decided to move to Baltimore for him. She'd followed through. She'd left the Club, with all its fights and panel discussions, where she'd learnt so much, become herself. She'd left Cedar Tavern and the Five Spot Café. She'd left all her friends, and left Frank O'Hara in the most dramatic way of all, writing a letter ending their friendship, telling him that it was hindering her romantic relationships.

Grace had been at the height of her career when she'd left New York, and her departure had destroyed it. Barbara Guest, at the time, felt that the decision was 'disastrous', that the arts community would never forgive it. Frank O'Hara, who had considerable power through his position at MoMA, and had previously used this to support Grace, published a negative review of her next show in *Art News*. Grace's sales slowed. She changed styles, changed subject matter, but an international reputation was no longer possible. Grace was ambitious and she couldn't satisfy her ambitions in Baltimore. She needed more.

I needed to apply for more jobs. I needed something to counter New Hampshire.

I was still hoping for Sally's job. If I got it, I would be able to stay in New York, close to Grace and Frank, and keep wandering through the galleries in the morning and watching films for free at night. I imagined taking weekend trips to visit Robert in New Hampshire; we'd both have the environment that we wanted and an excuse to trade it for another when we felt tired.

I emailed Sally, asking her if we could have lunch, if I might ask her advice on the application. I emailed Joanna, another curatorial assistant, to ask if she might have lunch with me, too. I opened up the draft of my cover letter, again.

I asked everybody, that week, for advice on my application. Lucy read three drafts of my cover letter and CV. She told me to downplay my academic achievements; everybody had a PhD and it didn't mean much. She complained about her own applications, about being *just a fellow*, and I felt drenched by her pessimism, though glad for her advice. I sent it to another friend, still in Boston, who told me that it was 'excellent!!!'

I adjusted and readjusted my commas.

'You'll definitely get it,' said Joanna, as we perched at the mahogany bar of Michael's Restaurant, on the ground floor of the Rockefeller Apartments on 55th Street.

I'd never noticed this restaurant until Joanna invited me for a drink a few months after I'd arrived at the museum. It was an old-fashioned restaurant, dimly lit with white tablecloths and beige walls, and I didn't think anybody, save museum employees and the residents of the building above, bothered to drink at the bar. We drank at the bar for historical reasons, as MoMA's first home was in the Rockefeller Apartments, and because it was only a block away. Michael's wasn't a particularly hip restaurant, and it was too expensive for us, but it was a place where we could commune with the museum's past while sipping wine and sharing gossip.

'I'm so glad you're staying,' said Joanna. 'How old are you?'

'I just turned thirty,' I said.

'That's good. I started at thirty-two, but thirty would be better. You can do the job for a few years and then, if you want a kid, you'll still have time. Oh, that reminds me – I do have some advice! If you're at any openings or anything before the interview, get a glass of wine and stand near the HR people while you drink it so that they know you're not pregnant.'

'Really?' I asked. 'Would they really worry that I might be pregnant?'

'It's also a good idea to imply that you're in a relationship with a woman,' she said. 'You should say *partner* rather than *boyfriend*, and suggest that your partner's not too ambitious, so that they definitely don't think you'll be the one to end up caring for a baby.'

I bristled at this. I referred to Robert as *my boyfriend*, most of the time, because I knew that I'd want to call a woman *my girlfriend*. I couldn't perform queerness, I thought, only when it served me. It wasn't the first time, though, that I'd heard this piece of advice.

Joanna sent me her salary, so that I'd have negotiating power, and a copy of the cover letter she'd used to apply for her job, in an email, the next day. She told me that she wanted me to stay, that I was sure to get the job, that nobody was more qualified.

I always wondered, though, if Joanna's friendliness was disingenuous; she was so generous and kind, in person, but she'd never followed me back on Instagram. I didn't know if this meant that I annoyed her or if she'd simply never noticed my account.

I asked Sally if she, having worked more closely with me than the others, had any feedback, advice on things that I could do better. I didn't really expect much, as Sally was shy and softly spoken, not the type to note my flaws, but I wasn't sure how else to have a conversation about the job that might offer insight. I'd scoured the internet for advice and found, mostly, that I should take any opportunity to ask for feedback, to solicit criticism and learn about my weaknesses. Sally looked startled by the question.

'Not really,' she said. 'I'm the one who could do better. I never really know what work to give you. If there's anything, I suppose, it's that . . . well, you're like me. You're shy. We could both be a bit more forward in meetings.'

I felt that rush of infatuation I'd felt at the beginning. Sally had paused and smiled, a little impishly, as she pronounced the words *like me*. I loved the idea that I might be like Sally. I knew Sally too well, now, to call my affection a crush. I felt, almost, that it was a desire to adopt her, to be adopted by her, to become her family. I longed to be her friend, but it seemed that the only person with whom she was close was her sister.

'What will you do after this?' I asked her.

'I'll probably do a PhD,' she said. 'I don't have one, you know.'

I had more conversations in the sculpture garden than anywhere else, as the offices were so quiet, and yet it felt, today, like a momentous setting. We were surrounded by marble as we spoke about endings and uncertain futures. It felt sombre, funereal, and the playfulness of Ellsworth Kelly's *Green Blue*, close to our table, was heightened by my recognition of this frame. I hated the idea that I could lose the sculpture garden, that it might be relegated to memory.

'It's like we'll be trading places,' Sally said. 'I'll be in graduate school and you'll be a curatorial assistant.'

'What will you study?' I asked.

'I won't have to choose a dissertation topic straight away,' she said. 'But Nancy Holt, maybe. Do you know that drawing where she charts her day according to whether she was a feminist, an artist or a mystic? I love that. I'd like to look at land art and mysticism.'

I spent my time, after I'd submitted the application, trying to make myself more impressive. I sent out a proposal for the book based on my dissertation, finally. I pitched a piece on artist biographies to *LA Review of Books*, reviewed exhibitions for *Hyperallergic* and the *Brooklyn Rail*. I sent my article on Joe Brainard, which I'd finally finished, to *Art History*. I had lunch with some of the curators, ostensibly 'before I left', and with a curator from Brazil who was on a staff exchange with International Programs, who told me that I'd made the right decision to focus on museums, that universities were dying, choked by neoliberal austerity politics. I thought of all my peers in universities, writing dissertations on MoMA's own neoliberal agenda, reading books on International Programs as an instrument of statecraft.

In early September, I had my first interview for Sally's position, with a woman from HR. We talked about my choice of graduate school, about my involvement in the university's feminist collective in Australia, about my experiences in the department over the last two years, about whether I'd miss the emphasis on research.

'Lastly,' she said, pen poised. 'What sort of visa are you on?'

I hadn't anticipated that the question might be so direct.

I blinked.

'A J1,' I said.

'Don't worry,' she said, smiling. 'We do sponsor visas. We sponsor visas all the time. We just like to know now, so that if you're hired we can start the process as soon as possible.'

'I'm on a J1,' I said, regaining my composure. 'But I'm engaged to an American, so I'll have that visa option, too.'

She smiled, again, like a cartoon wolf, and jotted this down.

'It was lovely to meet you, Sophia,' she said. 'I hope the rest of your time as a fellow goes well.'

34

It seemed, in September, as if all the couples in the city had grown closer, were starting to cling together for warmth. The light was beginning to hit at a different angle, so that the dust suspended in the air was illuminated, shimmering. I'd grown more solitary as I'd thrown myself back into my work, into my application. I didn't need anybody. I liked this, felt whole again for it.

I checked my email, on Tuesday, and saw Emily's name; she'd replied, finally, to the note I'd sent, and then completely forgotten about, weeks earlier.

I'll be in New York later this week, she'd written. *Can you do dinner?*

Meet me at MoMA at seven on Thursday, outside the Education building? I replied. *On 54th Street.*

I've changed a lot, Emily wrote, in her next email. *I'm a bit scared we won't get along anymore.*

I've changed, too, I replied, but I wasn't sure if it was really true. When I thought of my infatuation with Cara, and of the petty arguments I'd provoked after she said that she wanted only friendship, I felt disappointed in myself; I wasn't any more mature than I'd been at twenty-two. I wondered if Emily really had changed and, if so, if she meant that she'd matured and lost some of her idealism, or if she meant something else.

'Do you think people really change?' I asked Robert, who was in New Hampshire, over the phone.

'Only if we make decisions,' he said. 'Only if we really try things, take risks.'

'Do I take risks?' I asked.

'I don't know,' said Robert. 'Sometimes. You moved halfway across the world straight out of college. That's more of a risk than I've ever taken.'

'Hmm,' I said. 'It didn't feel like a risk. It was necessary, professionally . . . but it was cowardly, really, wasn't it? I was just running away.'

'You're too hard on yourself,' Robert said. 'You were running toward something, too.'

'That's true,' I said.

'Do you think I'm running away, right now?' he said. 'By hiking?'

It hadn't even occurred to me.

'Not at all,' I said.

'It's the same thing,' he said. 'There are so many different ways to see things. I'm afraid, sometimes, that I'm risk averse, too. I could be more decisive. I could take more risks.'

'I think you're pretty decisive,' I said. 'You decided you wanted to hike the Appalachian Trail and then you actually did it, before you even had a job lined up. You're adventurous.'

I didn't know what my own equivalent of hiking the Appalachian Trail might be. I wondered if I'd stayed the same because I'd been cautious, passive, afraid of pursuing inconvenient dreams. I thought of Grace, unafraid of living, marrying and divorcing, having and leaving a child, leaving New Jersey for New York, leaving New York for Baltimore and regretting it.

I didn't really know what Emily had been doing. I knew she'd moved back to Los Angeles a few years after I'd left Australia but I wasn't sure where she worked or who she lived with, what her life was like. Emily didn't use Instagram, rarely posted on Facebook, and her first name and surname were so common that a Google search revealed nothing. She was coming to New York *for a meeting*, she'd written. I remembered Emily, essentially, as a calmer, more glamorous version of myself. I pictured her in LA at parties beside swimming pools, wearing shimmering dresses as the sun went down, turning the sky behind the city purple and orange. She was less academic than me, more contemporary than modern, and so I pictured her working at Gagosian or the Broad, wearing a sheath dress and talking to collectors, her straight hair slicked back. I felt nervous about seeing her, afraid that she'd be disappointed in my shabbiness, that she'd wonder why she'd ever considered me her best friend. I imagined her, back in LA, in bed with Taylor Swift or some other bisexual starlet, recounting her disbelief that she'd ever had time for me, laughing with relief that we'd never really been more than friends. I knew these visions were unlikely, but they still seemed the most possible scenarios that I could conjure.

We went to Fuku+, which was the coolest place in Midtown that I could think of, though it still didn't seem cool enough for Emily. It was odd to see her, so familiar yet belonging to a different time and place. Emily had the same haircut and wasn't wearing any makeup. There might have been a new crease on her forehead, but I wasn't sure if I was inventing it, trying to make the distance legible, less jarring, through a physical hint of our time apart. If there was a wrinkle, anyway, it made Emily look sophisticated rather than weary.

I wished I'd suggested meeting downtown, taking her to Dimes or Mission Chinese. I wondered if the better option, given we were in Midtown, would have been the dumpling place where Robert liked to eat when he visited me at work; it wasn't pretentious, which possibly made it cooler than Fuku+, where the walls were lit in a bizarre pale orange and the acoustics were bad.

'Are you still with that guy?' Emily said, almost as soon as we sat down. 'What's his name?'

'Robert,' I said.

'I remember he was good looking,' she said.

I'd missed Emily, or missed, at least, having somebody who had known me for a long time, who had seen me from more than one angle, in more than one context. I told her how confused I'd been feeling about my relationship with Robert. I didn't downplay it as I had with Lucy. I described our relationship as if an ending was preordained, selecting the points at which people had told me that it wouldn't last. I told Emily about Cara. I told Emily that sometimes I didn't open Robert's letters until he asked about them, over the phone, and that I pretended that the postal service was slower than he expected. I told her that he had a job in Dartmouth, that I had hated the traffic on the Taconic, that I hadn't moved to the United States to live in Hanover, New Hampshire. Our chicken sandwiches had arrived and Emily had finished her first cocktail by the time that I finished detailing it all.

I wondered if I was emphasising the negative because I wanted to leave the relationship or because it was Emily that I was addressing, and she'd never liked it when I loved anyone else. I didn't tell her that I still loved falling asleep beside Robert, that I'd bought a wedding dress. I expected Emily to say that I didn't seem interested in him, that I was supposed to tear open Robert's letters, excited, and that it meant something that I didn't. I expected Emily to suggest that I didn't really want him, that I wanted somebody else instead.

'But relationships have never been your priority,' Emily said, instead. 'It's always been work. That's why you left me. If you've found someone who lets you put work first, that's a good thing. It doesn't sound like you'll have to move to New Hampshire, either. Lots of academics go back and forth with east coast cities.'

I wanted to tell her that it was a little unfair for her to say that I'd left her, given we weren't in a relationship and I'd just gone to graduate school, but I didn't want to start an argument. I'd left Australia, not Emily, I thought, though it wasn't entirely true. I'd left the country, in part, because I was tired of unrequited love. It was a bit hypocritical, now, for Emily to say that I'd left her when she'd been the one to leave me wanting more than friendship and meaningless hook-ups for years. It was a bit self-centred. I couldn't design my life around somebody who was, essentially, a so-called *friend with benefits*, even if she'd been my best friend.

I felt a small flare of anger, but kept it inside.

'What did you mean when you said that you'd changed?' I asked.

'Lots of ways,' she said. 'I'm very monogamous now, for one thing. I've changed my mind on lots of stuff, like . . . all those people we used to hang out with, I don't see them anymore, or wasn't seeing them, anyway, when I was in Australia. I'm still bisexual, obviously, but queerness . . . it's such a scene. Like, do you remember Emma? I told her I didn't want to sleep with her and then I was, like, shut out of the queer community after that. I'm kind of done with it.'

I wondered how much of this was just a matter of growing up, of the messiness of desire. I'd once borrowed my own opinions from Emily, but she sounded naïve now. Emily was blaming the ideologies she'd once subscribed to for something that seemed, to me, to be just a matter of human vulnerability, immaturity. It was silly to blame queerness or the queer community. We'd all hurt one another, left casualties on our paths to adulthood. It wasn't the ideas or communities that had failed.

'Are you still against marriage?' I asked.

I hadn't mentioned, despite talking about Robert for twenty minutes, that I was engaged.

'No,' she said. 'I've changed my mind on that, too. I hate post-structuralism now. I know everyone at Harvard or wherever loves it, all the academics, so you probably do, too, but we should be trying to make meaning, not destroy it. Especially in a world where kids already feel meaningless. And then they find a painting they love and art historians just tell them everything that's wrong with it, tear it apart.'

I remembered the world in which I'd known Emily, so different from the one in which I now lived, where paintings were hallowed, bathed in a cathedral glow. I didn't know many art historians who spent their time tearing apart paintings beloved by children. I recognised, still, a certain extremity of conviction in Emily. She'd changed her views, but she was still confident, forthright, and I, beside her, was much too passive. I just changed the subject to avoid arguing with her.

'Robert and I might get married,' I said. 'I'm not sure about it, though. I'm tired of people assuming that I'm straight.'

'People are always going to assume you're straight, Soph,' said Emily. 'You can be, like, wrapped in a rainbow flag and holding your girlfriend's hand and people will think you're just friends, just into bright colours. It's never about what other people think, though, Soph.'

I was comforted by Emily's certainty. She never began a sentence with *I think*. I had liked this when I was younger; it had been so easy to give in to her, to let myself be led. I wasn't sure, now, if I trusted or even liked her, if I found her too brash, but I envied the certainty and wanted it for myself. Emily was right about some of it, too. I was always so concerned with other people's impressions.

'How can anyone ever be sure about something as big as marriage?' I asked.

'You can't. But it's stupid to hesitate just because it might work out badly. You'll never know the future. It might work out well.'

'It feels as if everything's ending, though.'

'It's not like marriage means that you have to become a housewife.'

I was a bit disappointed with my chicken sandwich. I wondered what Emily thought of hers, hoped that she liked it. I wished, again, that I'd suggested the dumpling place. We could get pretzel soft serve from Milk Bar, afterward, here, at least. I knew tourists were usually excited about Momofuku Milk Bar, though I didn't know if Emily counted as a tourist or if David Chang's eateries had taken over LA, too.

'What about the girl you mentioned, though?'

'Cara,' I said. 'That's not really relevant. She's not interested in me.'

'That doesn't mean it's not relevant.'

'Well, it's totally separate. It's possible to have feelings for two people simultaneously. You can love multiple people at the same time. Isn't that what you used to tell me? I feel like I learnt that from you.'

'Maybe,' said Emily. 'But that doesn't mean that those feelings don't influence each other. You can't compartmentalise everything.'

I asked Emily about her work, shifting the topic again. We had leapt from distance to familiarity so quickly. I watched Emily's face as she spoke, trying to register, as I had earlier, some hint of the time that had passed, some sign she'd become a stranger.

By the end of dinner, I was tired of talking about myself, of dipping into the past and trying to figure out the future. I was tired of being tentative, of overthinking. I wasted so much time trying to weigh up every possibility before I finalised decisions. I'd told Robert that I'd marry him, but I wasn't acting as if I would. I was so risk averse. I wanted to act, now, to simply take a risk, and figure everything else out later.

'It's ridiculous that you're staying in a hotel,' I told Emily, after dinner. 'You could have stayed with me.'

'Work's paying. It's a nice hotel.'

'Well, you should come and see my flat, at least.'

'Okay,' she said, and followed me into a taxi.

We were both quiet for the ten minutes it took to drive downtown. I looked at the shimmering city, which I rarely saw through the back window of a car, and tried to translate some of my feelings into words, to figure out if I liked Emily or if

I feared her strength of personality. I didn't know if either of us had really changed. I paid the driver, when the taxi pulled up outside my flat, and unlocked the front door, climbed the stairs, and unlocked the door to the flat, Emily silently behind me.

I didn't know what Emily expected, but I kissed her as soon as I'd closed the door and she gripped my waist and kissed me back and we were both suddenly twenty-two again, almost fighting in our urgency to remove one another's clothes. I pushed her onto the couch and removed my shoes with my toe and heel, as she pulled off her jeans.

I was astonished by Emily's fluidity and abandon, which I'd thought, in the intervening years, that I'd imagined. She stood up to finish removing her jeans and I folded onto the couch beneath her, pulling her thighs toward my face as soon as she turned back to me, getting lost in the saltiness of it all. Her body, above me, was strangely hard to believe, so solid and three-dimensional. I knew Emily as a ghostly memory, but she was real, and I had my mouth on her and my fingers inside her. Emily let out some cries, as if she were about to come, but she didn't. Instead, her body shifted away from my face and past my torso so that our eyes met and we pressed into one another. Our legs wrapped around our bodies with a surprising grace, and I felt slippery against her, registering her pulse against my own. I couldn't keep my eyes open; my senses were overwhelmed. Emily's fingers were on the back of my ribs and behind my ear, and her mouth was against my mouth, breathing and kissing, messily, each of us eager to be closer, somehow, without wanting to pull apart to rearrange ourselves, without knowing if it were physically possible. I pushed Emily backward and kissed her breasts, and she sighed gently and let me linger, for a moment, and rearrange my hand against her, prompting a gasp, before she pushed herself upright, pushing me back into the couch, and the weight of Emily's body pushed her hand against and into me, and I tried to count her fingers, but I couldn't, and I dissolved into the intensity, unsure if I could withstand it, and then it was suddenly, too quickly, over.

It wasn't as I'd remembered.

We lay on the couch, breathing alongside one another, covered in sweat.

'I'm quite cold, actually,' Emily said, after a few minutes, and sat up to pull on her t-shirt.

35

We moved to my bed, lay beneath the blankets. I tried to shake my confusion, to hold off excavating things until the morning. I wrapped my arm around Emily and she turned toward me, her hand on my hip, and kissed me again.

'I know this was probably stupid,' she said. 'But I'm glad it happened. I've spent so much time trying to figure out why you were so cold . . . I mean, it's obvious what happened, you moved away . . . but we never really discussed it. You just left.'

'Right,' I said, but I couldn't really process what she meant.

'It was pretty cruel,' said Emily.

'We never really discussed anything,' I said.

'You knew that I loved you, though,' she said.

'As a friend,' I said.

'No,' she said. 'It was like . . . we were in a relationship and you just left. We didn't have to label it. It was so obvious. Or, well, I thought so. And everyone else thought so, too. But you never even broke up with me, officially.'

I must have been staring at her. I was confused.

'We were roommates,' I said.

'That's, like, the oldest euphemism in the book,' she said. 'It doesn't matter now. It was such a long time ago. But it took me a long time to get over it. It was an awful thing for you to do.'

'I didn't know that you felt that way,' I said. 'I thought . . .'

'You've always been so oblivious,' she said, and kissed my nose. 'You just left me. Like mother, like daughter, I guess.'

I tried not to flinch, though I wasn't sure if I was flinching at the tenderness of her gesture or at the casual cruelty of her words.

'I didn't mean to make you feel bad,' she said. 'I'm sorry.'

'I just . . . It would have been different if I'd known.'

I wanted to cry. I looked up at the ceiling, grey in the half-light, and blinked my feelings away.

'But of course you knew,' she said. 'You're not that oblivious.'

'I might not have left.'

'It was graduate school. You always would have left.'

I stared at the ceiling, feeling my arms sting, trying to identify my feelings. I'd been so sure that I'd meant very little to Emily, that it hadn't been a real relationship, but all I could remember, now, was my feeling of abandonment. I couldn't remember enough specifics to know if I'd created a narrative in retrospect to justify my actions or if Emily was the one doing this. If I'd been projecting, what had I been projecting? I couldn't understand how we'd seen the same situation in such wildly different ways. I wondered if I was crazy.

'It could have been long-distance, though, or something,' I said. 'I didn't think you cared.'

'We were so young, Soph. That wouldn't have worked.'

'Did you know that I loved you?' I asked.

'Yeah,' she said. 'But I also knew you'd leave.'

'I didn't think you cared,' I said, again. 'I didn't think you needed me at all.'

Emily seemed so comfortable in my bed. She fell asleep easily, quickly, while I lay awake, regretting our proximity. I felt as if I were twenty-two again and I learnt that I didn't like it; it wasn't what I wanted. I missed Robert, wanted him to comfort me, and the taste of Emily's body in my mouth filled me with guilt.

I'd spent so much time trying to win Emily over I'd never realised I'd actually done so. I still couldn't really believe it. I wondered if I'd seen everything incorrectly or if she was telling the story inaccurately, if she was trying to trick me to make herself feel better. I'd been so hurt by Emily. She'd never seemed close enough. I couldn't leave Emily, I'd thought, because she didn't want to be my girlfriend, but I'd never asked for that commitment. It hadn't been worth asking, I'd thought, because I knew she wasn't interested. It had never occurred to me that she might assume that our intimacies added up to something. I wondered, now, if it was all youth and semantics, if we'd loved one another for years, in our messy way, and if I'd been the one to end it.

If I'd suspected that my love was requited, would I have made the same decision? It wasn't really a question. I would have chosen graduate school over Emily, just as now I couldn't countenance leaving MoMA for New Hampshire, for Robert. It was possible, and painful, to fall in love with institutions, and I did it all the time.

But an institution, I thought, would never love me back.

I remembered how shaky I'd felt before I met Robert. I liked the security of our relationship. I liked that I always knew exactly what Robert and I were to one another, that I didn't need to fear losing him. I was hypersensitive to rejection, which I supposed was why I'd misunderstood my relationship with Emily; I'd ruined my friendship with Cara, too, because I'd been afraid she didn't want to be my friend. I'd felt the same way about Emily that I felt about Cara, now, as if my love were born of addiction, nothing wholesome, and might destroy me. I needed a little distance, in a relationship, so that I could comprehend things and didn't lose myself. I needed the sort of stability that I had in Robert, which I'd never really felt with Emily, and which I couldn't imagine feeling with Cara.

I was glad I'd gone to graduate school.

I was glad that I'd left.

I was frightened by everything that Emily had said. She'd seemed so calm and so certain as she disrupted my understanding of our shared past. If I'd misunderstood this, I thought, what else might I have misunderstood? I feared I was reading everything wrong. I wondered about the gulf separating my internal world from external reality. This was why I didn't trust my instincts, I thought. This was why I was cautious and overintellectual. This was why I needed other people to tell me that my decisions were the right ones.

It was disconcerting that Emily was asleep, so peacefully, beside me. She didn't seem troubled by any of this at all. I didn't want Emily back; I didn't want this feeling of confusion and powerlessness. I felt in thrall to her, as with Cara, when what I wanted was equality and stability.

I moved to the bathroom, quietly. I felt calmer there, with the light switched on and white tiled walls separating me from Emily. I checked my phone. Robert had sent an email to say that he'd decided to come back, briefly, over the next weekend. I replied that I was delighted and I really felt it, smiling as I typed, despite everything, and then I brushed my teeth, pulled on a t-shirt, and climbed back into bed, falling asleep alongside Emily.

I dreamt, that night, that Emily and I were still together, that I was staying with her family and washing dishes. I looked down and saw a hole in the floor, revealing that the house was built on sand. I went into another room, in search of a water glass, and found a fox curled on the sofa, and then I returned to Emily, in the kitchen, and slipped my arm around her, pressed my cheek to her cheek, kissed her ear. I felt, in the dream, tenderness and desire, the delight of proximity.

I woke and felt my eyelids tense, bracing against reality.

I felt guilty, at work, and I hated feeling guilty. It hadn't felt, when I kissed Emily, as if I were cheating on Robert. I'd been a little drunk, I supposed, though I knew that that wasn't an excuse. It had felt so natural that I hadn't stopped to consider that it was wrong. I'd felt the shiver of realisation after I'd orgasmed, as my body returned to room temperature, and I'd avoided thinking about it while Emily was in my flat, had smothered it with a blanket.

I knew that I was supposed to tell Robert, but the consequence seemed worse than the thing itself. I'd learnt from it, I thought. I'd never done anything like this before and I wouldn't repeat it. I knew, now, that I really wanted to marry Robert.

I wondered if the museum kept records of the phrases that we searched on incognito browsers. I went into the bathroom, intending to search *should I tell my partner that I cheated on him* on my phone, but found I couldn't type the word *cheated*, that my finger trembled above the *c*. I left the bathroom and slipped into the stairwell, feeling dizzy, and scurried down to the second floor and along the corridor, into the museum, and into the Tony Oursler exhibition. In its darkened theatre, nobody would notice the panic on my face.

I sat there silently for a long time. I decided to think about what had happened with Emily as a dream, because it had unfolded with the same bizarre logic as a dream. It hadn't really made sense. I had dreamt about Emily, anyway, that night, even if she'd been in my bed at the time, reading my copy of Grace Hartigan's journals as she waited for me to wake up. I flinched at the memory. We'd walked downstairs together and I'd kissed her and she'd caught a cab back to her hotel and she was, now, hopefully, on a flight back to LA. I didn't need to tell Robert, I decided, and I shouldn't. It had been a dream, and nobody wanted to hear about somebody else's dreams.

As I waited for the subway, I noticed a homeless man with a cardboard sign reading *TRYING TO SCRAPE UP $20 TO LEAVE NYC.* I noticed a woman with an avant-garde coat in black velvet and oversized spectacles balancing two large Dunkin' Donuts boxes on her arm. On the train, a man stood uncomfortably close to me as he ate an apple, holding the core between two fingers. I felt a sort of love, an affection born of familiarity, for the speckled floor and the smudged silver of the carriage doors.

I opened the windows of my apartment, as soon as I was inside, to air it out. I felt another guilty shiver as I sat down on the couch. Back in the apartment, Emily seemed too real. It all felt too recent, too visceral, to deny. This uneasiness reminded me of the minutes after waking from a nightmare, unable to distinguish the real from the imagined, and of the way that sleep itself, after such nightmares, seemed too terrifying to consider closing my eyes again. I reassured myself with this comparison.

I opened up my laptop and an incognito browser.

Should I tell my partn, I typed, and then stopped, deleted it.

Dreams about exes, I typed, instead.

I read that these dreams were often a sign of needing to move forward, that brides often dreamt of their exes immediately before their weddings, triggered by the distance that they'd travelled since these old relationships. It felt very true, I thought. I'd realised, after the previous night, that all my hesitancy about marriage was just a remnant of the past, that my desire for Cara had been a fantasy, like my desire for Emily, who I didn't really want anymore. I'd been longing for an idealised version of my youth, but my adult life was better than that. I loved Robert and I missed him. The dream of Emily was a sign, I decided, that I was ready to get married.

I thought of Grace, always throwing herself into everything. I needed to do the same.

I checked the time difference and called my father.

'When was the last time we got a call from you?' he said. 'You had an Australian accent, then. You didn't sound all American.'

'It wasn't that long ago,' I said. 'Do I really have an American accent?'

'Nah,' he said. 'You sound like Sydney University. Is everything okay?'

'Yes,' I said. 'I'm getting married.'

36

I was happy that Robert was visiting. I felt, now, that things might finally return to the way that they'd been before I'd met Cara, before I'd begun to topple toward irrationality. I'd realised, seeing Emily, that I'd been untethered, that my course needed correcting. Robert was almost done with the Appalachian Trail. He was in New Hampshire, which meant he had only Maine, with the Hundred-Mile Wilderness and then Mount Katahdin, to go, and then things would be as they had been in February, before he'd left.

I was still doing gallery checks for the 1960s show each day. In the gallery dedicated to 1961, there was a photograph by Richard Avedon entitled *Wedding of Mr and Mrs H. E. Kennedy*. It didn't receive much attention, sandwiched between the car that dominated the gallery, a navy roadster that I couldn't bring myself to care about, and the door that led to 1962. The Avedon photograph showed two middle-aged women, both in furs, greeting one another with a kiss on the lips while their husbands looked down from the edges of the frame. I'd never seen a kiss that was so obviously platonic; the lips of the two women were pursed as they touched and their bodies remained far apart, each holding their hands to their stomach as they craned their necks awkwardly. If there was any hint of sex to the image, it came from the two men that watched them enthusiastically, framing the kiss.

Since I'd begun looking, months earlier, I'd found plenty of artworks in the museum's collection that represented weddings. I'd saved images of them in a folder on my desktop. The artworks were photographs, mostly. The older ones, from the 1920s and 1930s, had something uncanny about them, and I wasn't sure if they were taken by Surrealists, pulling at the threads of the institution to reveal it as strange, or if they were simply ethnographic records made haunted by time. I thought of photography as such a self-conscious medium, but it was in these decades that artists had stopped dismissing photography as scientific and really begun to play with its possibilities.

There was also a wedding invitation that I quite liked, in the collection, designed by Edward Fella, for an event to be held in Los Angeles. In very small lettering, at the bottom of the page, invitees were given five choices for their RSVP: *a) can come; b) want to but can't; c) don't remember either of them; d) can't believe it; e) some combination of the above.*

Robert was in the White Mountains, now. I kept picturing this range in the shades of a wedding dress or the croquembouche

I'd promised Alice that I'd order, though of course the mountains weren't white at all in early September, but green and brown and grey, with pale mist rising from deep blue ponds in the early mornings.

I clicked through the images on Google. There were images of the landscape in winter, as white as its name, and in autumn, with foliage so orange, beneath the purple-grey mountains, that it seemed like a sunset reversed. These mountains had a grandeur that I'd never associated with New England; they didn't roll gently, but roared up, aggressively, toward the sky. There were sharp cliffs, shorn of trees, in every season, and often the photographs were taken from above or amongst the clouds.

I wondered why I'd been so dismissive of the Appalachian Trail, so sure that I'd find it boring. I suspected, now, that I'd simply been frightened of it. I was, after all, the sort of woman for which Benton MacKaye had intended this trail. I was, like Jessie Hardy Stubbs, a girl whose madness, or misery, could be read as the result of ambition or overwork. I genuinely didn't know if I was reacting to my circumstances, to a culture eager to classify my sexuality and evaluate my worth through my professional position, or if I was simply avoiding myself through examination of postmodern life. It was desire, after all, that was truly devastating for me, and I couldn't blame my crushes on late capitalism.

Benton MacKaye had described his wife, when she ran away at Grand Central Station, as 'stubborn,' and I was stubborn, too. I clung to the city, abandoning myself. It felt twee and sentimental to remark that trees, producing oxygen, made it easier to breathe, but it was also just true. I'd liked the Appalachian Trail, when I'd joined Robert for short sections, and I'd loved, throughout graduate school, our short trips away from the city.

When I was a child, I'd loved watching brumbies canter across the High Plains and I'd loved, when camping, looking up at the stars and identifying the constellations. I'd disavowed all this, I supposed, because it left me vulnerable in a strange way that I was still struggling to name.

If I didn't get Sally's job, perhaps I could hike the Appalachian Trail. I wondered what my trail name might be, considered how I could reinvent myself. I'd be stripped, hiking, of all my defences. It was grounding that I needed, and hiking might give me this. Robert gave me this, I realised, and I wondered if this was why I'd resisted the Appalachian Trail initially. I didn't need the Appalachian Trail, because I had Robert, and I didn't want the Appalachian Trail, because it was taking him away from me. I saw the world in such selfish ways sometimes.

I couldn't concentrate on work, impatient for Robert's visit, but this was fine as I didn't have much to do. I was wrapping up my fellowship, writing handover documents that I knew nobody would read, organising files in the department's communal folders. I went up to the library, sometimes, to scan books that I might need to consult in future. I found an excuse to catch the subway up to Columbia, renewing my reader's card in case my museum ID was taken from me, trying to forge an insurance policy in case I didn't get Sally's job. I was still too optimistic, though, to fully indulge my nostalgia; I didn't loiter in the sculpture garden during lunchbreaks.

Instead, on Wednesday, I stretched my break further than usual and went to meet Lucy near the Loeb Boathouse.

'We could have done this more often,' she commented. 'Just met somewhere in the park.'

'We should have taken lunchbreaks more often,' I said, half-joking.

'Do you know where you want to get married?' she asked.

There were always wedding parties in front of the Loeb Boathouse on weekends, which I supposed had prompted the question. I'd never actually been inside the Loeb Boathouse – I'd just seen it in countless films.

'Somewhere in New York,' I said. 'But everywhere's so expensive.'

'Won't Robert's parents pay?'

'Probably,' I said. 'I'd still feel strange about it, though.'

'I can imagine you getting married somewhere downtown,' she said. 'Maybe the Marble Cemetery.'

'Which one?'

'I didn't know there was more than one.'

'They're really close to one another.'

'Are you and Abby Willings still close?' she asked. 'Pull some strings and get married at the Frick.'

'I don't think Abby has that kind of power,' I said. 'She's leaving, like, next week, too.'

I'd found thinking about venues to be the hardest part of planning. I'd looked up the cost of the New York Marble Cemetery, accessed via a narrow passageway from Second Avenue, and it didn't look promising, particularly when considering catering and the chance of rain. I'd considered places in the Hudson Valley, too, but remembered, from my teenage years, that people drove home after drinking when there was no public transport or reliable taxi service. I was sure, though, that

Robert would have some good ideas, and I didn't have to do it all myself.

When I was back at the office, I noticed a new email from Human Resources. *Your Application for the P&S CA Position*, I read, before I opened it, and saw an invitation for a second interview, with Antoine, Doreen and Mark, scheduled for the following week.

I have another interview next week!!! I messaged Robert. *So we can celebrate!*

And you can give me interview advice, I added, in a second text message.

37

I ran to the door and kissed Robert when he arrived, but he was looking down at the floor, as if ashamed or embarrassed. I supposed that he was tired; he'd woken up early to travel down to the city. I wanted to talk about literature, to run some recent ideas I'd had about modernity past him. I'd bought bread, cheese and some tomatoes at Essex Market that morning, for lunch, but it was only eleven, so I started by making coffee in a plunger and carrying it, with two mugs and some milk, over to Robert, sitting on the couch.

'I'd forgotten your Australian coffee,' he said, looking at the plunger.

'I'm not surprised,' I said. 'You've been drinking instant coffee?'

'I haven't been drinking coffee at all,' he said.

I put my head on Robert's shoulder. I was feeling affectionate, acting like a cat. I wondered if I was trying to make amends for the ways in which I'd been a terrible girlfriend lately. I was just glad to have Robert back, though, really.

'I should probably have a shower,' he said.

Robert returned from the bathroom fully dressed, which was surprising. He usually draped himself in a towel and dressed slowly, in the bedroom, while talking to me. He looked worried. He sat on the opposite corner of the couch to me.

'We should probably talk,' he said.

I wanted an artwork about endings. I wanted to leave the scene, to focus on a beautiful image, to analyse something fixed, rather than experience life unfolding. I wanted to catch my breath, to swim out of my own mind and into a pool of coloured brushstrokes. I couldn't think of an artwork, though. I tried to conjure something from the museum, to run through a gallery in my mind, but I couldn't picture any of the paintings that I saw each morning. I could remember only *Grand Street Brides*, and I didn't want to think of those figures in wedding dresses, each hollow and alone, never looking at one another, all leering at me.

I felt sick, my stomach full with adrenalin, desperate to stop the conversation that Robert was attempting, but I was also confused, eager to reach the other side of it so that I might understand. He'd been talking, or we'd been talking, for half an hour, but I felt as if the whole scene was behind glass, beyond my comprehension, as if I was looking at a painting obscured by bad lighting, glare bouncing off the glaze. I hadn't even mentioned Emily. I didn't think Robert even knew that she'd visited. So what, I wondered, was causing this? I caught phrases like *I've been thinking* and *we're always fighting*, but Robert said them from the other end of the couch, and he wasn't holding my hand, and it didn't seem as if he was asking me to problem-solve.

'I don't know what's going on,' I said. 'It seems like you're breaking up with me, but—'

'I am breaking up with you,' he said. 'I'm sorry.'

It felt, speaking to him, as if he were slipping from my grip. I wanted to hold on, and yet I knew that he had already slipped away, that he had made the decision before telling me about it, that it wasn't possible to hold onto him. I kept losing my grip on the conversation, too, losing track of time, of what was said and why.

'You can't seem to commit, Soph,' he said. 'I want to get married. I want to have kids. I want to be with someone who's going to be in the same town as me. I don't want to wait a year for you to get your life together, to figure out what you want, and then have it turn out that you don't want me to be part of it. We're engaged, and you still keep saying that you can't make any promises about the future.'

'You've never said this before,' I said.

'I mean, I didn't realise it was an issue until I proposed,' he said. 'I tried to talk to you about it, both at my parents' house and in North Adams. I tried to ask about the future and you never said anything reassuring. You just kept saying that we couldn't know the future. You never wanted to tell me that things would work out, and it wore on me.'

'Why didn't you say that?' I asked.

'It just wore quickly,' he said. 'There wasn't time.'

Our chairs weren't empty. Our books were still mixed together. We were both here, in this apartment that we still shared, but

Robert seemed further away, now, than he'd seemed at any point on the trail. *Edward Hopper*, I thought, struggling again for an image; everything was flat and disconnected.

'Even when I suggested getting married,' he said. 'I wondered if we would be able to get through a wedding day without fighting over something stupid, about whether our families would get along.'

'I guess now we'll never know,' I said.

I didn't think that we fought often. I remembered intellectual conversations, questions about modernity, about literature and art, and only occasional brushes of irritation with one another. Robert told me to avoid drinking, to open my mail or eat more fruit, and I told him . . . I couldn't remember what I'd told him. I had always been kind and honest; I never left arguments until we had processed things, reached a consensus. I didn't say any of this, now, though. It might have led to another argument, one that wouldn't be processed, ever.

'I should have said something in North Adams,' he said. 'But I just couldn't. I didn't want you to have to drive back to the city like that, especially when it was your birthday.'

I felt more desire, upon losing Robert, than I had felt since we'd first met. I wondered if this was what I wanted: precarity, uncertainty and devastation, the repetition of childhood losses. We all say that we want to be happy, to feel secure, but do we, really? Or, rather, did I?

'I am trying to be kind,' he said.

I couldn't remember when I'd slipped off the couch, but I was lying on the floor, half my body beneath it. It was dusty, I noticed.

'Like Escher staircases,' I said, remembering Cara's analogy. 'Desires that don't match up.'

'You read Anne Carson,' said Robert. 'Finally.'

'What?'

'Your analogy. It's Anne Carson, isn't it? *Eros the Bittersweet*.'

I began to cry, again, only realising that the last set of tears had stopped flowing with the arrival of this next set. I'd thought the analogy so profound, and so profoundly sad, when Cara made it; I hadn't realised it had been from one of Robert's books, a book he'd mentioned to me, many times, until it was too late for me to appreciate this, appreciate all his erudite references.

'I'll stay with Jack tonight, then go back to the trail tomorrow,' he said. 'You can stay here until things are sorted out.'

I remembered, years ago, seeing a conference paper on a performance by an Australian artist, Anastasia Klose, who had wandered Venice in a wedding dress, wearing a sign that read *Nanna, I'm still searching* . . . She'd said that she was married to art, and that she didn't need a groom. She'd said, also, that she wanted to marry a stranger, to get a visa to live abroad, but that this wasn't possible in Italy. Klose had been a star, ascending, at that point, but afterward her career stalled. I kept thinking of the plaintive, pathetic tone of that image, that performance.

I imagined myself in my Comme des Garçons dress standing at an altar, waiting for Robert, in front of a crowd of people who offered worried glances and then went home, saying nothing. Even though marriage had never felt real to me, even though it had seemed frightening, seemed heteronormative, I hadn't hesitated before I said *yes*.

Robert had left after four hours. I felt he hadn't answered my questions.

'Can I call you?' I'd said. 'Can we talk about this?'

'I probably won't have reception on the trail,' he said.

After he left, my past mistakes crowded me, and I saw that Robert was the only person who would forgive me my failings. I'd thrown our relationship away by not being certain, always holding the door half open so that somebody else might slip through it. Instead, he'd slipped away. I'd received precisely what I deserved, but I'd expected to get more than I deserved. I wanted everything. I wanted to be in a relationship whilst learning who I was as an independent person, and the result was getting nothing. I'd always told myself that I was lucky and yet I'd taken my biggest stroke of luck for granted.

Robert was going, soon, to the Hundred-Mile Wilderness. I envied the poetry of processing a breakup in such a setting. He would be moving forward through something strange and unknown while I would just be tacking back and forth, past the Duane Reade, into the subway, circling the museum, going nowhere, stuck in my everyday life as it passed its expiry date. I lay there, still on the floor, imagining thin boards stretching through swampy valleys filled with sphagnum moss and bright ferns. I thought of fog sitting low over lakes in the early mornings, of the tangled roots of trees, of mice skittering across the floors of shelters at night. I'd googled the Hundred-Mile Wilderness, months earlier, when

Robert told me that it was meant to be the hardest section but that he was looking forward to it.

I kept rehearsing the things that I could have done differently, but the truth of the matter was that Robert wanted to quit loving me, if he hadn't already. This was the cruellest fact of all, I thought: that loving me was a bad decision, something that Robert did not want to do. It was a choice to love somebody and the easier choice, in this situation, would have been to continue loving me, which meant that he had to really want to stop.

He would have loved me if I wasn't me, I thought. *He would have loved me if I were a different person*.

I was still lying on the floor, unsure if time was working. I couldn't be bothered checking a clock.

I rolled onto my stomach and picked up my phone. I flicked across to his Instagram account. He hadn't posted in a week. He'd started the account for me, at my urging, and I wondered if he'd keep posting now that we'd broken up.

I scrolled through Robert's list of followers looking for some sort of clue. He had met somebody else, perhaps, while hiking. He had met a woman who lived in Hanover, in New Hampshire, with whom he could imagine a future uncomplicated by her ambition. He had met somebody who was sure of what she wanted, perhaps somebody who wanted, before all else, a secure marriage. He had met somebody warmer than me, more willing to commit. I saw my own failings thrown into sharp relief. I saw that he had one new follower and clicked to find a nameless private account.

If I had been a different person, it might have worked, I thought, again.

I didn't want to be a different person, though. I wanted to stay myself.

I knew that Robert would forget all the good things about our relationship. It had felt, when he was speaking, as if he had already begun to do that. He had accused me of crying so as to hurt him and not simply because I was hurt. I hated the thought that he would not remember me as I was but would picture, instead, a caricature of me. It wasn't possible for Robert to build a relationship with somebody else straight away while retaining his love for me; he would have to twist it inside out. Why was I assuming, though, based on one new Instagram follower, that he had left me for another woman?

I supposed that it was the easiest explanation to take.

I supposed that it was what I might have done if things had aligned differently.

Robert didn't seem to care that I was hurt. He was actively seeking not to know, asking me not to message him, refusing to check that I was okay. It revealed a cruelty that I hadn't known in him, which was perhaps why I was in shock. I refused to believe that Robert could be this callous. I remembered the adage that men cared only about women who were their wives, sisters, daughters or mothers, seen in relation to them, and never about women as people, as individuals. Robert had ceased to care about me as soon as he had decided that I was not his girlfriend, his fiancé, and would not be his wife, or at least it seemed that way to me.

I had behaved, looking back on everything, as if I were detached. I didn't think, now, that this had come naturally to me. I had cultivated detachment in order to deal with the time apart while Robert was hiking. I tried to protect myself from being hurt by persuading myself that I was unfazed. I was, now, clearly fazed.

I remembered the times that I had thought that if Robert broke up with me then that would save me from decision making, which was difficult, but it didn't feel that way now. It felt as if I should have rushed, as if in hesitating, in overthinking everything, I had thrown away my future. I felt, crying on the floor, closer to myself than I had in years.

I hadn't closed the blinds or the windows before the conversation began. I remembered, suddenly, the proximity of New York. I imagined my neighbours seeing me slip onto the floor, hearing me wail as Robert sat impassively on the couch, and felt suddenly less alone, as if my histrionics might be redeemed as entertainment. It was dark, now, and the streetlights cast shadows above me.

It was one am when I managed to cut a piece of bread from the loaf that I'd left on the kitchen counter, but I couldn't eat it because of the lump in my throat. I realised, stepping back into the living room, that the coffee plunger sat untouched on the coffee table.

I couldn't blame it all on myself, on my lack of commitment. I had, after all, said *yes* without thinking. Robert had hesitated – he'd never bought a ring. I had worried that I was staying too silent, spending too much time asking questions about marriage, imagining that he was content, following his path lined with white blazes, unwavering, telling his companions about me as they camped. It occurred to me, now, that perhaps he'd never told anybody on the Trail about our engagement; Robert had been turning the decision over, unknown to me, across hundreds of miles. I had worried that I was too silent, too uncertain, but I hadn't been the only one who was uncertain. I had thought that I was special, indispensable, but I was not.

Please, I messaged, at around three am, *just tell me why*.

He might regret it, one day, but I wasn't sure that that mattered.
His regret, later, would change nothing for me.

I had thought that I was special, but I was not.

38

It was daylight again and I hadn't eaten, hadn't slept. I had to leave the flat, full of Robert's furniture. It was too late in the year for sunglasses, but I wore them anyway, though the tears slipped down my cheeks and salt collected at the edge of each lens. My throat was sore and my jaw hurt. I bought an ice-cream, knowing that I'd have to eat it, that it would melt and drip all over me if I didn't, but the plan didn't work; my misery became a sticky mess and I felt like a caricature of sadness, holding the symbol of a carefree summer slightly too late. I threw the ice-cream in the bin and bought a bagel, then sat in the park and picked off the pieces of rock salt and pressed them against a break in the skin on my arm, trying to make the wound sting.

I was so tired. I walked around, crying, transforming the East Village into a blur.

When I spoke, I felt as if my ears were blocked. I felt as if the rumble of a washing machine or cars had replaced the thoughts inside my head. I noticed words vanishing. I thought of the person who checked vision. *Not orthodontist*, I thought. *Not orthopaedic surgeon.*

I felt, constantly, as if I were on the edge of collapse, but the release of falling never came.

I wandered back to the flat, eventually, exhausted. I remembered small kindnesses, like Robert carrying a suitcase up the flight of stairs that led to our apartment. I stepped inside and remembered his body on the couch. I shifted my eyes and remembered the way that he crouched, sometimes, to examine certain bookshelves. I noticed his coffee cup, from yesterday, and couldn't stand the idea of moving it. I felt, most freshly, the loss of Robert's body. It was too easy to remember what it was to hug him, the places where I'd positioned my arms, and I knew that I would not always remember this, that many more things than I'd lost now would be lost with time.

Optometrist, I remembered, finally, and fell asleep, fully clothed, on my own side of the bed, with Robert's belongings on his bedside table.

39

I calmed down, after a few days, and reassured myself with all the signs that I hadn't wanted Robert, anyway. I'd fallen in love with Cara; I'd slept with Emily. I'd willed Robert to leave me so that I wouldn't have to leave him. It became easier to think of him in past tense. It became possible to imagine, later that week, that a stranger might not realise that I had been crying. I managed to smile when the girl with the plait at Lucy's local coffee shop handed me my drink.

'Have a nice afternoon,' I said to her, as if I were living in an ordinary world, as if I usually bought coffee in Gowanus rather than Manhattan. I left the coffee shop and wasn't sure if I should turn right or left to find the subway. I tried to remember the block on which I'd seen *HOME OF THE RENEGADES* painted in yellow letters on a blue wall.

I had gone to stay with Lucy the previous day, unable to handle looking around the flat and knowing that all the furniture was Robert's, that half the books were Robert's, that the life I lived basically belonged to somebody who had abruptly broken up with me. I loved that life, that neighbourhood, that apartment, more than Robert loved it, and yet I couldn't afford to live on the Lower East Side without him. I'd been to Brooklyn before, of course, plenty of times, but it felt new, now. It felt as if I was embarking on some sort of adventure. I was exhausted from sadness, though. I didn't have the energy for an adventure.

In Gowanus, everything was bright against the grey sky. I noticed the richness of the bricks, red with iron, and the faded yellow of the stoplight's casing hanging above the intersection, the dark green of the sign reading ATLANTIC AVENUE like an abstract reference to the forest, taking me back, again, to Robert. There was a certain gloom to Lucy's apartment, too, on the lowest floor of a Brooklyn brownstone. I noticed the souvenir mug from the Atlanta Olympics sitting on the table, the teabag left draining in the sink, the way in which the cookbooks leaned gingerly against one another. I noticed the metal grates against the windows and the aging glass of the door. I imagined taking a photograph and filtering it in black and white, considered the shadows of the interior against the bright silver of that glass in the door. I couldn't be bothered taking any pictures, though.

It was strange to stay with Lucy. I was, after months of living alone, suddenly in close proximity to another person as I ate breakfast, cleaned my teeth, planned my clothing each evening for the following day. I'd expected to feel self-conscious about this witnessing of daily habits, this sense that I existed in relation to somebody else, but I realised that I'd missed these routine practices during my months alone. It wasn't a convenient time to realise that I longed for domestic intimacy.

'I think this a good thing,' said Lucy. 'It seemed like you were going off him. I never wanted to pry, but you'd stopped talking about him.'

'But I just feel, like, I didn't even know him,' I said. 'We'd been together for years and this completely surprised me. How could I have been so wrong about him?'

'The point at which you learn the most about a person is when you break up,' said Lucy. 'It's unfortunate.'

I flinched at my poor judgment. I hadn't seen any of this coming.

'I had no idea he was such an asshole, either,' said Lucy. 'I thought he was nice. I guess he's a relationship psychopath. This isn't how you treat somebody you've been in an intimate relationship with as an adult.'

It felt too predictable, this rallying, this taking-of-sides, this sudden disavowal of somebody who had been a friend to Lucy, too. I wondered what she would say to Robert, if she would say anything to Robert, and if somebody, somewhere, was telling him that I was the problem, that I was a relationship psychopath. We were both human, imperfect but probably not monstrous, and it was all in how the events were reported.

'How do you know it's not the way that I'm telling it?'

'No,' said Lucy. 'It's pretty clear . . . to say and act like everything's fine right before you break up with a person . . . He should have talked to you. This is traumatising. He seems like a bit of a narcissist, really.'

I wondered if every woman in a relationship with a man had a friend who declared, after the fact, that that man was a narcissist. It wasn't possible that all those men were narcissists.

I kept telling the story as if I were the victim, and yet I was in this position because I hadn't broken up with Robert first. I had thought about it, though. I suspected that I would have chosen Cara if I'd had the option. If I'd told Lucy about Emily, would she have seen me differently, felt that I deserved Robert's rejection? I could position myself as a victim, now, only because I'd been a coward, and so my melancholy was tinged with shame.

I had to go to work, and drifted through it. It all felt painful, now. I didn't know whether to write *their own* or *our own* when informally describing the museum's history. I looked at the departmental calendar and wondered why my departure was labelled as *Fellow's Last Day* rather than *Sophia's Last Day*. It felt like a cruel detail, reducing me to my position, and I wondered why the museum would make such a point of hiring people who paid attention to detail if they were going to hire other people who were either cruel or careless about it.

I asked Emma, in the cafeteria, if she was planning to stay in New York after we finished. She still hadn't found a job, either. I didn't think anybody had.

'No,' she said. 'There's too much hierarchy here, and everything's about work. It's always, like . . . you want to know where I work and what my position is before you decide if I'm worth talking to? I don't want that.'

I nodded.

'I'm so over MoMA, to be honest,' she said, moving forward to pay for her coffee.

I thought, silently, that I was over being a fellow, perhaps, and over precarity, but that I wasn't over MoMA, would never get over MoMA, would still love the museum long after I'd forgotten Robert. I couldn't stand the idea that this larger, more significant love affair might be ending while I was still in the honeymoon phase, still eager for more. I was not yet bitter or complacent, falling in love with other possibilities, ready to let go. I was trying to memorise the museum before I lost it, so that I might live in it later, or something, but the future was an abyss. I didn't know if I should steel myself and try to detach, in case I didn't get Sally's job, or if I should act as if I was sure I would stay here, investing in the institution that I hoped would invest in me.

Robert had rejected me unexpectedly, I thought, and so the museum might also. I imagined MoMA continuing without me, unchanged, unseen, like the world after death. It was embarrassingly believable. I thought of depictions of heaven in 90s TV shows; they weren't so different from the white cube. I wondered if the department would remember to send me catalogues for shows that I'd worked on, if a stranger – some new curatorial assistant, fellow or intern – would email me in a year, as I'd emailed those who came before me, asking for an address. I wondered if I'd still be invited to openings, if I'd want to go, if I'd be able to attend or if I'd have to leave the country, see the exhibitions on Instagram.

I didn't tell Sally, when she scheduled a last lunch for us, that Robert had broken up with me. We sat on a boulder in Central Park, having a hollow conversation about the future.

I remembered that Robert had told me, once, that these boulders were called *glacial erratics*; they were foreign rocks deposited by moving water during the last Ice Age, a disruption that forced us to switch perspective, thinking beyond the modern city. He'd compared me to a glacial erratic: forged in Australia yet living in the United States, shifting his view of the world.

'We should do things in Brooklyn or downtown,' Sally said. 'I'm a recluse, really. I never leave my house on weekends, but I should. We're both on the L Train, aren't we?'

I wondered if Sally really meant it, if she wanted to be friends beyond work, or if she was simply saying it because she sensed my sadness and presumed it was linked to her. I was too tired to feel the excitement at spending time with Sally, outside work, that I might otherwise have felt.

My syntax still stung with Robert's habits. *I'm soon going to work*, I'd say, rather than *I'm going to work soon.* I'd first noticed it during sex, years earlier. *I'm soon going to come.* I remembered, now, too, Cara's habits of phrasing. *It makes me crazy.*

I'd never picked her habits up, though. I'd only admired them.

I needed precise details, but these vanished, shifted in my memory. I wished that I had kept a diary. My relationship with Robert appeared as if it had been perfect when I scrolled back through it on Instagram. I'd almost never posted pictures of him, but I remembered him standing to my right in the Sargent room at the MFA in Boston, knew that he'd been opposite me in the library or our flat when I photographed the pages of books, teasing me about my need to document everything. He haunted the images; my happiness haunted them, too. I remembered Cara deleting pictures of Stacey, and of me, on Instagram, and knew that I could never do that to Robert, or to anyone. I wondered if this came from a kind of internal strength, a masochism, or a simple unwillingness to rewrite the past, to change a historic document.

Anthea suggested doing power poses in the mirror, though I wasn't sure it could make up for the fact that I'd spent more time crying than preparing for my job interview that week. It mattered even more, now, too, because my visa would depend on employer sponsorship instead of marriage. I ran up a flight of stairs to the library bathroom, so that I wouldn't run into anyone from the department, so that I wouldn't run into Mark or Doreen, who were about to interview me. I put my hands on my hips, as Anthea had instructed, and felt ridiculous. I could see, from metres away, that my eyes were still red and swollen.

I faltered, in the first five minutes, but then my adrenalin surged. I'd forgotten that I loved to impress people; I'd forgotten that I was actually good at doing it. I had so many ideas, and so many skills, and people were finally asking me about them. I loved the rush of job interviews, of crafting the perfect answer while in the process of speaking and watching the interviewers' reactions as my responses landed. I explained how I'd chosen my graduate school, told them the most effective ways to contact different departments and proposed artists for inclusion in upcoming shows. I argued when Antoine suggested that a fellow was more like a research assistant, really, and wouldn't have the requisite experience in logistics, listing all the curatorial assistant duties that I'd already fulfilled.

'Do you have any questions for us?' Mark asked, finally. 'It's fine if you don't, since you know the department already.'

'I do, actually,' I said. 'I've been here for a while, but I don't think I know the answer to this. What attracted each of you to the museum?'

'Wow,' Doreen said. 'That's a really excellent question.'

I sat there, smiling brightly, nodding enthusiastically, as each of the curators listed reasons that I really didn't want to leave.

Exiting Employee Memo, read an email in my inbox when I returned to my desk. I flinched and swallowed, feeling the muscles in my throat, and opened it, scanned the words. I hovered on the section about medical coverage, wondering if I should make a doctor's appointment before I lost it. I wondered if I should ask about going on antidepressants, just in case, but then wondered how I'd renew the prescription if I lost my health coverage.

'Back at your desk already?' said Mark, a few minutes later, as he walked past me, toward the elevator, and then he paused, lowering his voice. 'That was *brilliant*.'

'It was fun,' I replied, feigning lightness.

—

I hadn't thought beyond the job interview, and it was my last day, suddenly. I'd imagined that my last month at the museum would be a period in which I took advantage of everything, absorbed and recorded it all. I had expected to spend my mornings in the galleries saying goodbye to each artwork and my afternoons in the office, memorising the locations of the filing cabinets and the views from each window, the posters lined up on the wall. Instead, I'd let my final weeks drift by, in denial about the future, and then I'd spent my very last week fixated on Robert.

I'd been told in the interview that I was the first candidate that they'd interviewed, that I'd hear back after three or four weeks. I clung to the fact that Mark had said *brilliant*, that Antoine had arranged to keep my email account active *just in case*, and that Doreen, as she left the office on my last day, said *see you* instead of *goodbye*.

I had never seen the skyline as beautiful as it was that night as I crossed the Manhattan Bridge at sunset. The Statue of Liberty was subtly green against the highlighter pink sky; the strangers and stay cables on the Brooklyn Bridge were silhouetted in clumps and the only building glittering at this hour, neither early nor late, was a skyscraper under construction.

It was after Labor Day. I'd missed my last chance to wear white. I had joked to Sally, before that public holiday, that I would wear all my white clothing, in layers, all weekend. Labour Day in Australia was later, though, I remembered, vaguely. It marked the start of summer, not the end. I imagined taking my Comme des Garçons dress, no longer waiting for a wedding, outside, staining it with dirt and grass in Prospect Park. It wouldn't be white after that.

40

It's so necessary to one's work to have a calm, uncomplicated emotional life, wrote Grace, in 1953. She had worried, when Walt left her, that she would never have the comfort of a permanent relationship, but it was out of this tumult that her best work came, including *Grand Street Brides*. It had been her move to Baltimore, later, and the marriage that kept her there, that had pulled her from the spotlight. It had been, I supposed, the loss of Frank, of MoMA, of New York City.

I love the Essex St neighbourhood, she'd written. *The watermelons and pineapple slices on ice, the park filled with people. It was so hard combating Walt's hatred of all this, it left me no strength.*

I went back to the Lower East Side on the weekend because it felt natural to do so. I went to Magic Jewelry to have my aura photographed again, as a way of marking this moment in my life. I bought coffee beans at Essex Street Market, ate a scallion pancake at Vanessa's Dumpling House and saw *Merrily We Go to Hell*, alone, at Anthology Film Archives.

I was losing this neighbourhood, Grace's neighbourhood,

with Robert. I couldn't stay in the apartment, even though he'd be moving to New Hampshire; it belonged to his grandmother. I wondered who would live there, next, if it would be sold to some developer, eager to acquire the whole building, or if it would be rented cheaply to some other grandchild in graduate school. I had always loved the Lower East Side much more than Robert had; I paused on darkened corners to look at those bright fruit shops glowing in the twilight, wandered to the market to buy coffee and cheese, and knew that there was nowhere else on earth that I'd prefer to live.

I think boredom comes from the feeling that one would be happier some other place, Grace wrote.

I couldn't imagine being bored in New York.

After Walt left, Grace woke up at nine, listened to the symphony on the radio, drank juice and black coffee, read and talked to her friends on the telephone. It sounded peaceful, but the only place I could imagine this routine for myself was in Robert's apartment, in the East Village. I was a guest in Lucy's flat, saying *thank you* at each turn, keeping my belongings in a neat corner, taking walks when I needed to make phone calls. It was kind of her to say that I could stay, but I couldn't stay forever and I didn't know where I'd live next.

Grace and Walt reunited, but I didn't want to reunite with Robert. I'd had my illusions shattered. *I think that Walt loves me, but cannot bear my life*, she wrote in 1955, before they broke up again. I wondered if Robert could bear my life; I wondered if I could bear his life. I wondered how I'd ever manage to translate theory into practice.

I wondered if it was modern to cling to the past like this and decided that it wasn't.

On Cara's Instagram, I saw a picture of a green table, shot from above, with two plates of eggs and mushrooms on it, a pink flower in the middle. Alice was tagged as one of the plates. It felt strange, now, that Cara and I were following each another on Instagram. Cara hadn't liked any of my pictures since the first time we'd fought, despite the birthday dinner. I hadn't seen or heard from her since the following night. It felt intrusive to witness a life in which I wasn't welcome.

There was, I thought, a fairytale idea that what people wanted was comfort, marriage and children, but this was a disappointment after wilderness, whether that was an emotional wilderness or a literal one. I wondered if art might offer what relationships could not; I thought of Grace's unhappy relationships, and also of her paintings and diaries, still extant after four marriages dissolved, after she died.

I didn't know if Cara and I were still friends, if we'd ever really been friends. I'd avoided walking down the street where she worked for so long, now, that I'd forged new habits. I could have messaged her, apologising and telling her about Robert, but I wondered if everything was broken, now, if the power dynamic made things impossible. If I reached out to Cara, having seen no evidence that she wanted to hear from me, she'd respond simply to be polite and I'd feel, and look, pathetic.

Cara felt, now, like a remnant of a different life, further from me than Australia.

I clicked the 'unfollow' button.

I had to return to Robert's flat to pack my belongings. I felt almost like a character from a reality TV show, packing up in shame, forbidden from saying goodbye to the other contestants with whom I shared the house. I scanned the shelves, picking out the books that belonged to me – *Sleepless Nights* by Elizabeth Hardwick, Frank O'Hara's *Collected Poems*, dozens of heavy art books – and sliding them out, stacking them neatly in boxes. I had two copies of Grace Hartigan's diaries and I left the spare one on the shelf, for Robert, hoping that it might feel like a tiny blade, though I knew he saw knives as tools for hiking and cooking, not as weapons.

I looked at the bright orange couch, which belonged to both of us. I remembered buying it together from a furniture stall at the Brooklyn Flea Market; a middle-aged hipster had told us it came from a convent upstate and I'd considered the provenance romantic. I didn't know, now, what would become of it. The table, too, dotted with my sketches, was shared. Robert had never liked the idea of drawing on furniture, though he'd allowed it because he'd loved me. I wondered if he'd sand the drawings off, now, keeping the table, or if he'd replace it with another table.

I was so sentimental in this apartment that I bored myself.

I could leave it all behind, really. I needed my observations, perhaps, and my résumé, but it was fine if everything else splintered into a set of fragmentary memories, ephemeral and fugitive.

I thought of Robert on Mount Katahdin. I wondered if the end of the trail would, for him, be cosy or ghastly, if it would be characterised by cider and fires or bare, skeletal trees. I knew what the moment of summitting would look like; I had seen the photographs of hikers arranged around the sign, lifting their arms in victory, smiling. But what would the evening after that resemble? I wondered if it would feel like an anticlimax or another adventure.

It was like the dropping of old leaves, perhaps, to make way for new ones.

I walked east, with a full suitcase, toward the storage facility that hovered above the East Side Highway. I'd been twenty-four when I'd met Robert and I was thirty, now; I felt that my youth had vanished, lost with the relationship, though I knew it was less my youth and more the sense of possibility that had accompanied being twenty-four. The stakes, then, had seemed so low, and I'd made decisions without realising that they might add up to something, and now I'd realised that the stakes had been high, all along, because I'd been playing with my life.

The city smelt like wet wool, which I supposed meant that it wasn't summer anymore. It was the time of year when all the sunscreen on the shelves at Duane Reade was reduced to clear. I thought of Mark, taking his son to an orchard each autumn and bringing apples into work. I thought ahead to winter, when New York would be at its best, with small shops glowing alongside dark recesses filled with the scent of pine.

I wondered if I would still be here, then, or if I would be somewhere else. I remembered that Max Weber had written, once, that modernity was the disenchantment of the world. It was in disenchantment, though, that we were brought closer to our own nature. It was my errors of passivity, I supposed, that exposed the choices that I had. I felt bruised by the summer, but I didn't feel powerless, as if I were waiting for a museum to decide my future. I felt, finally, as if I might be an active agent in it.

Quotations from Grace Hartigan's diaries on pages 2, 98, 242, 243, 244, 316 and 317 are excerpted from *The Journals of Grace Hartigan, 1951–1955*, edited by William T. LaMoy and Joseph P. McCaffery. © Syracuse University Press, 2009. Reproduced by permission of the publisher. All rights reserved.

Grace Hartigan quote on page 23 from 'Oral History Interview with Grace Hartigan, May 10, 1979', Smithsonian Archives of American Art, Washington. The quote on page 163 from the Smithsonian Archives of American Art: https://americanart.si.edu/artist/grace-hartigan-2096.

Excerpt on page 242 from 'Abstract,' March 30, 1952, *The New York Times.*

'Poem Read at Joan Mitchell's', 'F.M.I. 6/25/61', and 'Poem (*I live above a dyke bar and I'm happy.*)' from THE COLLECTED POEMS OF FRANK O'HARA by Frank O'Hara, © 1971 by Maureen Granville-Smith, Administratrix of the Estate of Frank O'Hara, © renewed 1999 by Maureen O'Hara Granville-Smith and Donald Allen. Used by permission of Alfred A. Knopf, an imprint of the Knopf Doubleday Publishing Group, a division of Penguin Random House LLC. All rights reserved. 'Mayakovsky' © Grove/Atlantic.

Excerpt on page 262 from 'The Third Elegy' in *Duino Elegies* by Rainer Maria Rilke, translated by Edward Snow, North Point Press, 2000, © Macmillan.

Quote on page 73 from *Selected Diaries*, Virginia Woolf, Penguin Random House, 2008.

Quote on page 240 from *The Edwardians*, Vita Sackville-West, Virago, 2003.

Acknowledgements

I tend to believe that declarations of love and gratitude are best made privately, ideally when drunk at parties, but labour and its networks should be visible wherever possible; a book is made material by many people and their work.

I'm very grateful to Gaby Naher, my agent, for her warmth, wisdom and exceptional skill, of which I'm completely in awe. I'm very grateful to Ben Ball, Publishing Director at Scribner, for his attention, enthusiasm, insight and humour. I'm very grateful to Rosie Outred, Editor at Simon & Schuster, for her intelligence, friendliness and care. I feel very lucky to be working with Anna O'Grady, Fleur Hamilton and Lily Cameron. I'm thankful to Laura Thomas for designing such a beautiful cover. Thank you to Anne Casey-Hardy, Katerina Gibson and Laura McPhee-Browne for the kind quotations that adorn it. I'm also grateful to Anthea Bariamis, Elissa Baillie, Reilly Keir and Tricia Dearborn, and to everybody at and around Simon & Schuster who has worked on or supported this book.

It feels silly to say, as a writer, that I am struggling to measure my gratitude in words, but it's true: appreciation renders me imprecise, clumsy with language; there aren't enough synonyms for *lucky*. I could write that these people made a dream come true, but I've never allowed myself to dream that all this might work out so well.

I am grateful to Alex O'Sullivan and Roz Bellamy, who spent hours reading and discussing these words with me, as well as Imma Ramos and Kathryn Santner, who generously read an unpublished draft as if it were a real novel, providing vital encouragement and useful comments. I'm grateful, too, to Holly, Megan, Nora, Racheal and Susie for reading drafts. I'm grateful to books by Brad Gooch, Cathy Curtis, Lytle Shaw, Mary Gabriel and Robert Moor, to John Elder's tutelage in wilderness at Bread Loaf, to strangers detailing the Appalachian Trail on internet forums and to archivists at MoMA, the Smithsonian Archives of American Art and Syracuse University. Thank you to Chris, Damien, Hannah, Jean Michel, Laura, Lindsey, Nicholas, Sarah and Zara for significant conversations and field trips and to Leah for taking my photograph. I'm appreciative, too, of Tim, Richard and Pomelo. I am particularly grateful to Simon and Tracey, whose support and generosity made it possible for me to write a novel.

I don't know how to acknowledge my mother, whose absence shapes everything.

I am, obviously, deeply indebted to the Museum of Modern Art; I am grateful to my former colleagues in the Architecture and Design Department and elsewhere at the museum, particularly the interns, fellows and curatorial assistants. I'm also, more recently, grateful to those I've worked alongside at Writers Victoria and at our neighbouring literary organisations for their support.

I'm grateful to many more friends and relatives, along with writers, editors, booksellers and art historians, but I'll resist the urge to catalogue everybody. I always want sentences to be perfect, but gratitude is messy. I will end, then, with a reminder that there are, or will be, parties. I'll be awkwardly effusive there, too.

About the Author

Anna Kate Blair is a writer from Aotearoa based in Naarm. Her essays and short stories have appeared in *Cordite*, *Slow Canoe*, *Archer*, *Meanjin*, *The Big Issue*'s Fiction Edition, *Landfall*, *The Lifted Brow* and other publications. Anna has won awards including the Wyndham Short Story Prize, the AAWP *Slow Canoe* Creative Nonfiction Prize and the Warren Trust Award for Architectural Writing. She holds a PhD in History of Art and Architecture from the University of Cambridge and has previously herself worked at the Museum of Modern Art in New York. She is currently Program and Partnerships Manager at Writers Victoria.